HARD PRESSED

KATE CANTERBARY

VESPER PRESS

For best friends who scream obscenities in restaurants.

And Mary and Paul, and Mel and Sue.
On your marks, get set, bake!

1

ELASTICITY

n. Capable of recovering shape after stretching.

Jackson

FOR FIVE MINUTES EVERY MORNING, my life was pure agony.

On most days, I went out of my way to avoid her. I scheduled myself for early patrols or wellness checks on some of my elderly residents. Anything to get out of the station. It was a necessity. I couldn't see to the public safety of this town with my dick harder than a nightstick.

I knew because I'd tried. The squad was too small for briefings from behind a podium. When it came to positioning a clipboard or the sheriff's standard-issue campaign hat over my crotch, I could only hold that pose for a few minutes.

Oh, I'd tried to hide it, but the only solution was staying away from the station and the sweetheart of Talbott's Cove, Annette Cortassi. The bookstore she owned on Main Street was no more than fifty yards from my desk and I had a front row seat for her morning rituals.

Annette walked down the street as if surrounded by moonbeams and unicorns, her smile radiant. I didn't know it for sure, but I'd put money on her being the homecoming queen back in high school and Miss Congeniality, too. I'd also put money on her making it her life's work to torture and torment me. She was a devil in angel's clothing, I knew that to be fact.

Since my first days in this sleepy fishing town, it was the spunky brunette shopkeeper who'd stolen my attention. Annette knew how to wear the shit out of a summer dress. That woman's bare calves were a public safety hazard. And her ankles. *Fuck*. Since when were ankles sexy? They were bony joints, for Pete's sake. But all it took was the sight of her walking through the village in strappy sandals to turn me on.

As if the ankles weren't enough, her round hips swayed like a hypnotist's pocket watch. I couldn't avoid the sight of her sun-kissed skin or her waterfall of dark, wavy hair if I tried. More than once, I'd found myself gazing after her, hands clenched, jaw on the floor, and a puddle of drool beside it.

Annette was the brightest star in the Talbott's Cove

sky. Every time I caught sight of her, I was powerless to look away. And that was why I couldn't look *at all*.

I was a newcomer here, still working my way into the good graces of the natives. Bedding the town sweetheart wasn't the way to those good graces, no matter how much she enjoyed it. And she'd enjoy it. I wouldn't have it any other way.

But that didn't matter. For the time being, I was sleeping alone. A temporary vow of chastity was the right thing to do. The town deserved my full attention, and my predecessor had made it clear I was to lead by example. No boozing, no gambling, no skirt-chasing. Not unless I wanted a one-way ticket back to Albany.

I wasn't much of a boozer, gambler, or skirt-chaser, but I heeded the previous sheriff's warnings nonetheless. Getting this job was a big step up for me. It was an even bigger step *away*.

In the span of a couple of months, I'd left my job and sold my home in upstate New York and headed for this town on Maine's rocky coast. It was a bold move, but a necessary one. I wanted to find a different pace of life, and somewhere I could do important work and make some small difference.

I didn't say it in job interviews or mention it in conversation, but I also wanted to belong somewhere. Maybe, eventually, belong to some*one*.

I shot the clock on my SUV's dashboard a bitter glare. I'd already looped the town twice this morning, fielded complaints about a pair of foxes lurking around the Lincolns' chicken coop, helped the innkeepers fix a section of their back fence that went down last night, and mediated a dispute between fishermen over some missing buoys. So far, a productive morning and yet I still had fifteen minutes before Annette would be tucked inside her shop.

I'd only managed to speak to her a handful of times. It wasn't nerves that kept me away but a complete inability to look at her without wanting to step into her personal space and smell her hair. I didn't understand that reaction and a part of me resented Annette for surfacing it. Hair-smelling. What kind of witch was she?

Instead of doing or saying something I'd regret, I kept my distance. This small town didn't allow for any true distance but I didn't have to watch her scrawl the quote of the day on the shop's chalkboard sign or arrange and rearrange potted plants on the sidewalk.

Just the thought of her kneeling down to write in one of her gauzy sundresses drew a knot of want low in my belly. She was beautiful and alluring in the most simple, honest ways. Hell, she couldn't jot down a Dickinson quote without lighting a fire inside me from across the street.

But I couldn't get Annette messy and dirty. I couldn't make her scream my name. Not unless I was also ready to wife her up, and I wasn't sure about that. I couldn't casually date her with the entire town watching—and they would watch—and chances were good I couldn't casually fuck her either. She looked altogether too by-the-book for fuck buddies, and there was no room for a tomcat sheriff around here.

That left me killing time by patrolling the town's back roads and praying the lovely book mistress was on time today. My cock couldn't take any mix-ups this morning.

2

SCALD

v. To heat a mixture of liquid just below the boiling point.

Annette

THURSDAYS WERE GOOD SALES DAYS, especially in the summer. It was close to payday and people liked to stock up for the weekend. Sometimes the direct deposit was already burning up their bank account, and getting their hands on a beach read made the weekend seem that much closer. It was a mind game, of course, and I was the queen of those. I'd spent the better part of a decade pursuing a man who'd never want me. Not because I wasn't fun or smart or interesting or beautiful but because I was rocking a vagina and he preferred penis.

Not exactly the sort of thing I could fix with the right dress.

Yeah, I was the queen of mind games. Years ago, somewhere in the doldrums of being in my early twenties and frustratingly single, I'd convinced myself Owen Bartlett could be mine if I worked hard enough.

Silly girl, silly games.

On any other Thursday in July, I would've stayed open late and enabled those weekend dreams. The town's inn was fully booked, as were several rental houses and cottages within walking distance of my bookstore. Summertime in the Cove brought tourists and tourists brought money.

But it was close enough to closing time and I was shutting this place down because I needed hard liquor and wallowing. It wasn't every day that a crush I'd harbored for years—years!—blew up in my face. It wasn't just a crush. It was a dream—an *illusion*—I'd cultivated so thoroughly that it was my reality. I'd never stopped to ask whether I was operating on bad assumptions or shoddy information. Or playing a damn mind game with myself.

Instead, I devoted years to slowly pursuing a man who would never want me. I'd known this, of course, in the dark part of my mind where I hid truths too true to speak. I knew and I chose to ignore it until faced with him cuddling his boyfriend in my shop.

I wasn't surprised to see Owen with his new deckhand Cole in the mystery section, but I blinked several times as I saw him wrap his arms around Cole's torso. My brain couldn't make sense of this image at first and cycled through all the non-romantic possibilities. Bro hugs, back cracking, Heimlich maneuver, spontaneous team yoga session. All valid options. But then his hand teased under the waistband of Cole's shorts and I couldn't look away. Not even when Owen kissed Cole's neck and everything inside me turned to quicksand.

I wanted to scream, "What are you doing to him? What the fuck is going on?" but instead I sent up a prayer for a swift and graceful end to this visit and called, "It's my favorite fishermen!"

I wasn't sure how I managed that. I desperately wanted to know what the hell was going on, even more so when Cole let out an impatient sigh and dropped his head back to Owen's chest. That was the only acknowledgement of my presence. They carried on a whispered conversation as I rounded the counter and approached them.

I wasn't sure how I walked without stumbling. I wasn't one for theatrics but when Owen kissed Cole, my knees had the strength of jelly and a ten-ton boulder landed in my gut. I stood there, too stunned to speak, to look away as they shared this moment. There was no mistaking the intimacy they shared. It was true and deep, and it was a side of Owen I'd never known until now. Seeing him share it with someone else ripped me right in half. I grabbed the newest political tell-all off the shelf and pressed it to my chest just to keep myself intact.

"Hey, Annette," Owen said.

It took me a minute to find my words. In that time,

Owen didn't loosen his hold on Cole. It was as though he wanted me to see this, in all its crush-killing glory. He wanted to make his intentions clear.

"Good to see you, Owen," I said, forcing a smile I didn't feel. "You too, Cole."

"You have a great shop," Cole replied. "Awesome selection, fantastic layout."

I'm gonna have to talk now. I'm gonna have to play nice. And I'm gonna need a big bucket of vodka when this is done.

"Yeah, I try," I said, looking away as I rolled my eyes. I wanted to believe he was sincere but I was too busy hating this entire conversation. Hating everything, my bad judgment most of all. "Is there anything I can help you find?"

For the love of pinwheels and popsicles, please say no.

"I think we're good," Cole replied.

Thank you, thank you, thank you.

A second later, Owen said, "Cole wants a few mystery novels. Can you recommend some?"

Would it be wrong to say no?

"Oh. Oh, sure." I took a step forward, prepared to rattle off my standard mystery recommendations, but something snapped inside me. There was an actual snap, like a rubber band stretched past its limits, and every-thing it once restrained tumbled loose. The force of that snap propelled me forward and I whirled around the shop, plucking paperbacks as I went. "Let me pick out some books for your new boyfriend, Owen. That's what I do, make everyone else happy. Sure! Mysteries. Fantastic!

Everyone else gets their happy and I get to pick out books. Fabulous!"

Cole and Owen went on cuddling and whispering like they were cozied up on a picnic blanket, and they missed all the impatient glares I shot in their direction. A girl could only take so many hits in one day before trotting out some first-class sass.

"Mysteries. I love a mystery," I said, the edge in my voice sharp enough to cut stones. "Sometimes I think I live in a mystery. You know, the *what is happening in my life?* mystery. Because I sure as hell don't know." My arms were overloaded with books and I needed to get rid of these guys. I dropped my haul of recommendations on the counter. "Can I get you anything else?"

Please, please, please say no.

"No, this is plenty," Cole replied.

Of course, Owen asked, "Did that special order come in?"

Arggggh.

The damn special order. My deus ex machina. For years, we'd played the special order game. It'd served me well. Owen came in looking for a book, something old, obscure, or odd. Often, it was all three. And I got it for him, every time. He'd come in to pick up his newest read and we'd get to talking about books and history and everything else. To him, it must've been casual conversation with the book lady. For me, it was proof that we had something, even a little something.

Now, that special order was killing our little something with fire.

I sighed, and the effort pulled my shoulders down. I couldn't find a smile to save my life. "Yeah, Owen, it did," I said, annoyed with him, myself, everything. "I'll need a minute, okay?"

I didn't wait for a response, turning toward the storeroom and power-walking my ass behind closed doors. When I was alone and separate from the catastrophe on the other side of the wall, I brought my hands to my eyes as I choked out a sob. It was a gasp followed by tears that poured down while I gulped for air.

It was ugly, and it was gross. My makeup was melting off my face and my nose was running like a faucet, and I didn't even know why I was crying.

Yeah, I was hurt, but hurt for a hundred different, ridiculous, contradictory reasons. I couldn't even land on one reason and hold it up as proof that I was allowed to feel this way. Instead, I had a collection of missteps and mistakes, assumptions and inferences. It added up to a tiny disaster but it was coming down around me like a monsoon.

I could hear Owen and Cole talking on the other side of the door. Their happy little love fest was going on its merry way while I snot-sputter-laughed at the idea of sneaking out the back door. I'd do it, too. I could leave them there while I found that bucket of vodka to fade the warts and hairy moles of my life.

But I'd known Owen Bartlett my whole life and his

mother was my high school guidance counselor. Small town manners—and a long-standing fear of Mrs. Bartlett —had me snatching his special order off the shelf, wiping away the tears, and pulling myself together. I'd get through this sale and then I'd drown myself in vodka.

When I emerged, I found Cole and Owen with their heads bent together, whispering to each other in a way that squeezed my heart. I wanted to share that kind of intimacy with someone who adored me the way Cole adored Owen.

"Here we go," I said, slapping the paperback down. I wasn't trying to be ranty. It was just flying out of me too fast to pull it back.

"Annette," Owen started, "about all of this. I didn't mean to make you uncomfortable. If I did, I'm...I'm sorry."

His words were meant to smooth my obviously frayed ends but they only irritated me further. Owen didn't have to apologize for me being a fool. I did this all by myself.

I shooed his words away with both hands like they were annoying mosquitos. "No apologies needed. I wasn't thinking. I wasn't being smart." I glanced at the man beside Owen and felt the tears fill my eyes again. "I knew," I said with a vague gesture toward them, "but I still hoped."

Owen stared at me, his brow crinkled and his lips folded into a grim line. I stared back at him, my brows arched up in silent question, but he said nothing. I didn't have to be the love interest in his life to know he was desperate to make this better. I'd sat through enough town council meetings to know how he operated.

"This looks like something my mother would love," Cole announced, piling several copies of a local photography book onto the counter. "My sisters, too. My mother loves a good coffee table book."

He prattled on about his mother and several other things which I thoroughly ignored. I plowed my energy into ringing up their order rather than reveling in the newfound adoration they had for each other. I managed to ask a few rudimentary questions and charge Cole's black card—who the hell was this guy?—before shoving them out the door and flipping the locks. The lights were off, the front shades drawn, and I made quick work of stowing the cash in the safe before dashing out the back door.

I didn't bother fixing my makeup or cleaning myself up before heading to the village tavern, The Galley. It didn't matter tonight. If they weren't already, the people of this town would be abuzz with news of Owen's beau soon enough. They'd have something to say about him shacking up with a man and then they'd have something to say about me chasing after him since shortly after high school. Then they'd share knowing glances about me being thirty-three years old and having only this bookstore to call my own. Around here, there was always something to say.

I could almost hear it now. "Poor Annette," they'd coo.

"My heart just breaks for her. All those years she spent pining over Owen and come to find out, he's gay. What will she do now?"

"Vodka will solve this," I said to myself. "Vodka always comes to the rescue."

I pushed The Galley's heavy wooden door open and headed for the bar. The tavern was packed with people but I ignored all of them.

"JJ," I called, catching the bartender's attention as I settled onto a stool. "I need something strong."

"What d'you mean?" he asked, not looking up while he towel-dried a glass. "Like, a hammer? I don't got a hammer, honey."

"No, not a hammer." I sucked in a breath and blinked furiously to keep my tears from spilling over. Why was I crying? No need for that. I was a big girl with big panties and big vodka. "Some shots."

"Only shots I do are Jäger and whiskey. That whatcha want?"

The tears were flowing now, and I didn't care. I was furious with myself and hurt by my own hand, and I couldn't hold it all in anymore. "What about a German Chocolate Cake shot?" I asked, thinking back to my last foray into shots. Bachelorette party, Portland, blinking penis necklaces. "Or a Wet Pussy? Or a Slippery Nipple? Rim Job?"

He cracked the towel against the bar like a whip. "Try again, honey. None of that shit here."

I sniffled, and said, "A drink. I want a strong drink."

"Do I look like a mind reader?" He spared me a quick glance. "You're going to need to be more specific."

He was trying to break me, right here in front of everyone. I was sure of it. "Um, I don't know. Can you make me a cosmo?"

JJ went on rubbing his dishrag around the rim of a pilsner glass. "I can," he started, "but I don't want to. I don't do girly shit."

"For fuck's sake, JJ," I snapped. If I wasn't brimming with frustration at his refusal to give me the one thing I wanted right now—when nothing else in my world was working—I would've cried a river and floated away. Instead, I wiped my face and shot him an exasperated glare. "Shake up some vodka and some juice and keep them coming. If you can't deliver on that simple request, I'll hop behind the bar and do it for you."

JJ inclined his head, studying me with a surprised smirk for a second, and then shrugged. "Vodka and juice. All right." He set the pilsner down and reached for a martini glass. "Where are your girls tonight? Shouldn't you be mixing wine spritzers with Mitzi and Titzi? Where's Carley and Barley?"

"I don't have friends named after grains," I said. "You know that."

"But you do mix wine spritzers." He snickered as he filled a shaker with vodka and ice. "Where's Bam Bam?"

I reached for a cocktail napkin to manage the excessive tears-and-snot situation. It was woefully inadequate. "Brooke-Ashley doesn't like that nickname," I replied, reaching over the bar for more napkins. "I don't know where she is, but she told me this morning she was busy tonight."

He snickered again. "I bet she is," he said. He set the martini glass in front of me and stabbed a finger in my direction. "If your drunk ass gives me any trouble, I'll toss you out."

I rolled my eyes and scowled as hard as I could, which wasn't saying much. I didn't scowl too often. "You've known me your entire life, JJ," I said. "You know I have zero-point-zero trouble in me."

That earned me another snicker. "Famous last words."

3

DOCKING

v. The process of slashing or making incisions in the surface of bread or rolls for proper expansion before baking.

Jackson

THE CALL CAME in a few minutes shy of midnight, while I was checking out the high schoolers' usual late-night drinking-and-hookup haunts, and the request was quick.

"Could use your help down here, sheriff," JJ Harniczek barked, his Down East drawl as thick as always.

"Be there in five," I replied, pulling a U-turn as I spoke.

The barkeep grunted in response before ending the call. It was polite by Harniczek's standards.

When I arrived in town three months ago, Harniczek

made quick work of introducing himself and setting expectations. The man made it clear he was the unofficial law in these parts, and he kept the people—the drunks and everyone else—in line. He kept tabs on everything above board, under the table, and anywhere in between. He could handle most issues but if ever he called upon me or one of my deputies for assistance, he expected a prompt response. For a man in his early thirties, Harniczek knew his business and everyone else's too.

That made this call—direct to my mobile phone, no less—alarming.

Three months in a small town like this was nothing. I was a tourist as far as the natives were concerned. A few of them were doing their damnedest to test the boundaries, not unlike a rowdy group of tenth graders conspiring against the substitute teacher. They wanted to see what I'd put up with but the real test was whether I'd last. Others were more welcoming. Many paid calls to the station, offering their well-wishes on my new post or inviting me to their homes for supper. All in all, the people of Talbott's Cove were kind and gracious, if not a touch suspicious of the New Yorker taking up residence in their tight-knit community.

I'd only been summoned to the tavern on two other occasions, and one of them was to help trap a posse of raccoons out back. I trusted Harniczek, and I had no quarrel with his role around here. If anything, I was thankful for it.

The barkeep was an institution in small, insular communities like this one. I wasn't about to challenge that, or any of the other institutions. They needed me but I needed them just as much. Their approval and acceptance were critical, and not only because my job depended on securing the majority of the town council's votes each election year.

There was the harbormaster who doubled as the gossipmonger, old Judge Markham who puttered in his garden and yelled at seagulls, and the antisocial lobsterman who headed up the town council.

Another institution: Annette Cortassi, the beautiful book mistress busy twisting a long curl around her finger while she mouthed the words to Stevie Nicks's "Edge of Seventeen."

I made my way through the empty restaurant and toward the bar, my thumbs hooked under my tactical belt and my gaze on Annette. Her hair was a mess, half of it spilling out of the bun on the top of her head. Her eyes were shiny and red, with dark makeup was smudged on her cheeks. She'd been crying. I didn't like that. I didn't like any of this.

Something was wrong and I wanted to make it better for her. It wasn't my job, not the one I was sworn to carry out, but the one I desired more than I dared understand.

I glanced at JJ Harniczek, taking in his ever salty scowl. "What seems to be the issue here?"

"It's not a mystery, sheriff," he replied. "The girl's blitzed."

Turning my head to stare at the woman who drew me in like a force field, I watched as she propped her head on her hand. She mumbled the song's chorus while her eyes drifted shut for a long moment. She was a wreck and drunk as a skunk—probably twice the legal limit—and a minute away from sliding off the barstool.

"I can see that," I said, stepping behind Annette. I held my hand a few inches from the small of her back, prepared to catch her if she took a dive. "You don't call me up every time you overserve a patron, JJ."

"I don't overserve anyone," he snapped. "They don't know their limits."

I pinned him with a sharp look. "That's not my interpretation of the law."

Impatient, he shook his head and waved me off. "Just get her outta here. I got things to do tonight. I don't have the time to hustle her home or spend another hour listening to her cry over spilt milk."

I cut a glance toward Annette and then back to JJ. "Mind telling me more about this spilt milk?"

"Dammit, sheriff," he grumbled. "I said I don't got time tonight."

Nodding, I replied, "Understood. I'll have time to fine you for overserving, but you get where you need to be going."

He pivoted to shelve a glass, muttering under his breath. I didn't catch the entirety of the comment but it wasn't complimentary. Something about wishing my mother had swallowed me when she had the chance.

When he turned back, he said, "Best I can tell, Bartlett let her down easy and she didn't see it comin'."

"Um, no, I did not." Annette snorted out a laugh and reached for the martini glass in front of her. "Bring me the alcohols, JJ. All the alcohols."

I snatched the nearly empty martini away and handed it to JJ. "Let's get the lady some water."

JJ gave me a wan look while he shoveled ice from a bin under the bar top into a cup. "Yes, let's. There's nothin' I'd enjoy more than gettin' *the lady* another beverage."

"What's this about Captain Bartlett?" I asked, glancing between the bookseller and the barkeep.

Owen Bartlett lived on the far end of Talbott's Cove, made his living as a lobsterman, and was a powerful member of the town council. He'd asked hours of tough questions when I interviewed with the council for this job, and he was one of my biggest supporters now that I was sheriff. He led with his principles and believed in contributing to his community, and I admired those qualities.

But I couldn't square the idea of Bartlett and Annette. Not when I knew Bartlett was gay and living with internet billionaire Cole McClish. Mr. McClish seemed to be keeping a low profile this summer, and not splashing his fame or wealth around the Cove. I was thankful for that small gift. The last thing I needed was the media storming my beaches or news helicopters circling the harbor.

"He doesn't want me. No one ever wants me," Annette wailed. She tipped the glass of water back but grimaced when the liquid hit her tongue. "This isn't liquor and that is a problem."

"The sheriff is cuttin' you off," JJ announced. "Adios, honey."

With one hand low on Annette's back, I leaned across the bar toward JJ. "Kindly explain to me what the fuck is going on here."

He glanced at the wall clock and then back at me. "Are you payin' this girl's bar bill? If not, it's closing time."

I reached into my back pocket and thumbed out two twenties. "This should cover it for tonight."

"Barely," he muttered.

"Tomorrow we'll have an official visit to talk about overserving," I continued, tossing the cash on the bar, "and shaking down law enforcement. Good?"

JJ scooped up the bills and nodded. "Great," he said. "As far as I know, our girl here wasn't going with Bartlett but she wanted to be. They had words this evening. He told her it wasn't happening." He paced the length of the bar and switched off the overhead lights. "End of story, time to go, farewell and good night."

As the bar descended into near darkness, Annette wobbled on the stool and spilled the glass of water down my tan uniform trousers. "Oh, shit," she yelled.

I hissed as the icy cold seeped into my clothes and shocked my skin.

She lost her grip on the glass and it rolled down the bar, a wobbly, ominous echo in the dusk while she patted my crotch with a wad of cocktail napkins. Between the ice bath and the surprise fondling, my cock had no idea what to do. It was a true "Should I stay or should I go?" conundrum in my pants, and I was helpless to stop her. She had one hand braced on my thigh while the other worked me over, and the only reasonable response to this was sliding my palm up her spine to the back of her neck. Without conscious thought, my fingertips pressed into her soft skin, my thumb stroking the graceful column of her neck. A rush of newfound intimacy washed over me, hot and welcoming, and it was almost enough to forget everything else in the world save for Annette.

Almost.

In the distance, I registered a quick whistling sound. At the same time, I realized I couldn't hear the glass rolling down the bar anymore and—*crash*. It hit the floor and shattered, and JJ let out a string of curses laced with complaints about having better things to do with his night.

The crunch and clatter of glass shook me from my momentary paralysis. "Annette," I barked, reaching for her hands. The ones with enough knowledge of my anatomy to sculpt a perfect replica. *Jesus Christ.* This was wrong. I was in uniform and on the clock, and she was past the point of making informed decisions. So fucking wrong. Regret pulsed through me as I pulled her away from my crotch. Regret that I had to end this. Regret that I'd let it get this far. "It's good, it's fine. You can stop."

"You can both stop," JJ called. "Like I've said, it's closing time."

My fingers were still wrapped around her wrist and I wasn't inclined to change that. "Let's get you home," I said, peering down at her bright, wide eyes. "Are you steady enough to walk?"

She met my stare with a studious one of her own, dragging her gaze from head to toe and then up again. She paused on my face and I knew she was working to make sense of my features. It was a flicker, nothing more than a half second. Almost everyone did it, even people I'd known for years. My tanned skin and blond hair ran contrary to my most typically Chinese feature, my eyes. I didn't take offense. To the mind's eye, I was a curiosity.

And I didn't mind Annette's close study.

"Of course I can walk," she replied, hopping off the stool.

If I didn't have a hold on her wrist, she would've hit the floor when she swayed on unsteady feet. I yanked her closer to me and locked an arm around her waist. "Are you sure about that?" I asked.

"Right now," she started, her words punctuated by a hiccup, "I'm not sure about anything."

"Believe me," I murmured as I steered her toward the door, "neither am I."

Getting Annette out of The Galley was a challenge. She was a stumbling, bumbling disaster, all incoherent rambling and singing, and moments of weepiness that edged dangerously into full-on crying. Couldn't have that. I wouldn't be able to stand it.

It was dark, the empty streets illuminated only by the harbor lights. With my arm tight around her waist and my fingers splayed over her belly, I steered her toward Harborside Books. She lived in the apartment over the shop. "Sounds like you're having a rough night," I said. "Is that right, Miss Cortassi?"

"Owen and I have more in common than I thought," she announced. She leaned into me, her hand on my chest. I hated myself for reveling in her closeness. It was unprofessional and it was irresponsible to carry on with these thoughts while she was under the influence. I knew better and I had to do better. "We both like dick."

I let out a surprised laugh. I liked the way "dick" sounded on her tongue. It was bold and unashamed, and I was falling under this woman's spell. I couldn't help myself and I couldn't stop smiling down at her. "Do you now?"

"Oh, yeah," she drawled, pushing away from me. The second she was gone, I wanted her back by my side. She stood on the sidewalk, motioning both hands toward her mouth. I wasn't sure what she was doing but it loosely resembled her jerking off two guys. Or shaking a set of tambourines. Couldn't be sure. "I love dick. The bigger the better. All the dicks. I should call Owen and talk to him about dick. We can compare notes. And techniques! That will be fabulous. Dick, dick, dick."

I stepped toward Annette, not trusting her to stand on her own. That, and I was enjoying this more than I should. "Let's save that for another day. Okay?" She didn't respond. "How about we get you upstairs? Where are your keys, ma'am?"

"Oh, Lord," she said, groaning. "Don't ma'am me. My day's been bad enough."

I shook my head once. "I don't understand the objection," I said under my breath. "How would you prefer I address you?"

"Annette would be fine," she said. "Book Lady if you can't remember."

"How could I forget?" I asked. I gazed down at her, meeting her humor-filled smile with my serious stare. "I mean that sincerely, Annette. How could I forget?"

"I don't know," she said with a shrug. "It happens, or whatever."

She pushed away from me to study her reflection in a storefront window. Her hands lifted as she shook out her loose curls and I had to exert real energy to keep myself from walking up and smelling her hair.

"I wouldn't forget," I said. She wasn't listening. She was shoving her hands down the front of her dress and adjusting her cleavage. Scooping one breast up, plumping it in the cup of her bra, then delivering the same service to its twin. *God help me.* "I won't forget any of this."

"That's funny," she said, her voice flat. "I'm trying to forget."

"About that," I said, stepping to her side. "Time to go home. Lead the way and I'll follow."

She couldn't produce her wallet or keys, or any idea where she left them. The choices available to me weren't good. Either I was picking the lock to her apartment above the bookshop or I was taking her home with me. Neither situation was conduct becoming a sheriff.

On the off chance she'd left her door open—not uncommon in this town but worrisome nonetheless—I tried helping her up the back stairs without allowing my touch to turn into anything more than supportive. It would've been easier to throw her over my shoulder or cradle her in my arms, and I would've enjoyed it a lot more. But my hands hovered at her waist, barely there.

But the door wasn't open, and there were no potted plants or decorative bullfrogs hiding a key. Now we were faced with a trip down the stairs.

"I'll go first," I said, gesturing down the steep incline. "You stay right behind me. I don't want you falling."

"Yay," she grumbled. "The indignities of this day won't quit."

With my torso twisted toward her, I took several steps, my hand outstretched if she required assistance. "Are you doing all right?" I asked when she wobbled onto the next riser.

"I'm so far from all right, I'm all left," she replied.

I shifted to glance down at the stairs, and then a

petite pile of girl slammed into my back. Before I could make sense of this, her arms tangled around my neck and her legs around my waist. Her breath was warm on my neck, and when I moved just a twitch, her lips brushed over my skin.

"Careful there," I said. "You're too fragile to be launching yourself at people."

"I am fragile," she whispered. "Please don't leave me in the drunk tank for the night. Don't...don't leave me."

It didn't matter that Talbott's Cove didn't have a drunk tank, or that inebriated citizens who posed no danger to themselves or others were rarely arrested for public intoxication. The lady didn't want to be alone, and I wasn't about to contradict her desires. I wrapped one hand around her ankles and another around her wrists, the least I could do to hold on to her, and continued down the stairs.

"Okay then," I announced, mostly to myself. "You can sleep it off at my place."

"That's almost as bad as the drunk tank," she muttered.

"Not that bad," I replied with a laugh. "Is there someone you'd like me to call? Somewhere else I can take you? What about your fam—"

She cut me off with, "Nope. Going to your house in the middle of the damn village is less awful than calling my family."

"You're sure?" I asked. I stroked her wrist as I crossed the street, wanting her to say yes. She murmured in agreement, her head still on my shoulder.

When I first moved here, back before I understood much about life in Talbott's Cove, I rented a house near the town center. It seemed like a great location, with glimpses of the ocean and a short walk to the station. What I didn't account for was having the entire town in my front yard. Residents liked to pop in with a plate of pot roast and potatoes—not that I complained about that, of course—or to gather my opinion on Old County Road's traffic issues. Others simply made my comings and goings their business. It wasn't uncommon for me to step into DiLorenzo's, the local diner, and field questions as to why my lights were on past midnight. They wanted to know if I was sleeping well enough, if I had company, if I was tracking safety issues. Apparently, I was the only guy around here who fell asleep on his couch, not more than ten minutes into the local news.

I had to force all of that from my mind as I hiked up the hill toward my house with Annette Cortassi plastered to my back and her lips on my neck. I was thrilled to have a near-moonless night.

Once inside, I shifted her off my back and into a chair.

"You sit here," I ordered, unbuckling my duty belt. "I have to—uh—handle a few things."

First order of business: adjusting the erection hammering away at my trousers. Next up, pulling every curtain shut. That would probably set off alarm bells of its own with the locals, but that was an issue for another day. Once the house was adequately buttoned up and my gear and firearm were stowed in the safe, I poured a glass of water for Annette and snatched a banana from the fruit bowl.

That was when things went pear-shaped.

Annette wasn't in the living room anymore. She was right behind me, standing in the middle of my kitchen, bare-ass naked. My fingers tightened around the banana. "Annette," I warned. "What—what are you doing?"

"I might be fragile," she purred, swaying a bit as she stepped closer to me, "but that doesn't mean I always want to be treated like I am."

I was working hard at keeping my eyes above her chest. I had a peripheral awareness of her nudity but I'd yet to allow myself the kind of long, quenching gaze at her lush curves. Goddamn, I wanted to look. I wanted to drop to my knees and press my face to the soft lines of her belly, drag my fingers up her calves and grab her ass like I meant it. I wanted to feel her spine arch under my hands and her body tighten around me. I wanted to get lost between her legs and never, never find my way out.

Clumps of pulverized banana filled my palm, and I turned away. "I'll get you something to wear," I said over my shoulder. I tossed the fruit in the garbage and then rinsed my hands at the sink, but I knew she was watching me. I felt the intensity of her stare on my skin, and I wanted to give it right back to her. I wanted it more than anything.

Turning, I said, "Annette—"

She wasn't hearing it. She flew into my arms and pressed her lips to mine, and for the second time tonight, I was paralyzed. Dumbstruck and frozen in place. But then my body and brain returned to me in pieces. I sighed into her kiss, forgetting my job, my duty, myself. She tasted of liquor and juice, and something succulent and special all her own. I couldn't help myself. I curled my arms around her torso, backed her against the refrigerator, and rocked myself into the valley of her parted legs.

I stayed right there, trapping her between the hard lines of the refrigerator and my body while I drank in every ounce she offered up. I couldn't even process the glory of her naked skin under my hands. It was one gift too many.

Annette broke away first, turning her head a few degrees and hiccup-giggling against my cheek. Then her hand slithered down my back and she slapped my ass.

At first, I was stunned into silence. That was becoming my default reaction to this woman. But then I remembered she was sloppy drunk, and I wasn't the type of man who capitalized on that condition.

Her palm cracked over my backside again, and another hiccup-giggle rang out. "You're so...hard," she whispered.

I surrendered to her words rather than my judgment and rutted against her core. If she wanted to know something about hard, I was happy to illustrate. "You have no idea," I replied. "Not a clue."

She tipped her head back against the refrigerator and gazed up at me, her lips parted and her eyes unfocused. "Whoa," she murmured. So beautiful and so drunk. *"Whoa."*

Right then, my responsibility came down on me. It was lightning fast and there was no way I was coming back from it this time. Not tonight.

I tossed Annette over my shoulder and blocked out the sensation of her smooth thigh against my cheek. No, that wasn't true. I was keenly aware of her thigh. But I wasn't letting myself enjoy the thigh.

"Please tell me we're going to a bedroom," she called. "That would be fabulous."

"We're going to a bedroom," I replied, "and I'm putting you to bed. Alone."

"That's the story of my life," she whined, dragging her fingertips up and down my flanks. Goddamn, that felt good. I could die happy after nothing more than a night of her hands moving over my skin. "Me, in bed, alone. It's never my turn."

I wanted to argue with her, insist that she'd get more than a turn from me as soon as she sobered up. But it occurred to me that she was offering this information under drunk cover, and chances were good I wouldn't hear the same tune tomorrow. Annette had been pleasant to me since my arrival but hadn't given me much more than passing, platonic glances. She wanted someone right now, and I was that person only because JJ called me in to collect her. If he'd walked her home, he could be receiving the same treatment. He could've been the one getting her hungry kisses and gently demanding touch.

That idea did terrible things to me. *Terrible.* I tightened my grip on her thighs and gritted my teeth as I stomped through the house, barely fighting off the urge to throw her down and make her crave me the way I'd been craving her.

I could do it too. I'd lay her down on my bed. Make her comfortable. Kiss my way from those sexy ankles to her full lips, the ones that looked even more delicious now that I'd tasted her sweet smile. I'd skip the places she wanted me most. I'd make her wait the way I'd waited for her. She'd ache and squirm and beg, and then I'd hike her legs over my shoulders and show her everything I'd held back. And then she'd know. When I was deep enough to steal her words and everything else save for screams, she'd know I'd wanted nothing but her for months.

Instead, I set her on my bed and only allowed myself an extra moment with my hands on her body before turning away. I couldn't meet her hungry, needy gaze again. Not without tearing my pants off and feeding her my cock. I moved toward the door but couldn't leave. I stood there, my hands gripping either side of the doorframe while I stared unseeing down the hall. I needed this moment to gather myself, pull the loose threads of desire tight and sew them up. Set aside the urge to forget myself and take everything she was offering.

"Where are you going?" she asked. Her voice was small, almost childlike. "I want you to stay with me. You're not leaving. Are you?"

Go ahead and flay me open, woman. Go right ahead and gut me where I stand.

"No," I choked out. There was no way in hell I could walk away now. "Just going to grab some water for you." I shot her a glance over my shoulder. That was a huge fucking mistake. She was tucked back against my pillows, her knees drawn to her chin and her ankles crossed. It was a modest pose, her most private places covered, and I didn't believe there could be anything more intimate. Or anything that could make me want to crawl to her on my hands and knees more. I wouldn't be able to look at those pillows again without wanting her right there, exactly like that. "Put your head down. I'll be right back."

I stood in the kitchen for several minutes, my hands curled around the lip of the countertop while my cock thrummed against my zipper. I had to remind myself I didn't know Annette, not beyond her reputation as the town sweetheart and everyone's favorite book mistress. But that bright, joyful woman, the woman who had a smile and buckets of patience, wasn't the one begging me to join her in my bed right now. The slightly heartbroken and fully drunk woman was asking, and there was a world of difference between the two.

With a growl aimed at any number of frustrations, I grabbed the glass and headed back down the hall. I was busy playing out several scenarios in my head and finding the side of right in each one. I could hold her for a bit, and kissing wasn't off the table, but it couldn't go any farther until she was sober. If she really wanted something more, well, I'd just handcuff myself to a chair, tell her what to do, and watch from a distance. It would probably result in a broken wrist and equally broken chair, but I'd do it if it kept that lonely, vulnerable bite from her voice.

I was so busy with those plans that I missed the sound of Annette snoring like a chainsaw. Water sloshed over the rim of the glass as I stuttered to a stop at the door, and I choked down a laugh. This woman was something else. Within minutes she'd gone from the picture of sweet sin to classic drunk chick. Her hair was tangled around her face like a veil, one leg was over the blankets, and her hands were pillowed under her head. She was just as alluring as always, but now she wasn't Miss Congeniality or the white-sundress-wearing book mistress of my fantasies. Now she was a real woman, raw and flawed, and miles away from the pretty girl on the town's pedestal. If it was possible, I liked this version even more because she saved it for me.

That was the story I was telling myself.

I set the water on the side table and tucked a wastebasket next to it in case that liquor came back to haunt her, and then pulled the quilt over her shoulders. The breeze off the water was cool and damp tonight, and I didn't want her waking up with a chill. I did my best to brush her hair from her face but sensed I was doing it wrong when she batted my hand away between snores.

"Sleep well, Annette," I whispered. "See? I told you I'd remember."

With a t-shirt and pair of athletic shorts in hand, I left Annette in my bedroom. It was odd stripping off my work clothes in the middle of the living room but it was one more thing I was ignoring for the time being. This entire evening was odd but while I collected her abandoned clothes and set them in my bedroom, I kept telling myself I was doing the right thing. Even if we both wanted me in that bed right now, it was best for me to find rest elsewhere.

My couch wasn't meant to sleep men like me. Not intentionally. It was too short, and the arms were bad pillows, and the fabric itched the patch of skin exposed when my t-shirt rode up. Worse than all of that was the erection throbbing against my belly.

Since I couldn't do anything about it—I mean, I *could*, but I wasn't going to—I folded myself into a tolerable position and yanked an afghan over my legs. Nothing to kill a boner like Gramma's orange and blue afghan. That lady never quit with the Syracuse pride.

And the blue, it was especially fitting.

4

RECONSTITUTE

v. To restore to a former condition by adding water.

Annette

I WOKE NAKED. That was my first clue that my evening had gone horribly, horribly wrong. The second clue was that I had no idea where I was.

My hair was a ratty disaster and I could smell the vodka seeping out of my pores. When I sat up to take in my surroundings, the contents of my stomach sloshed like a snow globe and I reconsidered ever moving again. I could stay here, in this strange bed, and make a new life for myself. Easy peasy. No need to account for my mistakes.

Carefully, I turned my head to glance at the framed photographs atop the dresser. I couldn't make out the fine details from this distance but I knew I was looking at a graduation photo. It wasn't a simple cap-and-gown setup though. It was military or...Oh, shit.

That was a police academy graduation photo and I was naked in Sheriff Lau's bed and oh my god how did I bring this many disasters upon myself in a twenty-four-hour period without earning some kind of medal? Where were the roses and cupcakes for being a prize train wreck? Because I wanted both, and the sash, too.

My only consolation was that I was naked and alone, and yes, that was better than being naked with Sheriff Lau. Only vodka used my body last night, and that was preferable. It was bad enough Owen dumped me...or whatever it was that went down between us...but I'd have to pack up and move to a new town if I'd drunkenly bedded the new sheriff. I didn't drunkenly bed anyone. Ever. I didn't possess the language to make those kinds of advances or negotiate those terms.

Then I caught sight of my sundress. It was neatly folded on the dresser, and my bra and panties sat right beside it. I stared at my clothes for a minute, wondering where I'd left my purse. As I dusted off hazy memories of yesterday, every minute of last night came rushing back to me. The bar, the cosmos, the water down his pants, the piggyback ride to his house, the kiss, the ass slapping —my god!—the way I'd begged him to take me to bed. The way I'd begged him to stay.

My embarrassment was much larger and far more powerful than my hangover, and it propelled me out of bed in a flash. I finger-combed my hair, threw on my clothes, and made the bed. I couldn't leave an unmade bed behind. I couldn't do it at my apartment, and I couldn't do it after inviting myself into the sheriff's bed. With the stealth of a cat burglar, I flattened myself against the hallway wall and tiptoed toward the door. I knew the sheriff was going to be around here somewhere, but I wasn't prepared to find him washed up on the couch.

He had one arm bent over his head, the other under his t-shirt, flat on his belly. Dark golden skin peeked out from where his t-shirt was rucked up and I spent a solid minute studying the muscled cuts on his torso. I thought those things only appeared while flexing but Jackson was as loose as linguini this morning.

His sandy blond hair was roughly tousled, as if he'd spent the entire night running his hands through the thick strands. He was a tall guy, too tall for this couch by at least six inches. Both legs dangled from the arm at angles I couldn't imagine were comfortable. There was a truly hideous blanket tangled around his legs but I couldn't spend a second wondering why anyone would knit such an atrocity after I caught sight of the tent in his shorts. At first, I didn't believe it was an erection. I'd never seen anything that, *ahem*, proud. I assumed it was something else. Maybe he had a cell phone in his pocket or...some zucchini. Sure, those were crazy options but no crazier than the possibility he was working with *that* kind of equipment.

As I stared at him, I was reminded of him pressing me against the refrigerator and fitting himself between my legs. His long scoop of his dark eyes had clouded over with need when he ground into me. I'd felt every inch of him then, and I'd—I'd slapped him. Yes, I'd slapped this man's ass and I'd done it more than once.

"Oh my god," I breathed.

With a shake of my head, I slipped out the front door. It was early, even for a fishing community that lived and died by the dawn. I had to pick my way through the woods ringing the village to get back to my shop. It wasn't the most direct route, but I couldn't risk a walk of shame past the docks. Also, I had to stop every few minutes to vomit into the bushes, and that kind of local news would make it back to my parents in nine seconds flat. My mother would be on her knees at St. Cecelia's, lighting candles for the salvation of my soul. My father would threaten to pack up my apartment and move me back home. Somehow, I couldn't have that.

I made it back to my apartment and fished the extra key out of the loose cedar shingle near the door. I had several hours before I was due to open the shop for the day—I wasn't even going to think about the condition I left it in yesterday—but I was too edgy and overwrought for sleep. That was the smart choice but it was too late to start with that now. Not when I could flip on *The Great British Bake Off*, drool over baked goods I'd never seen before, and tune out the world. I needed to forget a few things this morning.

I happened upon the Bake Off last winter. I didn't watch much television and couldn't justify spending money on a monthly cable bill, but I'd turned to public television after three weeks of mega snowstorms that shut down the seacoast. I was out of books to read, as impossible as that seemed, and I was going crazy in my little attic apartment. I found this charming import from the BBC that featured a dozen amateur bakers competing in a trio of challenges each week. It lacked all the snark and sass of most reality programming and focused instead on the baking itself.

To that point, I hadn't baked more than some Duncan Hines brownies on my own. I was Italian-American and I bled my grandmother's red sauce, but the kitchen had never interested me. It always felt like an event that belonged to my mother and older sisters, and never me. I was always too young to help, and when I wasn't too young, I was too clumsy, too disorganized, too something. If ever I was involved, they made sure I knew what I was doing wrong.

My mother and three sisters had their world, and I had mine. I didn't begrudge them anything, but that was always the way of it. That was the strange price for being the youngest by eleven years when my sisters had a year or less between them, all born before my mother's twenty-first birthday. If anything, they'd all grown up alongside my mother and spoke in a shorthand I didn't understand. How could I? They shared too many common experiences for me to reach their level. They were English teachers at the regional junior high school, their classrooms all together in a row. At one point or another, every kid in this area had one of the Cortassis.

But it was more than the years between us and my decision to get a degree in teaching but never use it. My parents had three girls in quick succession and they wanted a boy. My dad had taken over the family plumbing business from his father, and while he'd never turn one of us girls away if we wanted to partner up with him, he had it in his head that he'd pass the business on to his son. Cortassi and Son. That was how it went. Except...it didn't go that way at all.

They waited until they could afford another kid, an addition on the house, and a year off from school for my mother. They waited for a boy and that was one challenge I'd never best.

To be fair, my parents didn't lock me in the cellar because I didn't come with a penis. They didn't do much of anything. I wasn't abused or ignored, but I wasn't what they'd hoped for and that was plain to see. They cared for me and loved me in their own stilted, unsatisfied ways, but even when I was a child, I had the sense I was a consolation gift...and a problematic one at that.

They looked at Nella, the oldest, with pride and affection. She was smart and well-spoken, and even though a thick mean streak ran through her, she was always ready with clever ideas.

Then there was Rosa, the one they often called the middle child, and she was beautiful. She had other qualities but she didn't need them. She could live a long, happy lifetime on her appearance alone. That knowledge left her a bit vain, a bit self-absorbed, a bit cruel.

Lydia was the youngest of the original three, and they adored her feisty, outgoing nature. She could strike up a conversation with anyone and make that person feel like the center of the universe. But Lydia was terrible to people behind closed doors, tearing them to shreds over the slightest offenses.

My parents had a smart one, a pretty one, and a chatty one. That left me as the difficult one. I wasn't explosively rebellious or anything, but I had ideas that differed from my sisters' and parents'. I preferred getting lost in books to anything else, and my sisters went to book club gatherings for the wine. I had to make my own mistakes, and my sisters were content to take direction and advice without question. I liked the rustic village of Talbott's Cove, and my sisters and parents were quick to move several towns away for newer construction, Dunkin' Donuts drive-thrus, and better shopping. I wanted to be my own boss, and my sisters and mother believed I was denying my destiny as an English teacher. I rotated between preparing the same four meals for dinner every night, and my mother and sisters once compiled a cookbook based entirely on family recipes for a church fundraiser.

Anything from the kitchen was the domain of Mom, Nella, Rosa, and Lydia. It was surprising, then, that I'd latched onto the Bake Off. But it was a distant relative of my mother's ricotta cheesecake or tiramisu. This show was about slightly obscure tortes and unusual pastries, and other creations that didn't know a home in my mother's Italian kitchen. It sucked me in, and not long after those winter storms cleared, I started experimenting with recipes. My apartment had a postage stamp of counter space but I made the most of it. I'd gained a few pounds in the process, but I considered them fun, happy pounds.

I watched as the bakers organized their ingredients for a new challenge but couldn't keep my mind from wandering back to Jackson. I had to *do* something about this. About him. He'd come into the shop a few times since his arrival this past spring. He was polite but reserved, like he was only coming in to make sure I wasn't cooking meth in the storeroom. We'd talked about books—he liked sports memoirs—and he'd always left me with some pointers about security or safety issues he'd noticed. It was easy and free of complications such as unwelcome ass-grabbing or stripteasing.

Of course, I'd noticed he was attractive. He went running on the beach at sunrise. Shirtless. It was impossible to miss him and his orange shorts. And it wasn't just me, it was everyone else in a thirty-mile radius.

Sheriff Lau was the topic of conversation at my mother's Easter dinner after he'd visited the junior high to speak to the students about the dangers of four-wheeling in the woods. The way my sister Antonella—she went by Nella with family, Antonella with everyone else—told it, teachers were swooning left and right. Some of them were contemplating low-level crimes to get his attention. It was generally agreed upon that Sheriff Lau could stop and frisk any of them, any time.

But he wasn't *just* attractive. Anyone could be attractive. That didn't make them kind or respectful or compassionate, and Jackson checked all those boxes. I hadn't put conscious effort into cataloging his qualities because I'd had my eyes on Owen and other dead ends, but my entire life revolved around this town and the people in it. I knew Jackson mowed Mrs. Mulcahey's lawn when her husband broke his arm two months ago, and her grandson couldn't do it until after his college final exams. I knew he helped the Fitzsimmonses get their son into one of the good opioid treatment programs in Portland. And he took me to his home when I was drunk and sad.

"Muffins," I said to the empty room. "I'll make him some muffins."

I had blueberries because it was July in Maine and everyone had a barrelful of blueberries right now. Two bushes grew wild in the space behind my shop, and I wouldn't be able to eat them all if I tried. But I could cram them into these muffins until they were more molten blueberry, less cake. And there was nothing sexy or suggestive about a blueberry muffin. Not even a perfect blueberry muffin. They were safe and simple, and the most neighborly of the muffins. Neighborly was the closest thing to "sorry about sexually harassing you last night" as I was going to get with blueberries, flour, and sugar.

I threw myself into baking, first doubling and then tripling the recipe as I decided to load up a basket with muffins and walk it over to the station. It wasn't a gesture for Jackson's benefit alone but all the law enforcement officers and firefighters there. They were going to be double-fisting those muffins and all would be right with the world. Maybe then I'd be able to stop thinking about his lips on mine, and the way it felt when I was certain he was kissing me just as much as I was kissing him.

Drunk memories were liars. They told stories and invented truths, and I couldn't rely on them. But...he'd pressed me against the refrigerator—maybe a cabinet or a wall, I wasn't sure—and *kissed me*. Really kissed me. Like he'd wanted to kiss me and he wasn't merely putting up with crazy drunk girl antics. He'd held me, too, and more than the steadying hand of a man who dedicated his life to looking out for others.

Drunk memories were liars but Jackson Lau's touch was the truth.

When the last tray of muffins went into the oven, I stared at the mountain of dirty dishes in my sink. It should've been a reminder that for every action there was an equal and opposite reaction—and I had to deal with my damn reactions—but all I could think about was caramel sauce. Sauce meant for drowning thick, chewy, cinnamon buns. With pecans. And caramel sauce, too.

Without giving another thought to the dishes, I dug into my refrigerator for the chunk of dough I'd left in there a few nights ago, and then cleared off my two-seat kitchen table. It wasn't ideal for stretching dough the way good buns deserved, and neither was storing dough indefinitely, but they did the job well enough.

I didn't have enough dough to make a full pan, but I was happy with the limited edition. If the muffins were for the first responders, the buns were all for Jackson. The thought made my heart leap with anticipation, and I had to fight back a grin while I coaxed the sugar into caramel. I wanted him to have this, something I'd made all by myself, and I wanted it to say a million different things.

Thank you for giving me a soft place to land. Sorry about rubbing my ass all over your house. I hope we can be friends even though I attacked you. Thank you for shutting down all of my attempts at seduction. Have a muffin; now please forget all the things I said when I was drunk. Did you mean to kiss me back? Would you do it again?

While the muffins and buns cooled, I stepped into the shower. Like everything else in my apartment, it was tiny. This space was little more than a converted attic but it was plenty for me. I didn't need a soaking tub or proper closets or full-size windows. Those things were all nice to have, much like retirement plans and stand mixers. But I could make do with what I had.

When I was finished, I toweled off and wrapped myself in a short robe printed with flamingos. With my damp hair falling across my face, I thumbed through the greeting cards I hoarded in an old boot box. I had a serious compulsion where cards were concerned. If I saw something cute or thoughtful or punny or emotional, it didn't matter whether I had a need or purpose. I had to have them.

Of course, there was no greeting card appropriate for my current situation. Not even the blank ones with art or photographs on the front were right for this. Every card invited too many opportunities for accidental symbolism. Flowers were too sensual, too suggestive. Driftwood on the beach was just as bad. The one with a bowl of glistening cherries and a wooden spoon made my cheeks heat with embarrassment, among other things. Abstract art was out of the question.

Close to losing my patience and ready to blow off the entire muffin plan, I found a package of recipe cards. I wanted to believe I'd get into the habit of writing recipes down on nice, orderly cards rather than scribbling notes on the side of printouts or relying on my phone, but I'd never followed through on that plan. Now I had one hundred cards trapped behind shrink wrap, waiting for a reason to exist.

Kinda like my vagina.

Blowing out a heavy breath, I tore into the plastic and carefully slipped one card free from the deck. Then I thought better of my ability to get it right on the first shot and pulled out two more. With my flamingo mug filled with coffee and sugar, the cards, a pen, and a hardcover book in hand, I climbed out the window and settled onto my sliver of a deck. It was big enough for me, a beach chair, and a handful of terra-cotta pots. I'd only managed to keep the mint alive but I was still calling this a kitchen garden.

This narrow parcel of outdoor living space was perfect. I could see for miles out here, and there was nothing better than an ocean breeze. And early sunrises followed by impossibly late sunsets were the best parts of summertime in Maine. The sun was bright, and already far above the horizon, though the day was young. The shop wasn't due to open for another two hours and the sheriff didn't settle into his desk until after his morning patrol for another three hours.

I knew that only because my shop was on Main Street, a stone's throw from the station, and I couldn't *not* notice. It wasn't just the sheriff; I noticed everyone's routines. Maybe that made me the town creeper but I didn't care. I'd rather be the kind of person who noticed everything than the kind who noticed nothing. That was my little way of being the change I wanted to see in the world. I wilted a bit whenever someone forgot the details I'd shared in our last conversation or asked the same questions every time we talked. Those exchanges always dimmed my shine and I always walked away wondering why I wasn't memorable.

Considering I made good observation my corner of the market, it was shameful that I'd failed to notice the most basic things about Owen Bartlett. It seemed I could

notice things as long as they didn't impact me. And that
—*that* was the wound I was feeling today. I wasn't aching
over the loss of Owen as a love interest, probably
because he'd always existed as a future prospect, a hypo-
thetical. I should've stepped back and examined my flir-
tations with him ages ago, but it was easier to soothe
myself with the idea that I'd always have Owen. Even if
he was never mine.

I sipped my coffee and wished I'd brought a muffin
with me, but I wasn't putting everything down and
monkeying my way back inside now. Climbing out here
was no simple task and I had a history of spilling coffee
or cocktails in the process. And I was stalling. Putting off
the sorry-and-here-are-some-muffins note I had to write.
If I didn't, they'd be mystery muffins and the sheriff
would march on over to my shop and demand to know
the meaning of all this. Or he'd read all the way into
those *muffins* and *sticky buns*, and we couldn't travel
down that road today.

I'd sample my creations after I found the right words
for Sheriff Lau.

My first attempt wasn't awful but it wasn't awesome
either.

Sheriff Lau,
My deepest apologies for my behavior last night. I wasn't
myself. Thank you for coming to my rescue. The town is
lucky to have you.

The least I could do was bake some muffins and rolls for you
to show my appreciation.
Best wishes,
Annette Cortassi

I REREAD the words with a scowl. They weren't *right*. They met the basic criteria for an apology note, and the overall message was appropriately concise, but the whole thing tasted bitter, like an over-ripe cucumber.

And that brought to mind the feel of Jackson's body pressed against mine, the hard planes of his chest, and the undeniable ridge of his erection.

I realized I wasn't scowling anymore. A breath parted my lips as I shifted through foggy memories of his hands on my naked body, his ragged breath in my ear, his hips rocking against me as he searched for a small dose of relief.

I did that to him, all of it. I'd also stripped down to my skin and thrown myself at him. I wasn't sure how much feminine pride I was allowed in this situation. He was a man, and as much as I loved and respected men, most were consistently reliable in their reaction to bare breasts. Hell, my tits were terrific. I would've been miffed if he hadn't popped some wood.

A small part of me wanted to acknowledge it. I wanted to signal to him that things took a turn for the intimate for both of us and I wasn't one hundred percent clear on my feelings there. I knew I was zero percent clear on his feelings.

On the one hand was the erection, the way he touched me, the way he kissed me back.

On the other hand were drunk memories, and they were liars.

"None of this is helping," I muttered to myself.

Shuffling the next card to the front of my pile, I started a new note. I was aiming for a personal tone, something that quietly said, "Hey! You've seen me naked! Maybe you liked that?" but striking that balance was tough.

Dear Sheriff Lau,

Thank you for escorting me home last night. Unfortunately, it seems that I didn't make it to my home and I am sorry for any difficulty I caused you. I had a bad day and drank too much, and somehow that became your problem. I apologize for that. I don't like being anyone's problem.

I know muffins and rolls can't solve everything and they probably won't make you forget any of the inappropriate and invasive things I said and did last night, but they're the best I've got. I hope you enjoy them and I hope we can put this weird night behind us. I know you haven't been in town long but I can promise you, I don't get sloppy-and-stripping drunk very often. Or, ever.

I'm a grown-ass lady and I can handle my liquor except for when the guy I thought I'd marry (eventually) shows up at my store with his boyfriend. It's not fair to say I thought we'd get married. It was more like a backup plan. Like, a back-way-up plan. I thought we'd get together at a certain point if neither of us were married or in a serious relationship, but I'd never run that plan by him. I didn't want to be his problem. I wanted to be the girl who was there if he wanted me.

That sounds pathetic. That's even worse than sloppy-and-stripping. I'm not pathetic and I can handle my liquor. It was a bad day and I learned many things I'd been ignoring or pretending I didn't know. Thank you for being there when I needed someone, even if I don't like needing people. I doubt that matters to you. I was a hot, drunk mess and you kept me safe. I imagine this is all part of your job description and just another day at the office for you.

Enjoy the muffins.

Annette Cortassi

I BARKED out a mortified laugh as I read over this draft. This was personal but it was also awful. I could be embarrassed without being a sad, single girl cliché. And this was the saddest.

Staring out at the sparkling blue ocean, I drank the rest of my coffee and debated short and sweet notes like, "Thanks for all your help!" or "Sorry about all the trouble last night. Enjoy some baked goods." Those were much easier approaches. I wasn't lacing anything between the lines and he wasn't getting the story of my life.

But I couldn't get over the feel of him, the pressure. Even through the heavy fog of vodka, I remembered his touch. It wasn't a cautious hold, as if he was preventing me from falling over. It wasn't friendly either. It was purposeful, as if he was telegraphing his intentions. His desires. No man had ever touched me that way.

I'd embarrassed the hell out of myself and probably Jackson, too. And I owed him an apology. Somehow, I had to wrap each of those sentiments up and tuck them into a bakery basket.

Leaning forward on my rickety little chair, I caught sight of the clock inside my apartment. I had half an hour to finish this damn note, get dressed, drop off the basket at the station, and then open the shop. That was all the motivation I needed to get it right this time.

Dear Jackson,

I'm leaving you this note because I know you're very busy and I don't want to waste the town sheriff's time. Lord knows I've already wasted enough of it.

Thank you for taking me home last night...and everything else. I made you a basket of wild blueberry muffins for your trouble. That seemed like the appropriate baked good for getting naked in your living room.

I wasn't myself last night. I didn't mean to kiss you or fondle

*your backside or ask all those intimate questions. Thank you
for pretending to enjoy it.*

*It was very noble of you to sleep on the couch while I was
starfished on your bed. I couldn't help but notice it's quite
large. The bed, that is. I swear I didn't notice anything else
when I let myself out this morning.*

*As you know, Talbott's Cove is a ridiculously small town and
there's no chance we can avoid each other. Not that I'd want
to avoid you, of course, but I'm not sure I can look at you
without thinking of the forty different ways I made a fool of
myself.*

*Instead of avoidance, let's try to be friends. We'll forget all
about last night...if that's what you want.*

Please burn this note after you read it—

Annette

*p.s. I whipped up some cinnamon buns, too. Please enjoy
them. I'm not sure why, but I couldn't get buns out of my
mind today.*

I DIDN'T ALLOW myself the time to reread this draft,
instead folding it in half and penning his name on the

front. I returned inside, marched straight for the basket, and set the note right in the center. The other drafts I slipped inside the hardcover book, and left it on the counter.

The morning sun and ocean breeze had dried my hair, and I pulled on the first sundress I found in my closet. Dresses were my favorite. One piece of clothing, no worries about matching tops and bottoms. It didn't get any better than that. Then again, dresses that required neither dry cleaning nor ironing were better. I didn't mess with either of those chores.

I slipped into a pair of cute sandals, grabbed my spare set of shop keys, and hooked the basket around my elbow.

I didn't allow myself any time to reconsider the muffins or the note, instead greeting other shopkeepers and neighbors as I walked down Main Street. It wasn't strange for me to come calling with an armful of goodies. Ever since I'd started watching Bake Off and teaching myself how to prepare pastries, I was always delivering something to someone.

"Good morning," I said when I reached the station's front desk. "I made some muffins this morning and couldn't possibly keep them all to myself. I thought the new sheriff might like to try some wild blueberries."

"Of course," Cindy, the station manager said. "He'll be in by ten. He does morning patrol first, then paperwork."

She went to high school with my grandmother. They played bridge together every Thursday and she came into the store each week for a new stack of romance novels, the smuttier the better. That was small town life for you. It was a wonder she didn't mention how grown-up I looked these days or that she was happy my teenage acne had cleared up so nicely.

She gestured to the corner office, and then swiveled away from her desk. She tapped a cane against a thick plastic boot on her leg. "Take that back to his office, wouldya, dear? I had bunion surgery last week and I'm slow going."

"No problem," I said, plucking two muffins from the basket and setting them on her desk. "Let me know how these turned out."

"I'm sure they're outstanding," she called as I walked through the station to Jackson's office.

I didn't allow myself to think about being in his space, instead smiling and greeting officers and fire-fighters on my way. The door to Jackson's office was ajar and I elbowed my way through. It was sparse and tidy, not unlike his home, and it smelled like him. I didn't know how to describe the scent—woodsy? male? were there any words that didn't remind me of erections?—but I liked it.

I liked it enough to know I had to put the damn basket down and get the hell out of his office.

Something about this man made me want to take off my panties.

5

KNEAD

v. To combine dough by hand on a hard surface.

Jackson

I READ the note once more but not for content. No, I knew what it said. I'd read it forty times if I'd read it once. This time through, I focused on the line and swoop of her letters. Her penmanship was simple, direct. No time wasted on flourishes like dotting the *i*.

I wasn't going to let this note—or last night—go unaddressed. But more importantly, I wanted to see Annette again. Hell, I'd wanted to see her this morning but she foreclosed that possibility. Not that I blamed her. It grated on me and it drove me mad with worry but I understood her reaction. If the tables had been turned and I woke up after a night like that, I'd probably tuck tail and run, too.

I didn't have to glance out the windows to know evening was settling in and it was long past quitting time for me. My inbox was as empty as I was going to get it today and my deputy was on duty for the night. By all accounts, I should've been kicked back on my patio with a beer by now.

But I couldn't go home. Not yet. Not after Hurricane Annette left her mark all over my house. Not after suffering several heart attacks when I found her gone this morning. Not after receiving the best blueberry muffins in the world—or so I was told—and a note loaded with mixed messages.

And I didn't have to look in the direction of Annette's shop to know the door was open and the lights were on.

I hadn't been able to keep myself from staring across the town center all day. I'd wanted to go to her the minute I arrived at the station and found the treats she'd left for me, but I knew we required the type of time and privacy that a busy Friday morning in July couldn't deliver. So, I waited. I paced my office, gazed out the window, went on unnecessary patrols around town, always looping past her shop.

I hated that she'd left my house before I woke up this morning. I'd barely slept on that rigid torture device of a sofa and I couldn't fathom how she'd snuck out without my notice. Discovering she was embarrassed about last night

—and thinking I *pretended* to enjoy her—was another round of torture. We couldn't have that. It took everything in me to keep from marching across Main Street and setting her straight. It was a damn good thing I'd been due in court this afternoon. I needed every distraction I could find.

But through it all, I was conflicted. Annette's head and her heart were all over the place. I couldn't blame her for that. As recently as twenty-four hours ago, she had romantic feelings for Owen Bartlett. Even if he'd closed the door on those possibilities, it wasn't right to assume she'd shed that skin overnight. Any advances she made toward me were a product of Owen's rejection rather than an attraction toward me.

But I couldn't deny the way she set my pulse racing every time she smiled at me. I couldn't deny my attraction toward her, or that I'd felt it since my first day in Talbott's Cove.

I glanced out the window around sunset and caught sight of Annette through her storefront. She was with a customer, her hands doing all the talking. With a smile, I read the note again.

We'll forget all about last night...if that's what you want.

I tapped the card on my desk, nodding to myself. I didn't want that.

With that decided, I pushed away from my desk, grabbed the empty basket, and strode through the station. A wall of hot, humid air hit me when I stepped outside. Thankfully, I'd left my suit coat in the office. I wrenched my tie loose, flipped open the buttons at my collar, and rolled up the sleeves of my dress shirt. Before coming here, I'd believed coastal Maine enjoyed mild, breezy summers. That was occasionally true. It wasn't true tonight.

As I walked toward her shop, I watched two customers exit with bags in hand. They didn't notice me as they chatted about their purchases and headed toward The Galley. I'd devoted too much time to staring out my window today to have that talk with JJ about overserving his patrons, but I'd make time soon.

I pushed open the door to Harborside Books, a small bell tinkling overhead to announce my arrival.

"Just one second," Annette called from behind the counter. She was crouched down low and I couldn't see what she was doing. "Just plugging in my phone. I forgot to charge it today—and last night, for that matter—and I just remembered that now. Actually, I just found my phone now. I guess I'd left it in the receipt tape box. Funny, I don't remember going in there yesterday. I hope the world didn't fall apart today. If it did, it couldn't have been that bad since we're fine but you never know. Anything I can help you find this evening?"

I set the basket on the counter and planted my hands on the wooden surface. I couldn't begin to catalog the number of worries she just invented for me. Instead, I studied her dark curls as she wrestled with an over-loaded power strip. That was the first thing I'd noticed about her—I was obsessed with her legs but her curls straddled the line between damn cute and fucking sexy.

"You can help me find the woman who made the most incredible cinnamon buns I've ever tasted," I said. "I'd like to thank her for her generosity, among other things."

"The—oh," she stammered, her head snapping up and connecting with the edge of the counter. "Oh, shit. That hurt."

"You're a whole lot of trouble, Annette," I muttered as I joined her on the floor. I brought my hands to her face, squinting at the red mark on her forehead. "How bad is it?"

"Not bad," she replied, her eyes cast down. "Just took me by surprise. I'm all right, sheriff."

"Jackson. You call me Jackson," I ordered. I wanted the openness and honesty of last night. I didn't want the nice girl who said all the right things and lathered everyone in cheerful platitudes. I didn't want her at all. "Now, tell me. Where do you keep the ice around here?"

She turned her head, silently forcing my hands away from her face, and pushed to her feet. She put several steps between us and busied her hands with a small flower pot filled with pens. I almost laughed at the idea of her being shy around me when she'd stripped down and stood naked in my kitchen last night, but this was the side of her I was getting today. Shy, and jumpier than a cat in a roomful of rocking chairs.

I hated it.

"No need for ice. Just a little bump. It won't even bruise," she said, still focused on the pens. They had softball-sized fake flowers attached to the ends. I didn't get it but I wasn't about to ask. I knew something about sticking to my priorities. "I'm glad you liked the rolls. I made the caramel myself."

I was a modern man. I believed in equal pay for equal work and every one of women's rights and choices. I didn't entertain any notions of women belonging in the kitchen. But something about Annette announcing she'd made the caramel herself sent a ripple of rightness down my spine. I'd kneel at her feet if it meant I'd get a taste of her fresh caramel.

"I *loved* the rolls," I corrected, brushing my palms down my thighs as I stood. "The guys demolished the muffins before I could get a hand in there but I heard they were also exceptional."

Finally, she glanced up and met my gaze, a smile pulling at her lips. "I'm happy they went over so well," she said.

I shook my head and stepped closer to her. "Let me be clear, Annette. Grown men were shoving muffins in their face as if they hadn't eaten in weeks. A fistfight almost broke out in my bullpen over those rolls. The rookie resorted to picking crumbs out of the basket. It was mayhem. I almost turned the fire hoses on them."

Laughing, she abandoned the pens. "I'm sorry you didn't get a muffin. The wild blueberries are amazing right now. I should've made more."

I wagged a finger at her. "Don't say that. Don't take

the blame when you haven't earned it. You had no way of knowing my staff was full of heathens."

She lifted a shoulder and let it fall. "I saved a few muffins. I might have some stashed in the storeroom if you'd like."

I spread my hands wide in front of her. "Would I like? I'd fuckin' love. Lead the way."

Her pale blue dress swirled around her legs as she moved toward the back of the shop. The fabric looked soft, maybe a bit stretchy, and all I could think about was dragging it up her thighs. I'd bend her over the counter, shove that dress up to her waist, discard her panties, and then fill her with one glorious thrust. I could see her lips parting on a sigh, her eyelids drifting shut, her cheek pressed flat against the surface.

"Jackson?"

"Wh-yeah?" I asked, the majority of my brain busy cultivating my newest fantasy.

I blinked twice and glanced around the storeroom. It was a compact space with floor-to-ceiling shelves, a battered kitchen table, and a small desk up against the far wall. I'd expected a mountain range of books but this was painstakingly ordered.

She grinned and seemed to gulp down a laugh. "I asked if you wanted any coffee," she said. "I have tea and water, too."

"Water," I croaked. "Water would be great."

Annette gestured toward the table. "Have a seat," she said.

I heeded her request but sitting only consumed a handful of seconds. After completing that task, I didn't know what to do with myself. I couldn't pin her to the table and claim her panties as my prize. Not yet. Not until I drew out the woman who slapped my ass like the vixen I knew she was last night.

"Annette, I—"

"Did you finish that basketball book? The one about the Larry Bird-Magic Johnson rivalry?" she asked, blowing right past my attempt to revisit the events of last night. "I've sold that book to a couple of people, and always heard positive things about it. The author has several other titles if you'd like me to order them for you."

Annette set the glass of water and a plate in front of me, a fist-sized blueberry muffin in the center. Then she joined me at the table with a mug. "No muffin for you?" I asked.

She waved off my question. "I'm good. I had one before the evening rush."

"Okay." I shrugged as I broke the muffin in half. "I haven't finished that book yet. I'm sorry. I have it on my bedside table—"

"I know," she interrupted. Her words were quiet and husky, just as I imagined they'd be when I pushed inside her and she told me how full she felt. "I saw it there. That's why I asked."

I stared at Annette, my heart hammering as I stood at

this crossroads. I didn't want to make the wrong move and I didn't know what she wanted.

"I'm sorry about last night," she continued. "I'm sorry I wrecked your evening and I'm sorry I was such a mess."

"Don't be," I replied. She started to interrupt but I held up my hand. "No, Annette. You can apologize for sneaking out of my house without saying goodbye and that's about it."

"Then I'm sorry for sneaking out," she said, laughing. "But I know you didn't have to bring me home with you and put me to bed. You could've—I don't know—done something else. I'm sure you don't take every drunk chick in Talbott's Cove home with you after last call."

"You're right about that," I said. "I don't take women home. You're the first woman I've had in my house. I could've sent a deputy to The Galley to pick you up and get you settled for the evening."

"But you didn't," she said.

I nodded. "I didn't do that. I wanted to take you home."

"You wanted to take me home," she repeated.

"Yes, Annette," I replied. "I wanted to take you home. I don't regret anything and it kills me that you're upset about it."

She sat back in her chair, crossed her arms over her chest, and glared at me for a long, uncomfortable beat. I had no idea what was going on.

"You're placating me," she said eventually.

There were many things I'd expected Annette to say

in response. That wasn't in the top one thousand. "I'm—I'm what?" I asked.

"Placating me," she repeated. "You know all about my personal drama and you're using it against me."

"I-I-I, uh...what?" I stammered. I couldn't stop shaking my head. "No, that's ridiculous. If anything, I've spent the past twenty-four hours trying to pretend you weren't lusting over the lobsterman."

"And why is that?" she asked.

She had no idea. Not a fucking clue. Even after insisting I'd wanted to take her home, she still didn't get it. That I was starved for the mere sight of her. "For one, it's a waste of your time and energy," I said, spreading my hands out before me.

Annette flinched, bringing a hand to her chest and rubbing the exposed skin above her heart. "Ouch."

That gesture had the unfortunate consequence of directing my attention to her breasts. Her gorgeous, slightly more than a handful breasts. The ones swaying against the soft fabric of her dress as she rubbed. I wanted to reach in and stroke my thumbs over her nipples. I was damn near salivating at the thought.

"I don't say that to add insult to injury," I continued. "I'm sorry."

Glancing away from me, Annette said, "It's fine. What was two?"

"Two?" I repeated.

"You said wasting my time and energy on Owen was your first point. Surely, there's a second point that you're looking to present. If not, thank you for returning the basket and have a good evening."

Her ankles were obscene. Her hair was soft and wild all at once. Her big, dark eyes were straight out of an animated princess movie. Her dresses launched the filthiest dreams of my life. But it was her mind—the one thing I hadn't been able to watch from my office—that had me twisted ten ways to Tuesday.

"You're right, I do have another point," I admitted. "I don't want you lusting over the lobsterman and I don't want to forget about last night."

Annette's lips parted as she blinked at me. "I don't want any romantic pity," she said. "I don't need it, thank you very much."

"Pity?" I repeated.

She nodded. I shook my head in earnest. She nodded again.

I picked up the forgotten muffin and pointed it toward her. "I'm gonna eat this while I try to make sense of you. I need a quiet moment with the muffin. Okay?"

She rolled her eyes and re-crossed her legs, and I couldn't believe this was the same shy woman who couldn't look at me minutes ago. Or the same seductress who'd pushed the limits of my restraint last night. There was far more to the town sweetheart than I'd realized. And I liked all of it, even if she was driving me mad with this argument.

I bit into the muffin and promptly discovered a new level of ecstasy. "This is fucking amazing," I said around another mouthful. "This is blueberry muffin heaven. It's not even a muffin. It's a blueberry acid trip orgasm."

The scowl and angry glint in her eyes melted, and a warm smile took its place. "Yeah?"

"Fuck yeah," I replied. "Now I understand why the guys went crazy. These things are life altering. It's like I've just now learned what a muffin should be."

Annette threw back her head and laughed at that. "That's a bit much, don't you think?"

I devoured the other half of the muffin and she was quick to set another on the plate. "Not at all," I said. "I'll never again waste my time on inferior muffins. Not when I can knock on your door and beg for more."

She stared at me for a moment and her gaze dropped to my mouth. She started to say something but then pressed her fingertips to her lips and glanced away.

"What?" I asked. "After last night, I think we should be comfortable with each other."

"Easy for you to say," Annette replied. "You were fully clothed."

"Yes, well," I started, shooting her a pointed look, "it sounded as though you got an eyeful of something on your way out. Or did I read that wrong?"

Shrugging, she offered an innocent smile. "Maybe a little something."

"Maybe not so little," I said, leaning back in the chair and manspreading like it was my job. "Whatever you want to tell me, I want to hear."

"You're wearing a suit today," she said, tipping her head toward my navy trousers.

"You like?" I asked between bites.

Her curls rustled as she shook her hair. "It was just an observation. It doesn't matter what I think about your clothing."

"No? Not at all?" I asked as she continued shaking her head. "It matters to me."

She tossed up her hands with a frustrated grumble. "It's not what you usually wear. That's the only reason I brought it up."

"I was in court this afternoon. It was a short hearing so I gave the suit a shot." I shrugged, aiming an easy smile at Annette. Her lips turned up in a grin but her gaze dropped to my mouth and I had to stifle a hungry groan. It was all I could do to smother the desire to drag her into my lap and finish what she started last night.

"It works for you. The suit." Annette leaned forward and gestured toward my face. "You have a little something," she said, staring at my mouth again. "Some blueberry."

I jerked my chin toward her. "Get it for me."

She hesitated but then edged closer. Her thumb passed over the corner of my lip and I couldn't stop looking at her mouth. I wasn't sure who moved first but her hands were in my hair and my arms around her waist, and then she was in my lap and our lips crashed together in a frantic rush. Every second throbbed like a strobe light. My tongue stroked over hers and my hands were sliding up her flanks, her thighs, her ass. But it wasn't enough.

A quiet thought spiraled up from the back of my mind, one that nearly dragged me right out of the moment. *I'll never be able to have enough when it comes to Annette.*

"Does this feel like pity to you?" I asked, rocking my erection against her. "D'you still think I'm placating you?"

She dragged her teeth down my neck and stars sparkled behind my eyes. I'd never wanted to rip a dress or any article of clothing before but I needed it like I needed oxygen. *Annette, naked, now.*

"I don't know what I think," she whispered against my skin. Her hands traveled down my shoulders to rest on my chest, and after a breath, she pushed me away. It was the slightest push but there was no mistaking it. "I don't even know you."

I gazed at her, my hands still gripping her ass, and waited for direction. I knew what I wanted and I had a good idea what she wanted, too, but I wasn't about to announce that. There was no reason to bully my way into her panties or insist that she surrender to my wishes because I'd make it good for her. It didn't matter whether she was sorting through some complex issues right now. To my mind, a real man waited for his woman to be ready and willing. There was nothing sexy about cajoling a woman into something, even if she enjoyed it in the end. Even if she loved it and begged for more. Sex wasn't about saying "I told you so." I wanted my woman how and when she was ready for me, and nothing less.

"That's all right," I said. "There's no rush to—"

Annette grabbed my shirt and yanked me to her, her knees squeezing my waist as her mouth found mine. I held her close and kissed her until we were breathless. When she edged back again, I knew it was time to go.

I brushed her hair off her forehead and kissed the corner of her mouth. "I like you. I've liked you for a long time. I don't think it's crazy to say you like me, too. When you're not hollering at me, of course. But you're figuring things out and you don't need me pawing at your ass right now."

I kissed her again because—for this fleeting moment —I could, and I couldn't stay away from her.

"I want to know you, Annette," I said, my forehead pressed against hers.

"I was naked in your kitchen last night," she said, laughing. "How much more do you need to know about me?"

"Naked is only one form of knowledge," I replied, "and I'm sure you're an opponent of judging books by their covers."

"You want to get between my pages?" she asked, her eyes sparkling.

"Like you wouldn't believe," I said. "But I also want to be your friend, Annette. Let me do that."

"What kind of friend, sheriff? The kind with benefits?" she asked. "Or something else?"

"Is that what you want?" I asked.

Annette started to respond but bit her bottom lip instead. Then she said, "I'm not sure."

"When you figure it out, let me know," I said. I wanted to kiss her again but I knew I wouldn't stop if I did. Instead, I brushed my lips over her forehead. "I should go. Keep that cell phone charged, would you?"

"I'll work on it," she said, settling back in her seat.

"Good," I replied. "Lock the door behind me."

I didn't allow myself another word, instead dragging my gaze over her body and shooting her a heated smile as I backed out of the storeroom. When the front door bell chimed overhead and I stepped onto the sidewalk, my chest lurched at the reality of leaving her.

I'd never felt starved and sated all at once.

6

CRIMP

v. To seal the edges of two layers of dough with a fork, tool, or fingertips.

Annette

I DIDN'T LET myself think about Jackson while I baked that night. Instead, I plowed my focus into my pie crusts and fillings, and the Bake Off reruns playing in the background. That combination soothed my senses and lulled me into a Zen state where the implosion of my romantic life didn't seem too bad. And I couldn't dwell on my desire for Jackson when I was busy folding butter into dough.

But I didn't have to think about Jackson to know why I pushed him away when his kisses were heaven and his eyes were hunger. I pushed him away—*twice*—because I didn't trust myself anymore.

I used to be chock-full of confidence. I knew what I was doing and where I was going, and the path was clear. Striking out on my own, opening this shop, putting everything into making it a success, and...Owen. Confidence struck again, telling me I could have anything—and anyone—if I worked hard enough. Never once did I stop to ask whether I should be doing that work. I believed the world was mine for the taking, and with that arrogance, I took a man who'd never belong to me.

I didn't know what to believe anymore. I'd allowed myself to believe Owen harbored feelings for me—small, sapling feelings that would require time to grow, but feelings nonetheless. But that was a lie perpetrated by my boundless belief in myself, one that succeeded at forcing Owen into an awkward position and humiliating me.

It was a belief in myself but also a slow-rumbling awareness that I had to take anyone I could get, regardless of how poorly we fit together. When I stepped away from the awkwardness and the humiliation, I was forced to see some unpleasant truths. Owen wasn't meant for me and I knew that. I'd known it for ages but I'd allowed myself to believe there was a chance for me because I hadn't seen him date anyone, ever. Aside from grossly disregarding his preference, I was also telling myself I was only worthy of the scraps. That I could live with a love that came from me wearing someone down rather than authentic affection. That I didn't deserve someone who wanted me enough to pursue me.

I wasn't sure where any of that came from. Maybe it was my upbringing; maybe it was something I created. Maybe it was both, or neither. I'd spent so long hustling to make my way and do everything on my own that I didn't know how to accept anything that came without concerted effort. It seemed too good to be true.

Now, I couldn't trust my reaction to Jackson. I didn't know how to abandon the world I'd built around Owen and then construct a new one around Jackson, and I wasn't convinced I should. It was easy to force him into the space Owen vacated, but that seemed like a recipe for disaster. As if disaster wasn't a big enough problem, I didn't *want* to slide Jackson into Owen's slot. They weren't interchangeable cogs but creatures with their own shapes and angles. Jackson would never take Owen's place and he wouldn't fit if I tried.

If I was hopping on the truth train and riding all the way to revelation station, I'd see that I didn't know what I wanted or needed. I knew these little pies were delicious and there was a good chance I'd be wiping some wild blueberry filling from Jackson's lip tomorrow, but I didn't know anything beyond that. I couldn't get myself to choose past the point of my thumb brushing over his lip. I saw all the paths—friends, fuck buddies, dating—but I was afraid the ground would collapse beneath me if I took a step forward.

But if Jackson took that step, I knew I'd follow him

down whichever path he chose.

I slipped two trays of mini pies into the oven and set the timer. Again, I ignored the dishes, flopping onto the sofa with my phone instead. It was charged, as per Jackson's request. I didn't spend much time on my phone. The cell signal in this area was wobbly and I hated notifications with the fire of a thousand suns. My social media energies were reserved for the shop, and I was a lazy texter, often forgetting to respond to messages for hours.

Case in point: a truckload of messages had piled up from my friend Brooke over the past two days. Brooke and I went to high school together but we barely knew each other back then and didn't become friends until she moved home to Talbott's Cove after a decade away. She lived at her childhood home with her father, Judge Markham. He'd retired from the bench years ago but he was still Judge Markham around here, much in the way many of us gave directions based on landmarks that no longer existed. "Turn right where the Zayre's used to be," or "Around the corner from the old Market Basket, the one they turned into the sporting goods store but that went out of business and now it's Planet Fitness."

Brooke, or Brooke-Ashley as she was known in high school, was my opposite in every way. Tall, blonde, slim, super stylish. If I was the kind of lady who used the word *chic*, I'd use it to describe Brooke. But beyond those basics, she was bold and brash where I favored subtly subversive. She was salty when I leaned into killing with kindness. She lived for big risks and bigger payoffs, and I found owning a small business to be more than enough risk.

The one thing we had in common was our single lady status. At the ripe old age of thirty-three, we alternated between wanting to get married right-fucking-now and giving convention the finger. Brooke was a pro at shutting down the well-intentioned fix-up attempts by everyone in this town with an eligible son or grandson. I loved the girl through and through.

I'd never expected to claim Brooke-Ashley Markham as my best friend but I wouldn't have it any other way. Unfortunately for her, I was a terrible texting partner.

Brooke: Could it be any more humid and miserable around here? This weather actually makes me miss NYC subways in the summer and those smell like piss and corn nuts.

Brooke: Okay. Fine. We don't have to talk about the weather.

Brooke: Do you want to get lunch this weekend? We could wear complementary Lily Pulitzer dresses and drive down to Kennebunkport and drink wine and call it lunch. As you do.

Brooke: To be clear, I want the wine. Food is unnecessary.

Brooke: Excuse me, ma'am, but did I just see your cute ass walk of shame its way down the street?

Brooke: I need an explanation for this. If I don't get one, I'm going to start inventing my own.

Brooke: Nope. Can't do it. I tried but I can't figure out why Little Miss Angel Cake would be sneaking home before dawn. That is not your operating system.

Brooke: Serious question, no judgment: do you need some Plan B? I stocked up before I left NYC because I wasn't sure rural Maine had its women's health shit in order.

Brooke: I've done some light recon but no one has any intel for me. I'll never understand how this town can alternate between high-powered rumor mills and cones of silence.

Brooke: I mean, they'd cone of silence all over you. You're like the town mascot.

Brooke: No, you're not a mascot. Mascots are weird. You're more like our Good Witch.

Brooke: Or something like that. You're just pretty and happy and everyone loves you.

Brooke: Does that make me the Wicked Witch?

Brooke: Shit.

Brooke: Now that I think about it…I kind of hate you. We can't be friends.

Brooke: In other news, Dad wanted meatloaf for breakfast, lunch, and dinner, and he insisted I serve his mashed potatoes with an ice cream scoop so I'm going to need you to talk me through this walk of shame situation before I start eating the wallpaper.

I PRESSED the phone to my chest and laughed for a solid minute.

Annette: So many questions but let's start with this: why were you awake and watching the streets at 4:30 in the morning?

Brooke: Because I'm a muthafuckin' beast?

Annette: Yes, but also...?

Brooke: Hong Kong's market closes at 4 a.m. EST. Singapore at 5.

Annette: Oh, right. I don't understand how you keep those hours.

Brooke: Funny story because it seems like YOU keep those hours, too.

Annette: It was just the one time and it won't happen again.

Brooke: Wait a hot second. Why isn't it happening again? It should definitely happen again!

Brooke: Also it would be wonderful to grab some details like who, where, how it was, length and girth. The basics.

Annette: Because I wasn't being smart. I made some bad decisions.

Brooke: Was it bad-bad decisions or bad-very good decisions?

Brooke: No, don't answer. Just tell me the damn story before I get an eye twitch.

THE OVEN TIMER trilled and I abandoned my phone to collect my little pies. Dark purply-blue liquid bubbled up between the crust's lattice lines and the scent of sweetness filled the air. I'd prepared a small batch this time and they were just for Jackson.

When I had them seated on the cooling rack, I returned to the sofa and Brooke.

Annette: Sorry about that. I had to take some pies out of the oven.

Brooke: How the holy fuck are you baking in this weather? Dad's house has central air conditioning and I'm still sweating like Whitney Houston on stage. I have to wear a bra just to keep the tit sweat under control.

Annette: There is such a thing as oversharing, dearie.

Annette: I have a breeze off the water. It's not much, but it helps.

Brooke: Back to the story and make it snappy, please. I'm due for my two hours of sleep soon.

Annette: I got drunk at The Galley, Sheriff Lau took me home, I stripped in his living room and did rude things to him, and then passed out in his bed.

Brooke: YOU FUCKED LAU?!?

Brooke: Well done. I knew we'd make a hunter out of you.

Annette: I didn't fuck him. I was really drunk and really stupid, and I kissed him. And then I spanked him.

Brooke: I'm going to need some time to process this information.

Brooke: Processing finished. Tell me about his cock. It's huge, right? It's gotta be.

Annette: I was the only one naked, but based upon certain interactions, yeah, I'd say it's huge.

Brooke: YESSSSS. So, what's next? When are you seeing him again? I need this kind of live action drama in my life.

Annette: I don't know. He's so polite and respectful, it makes my teeth hurt. He wouldn't fuck me when I was drunk, and when I saw him tonight he made it clear he wasn't going to fuck me until I had my head on straight. Which it is not. So it's probably a good thing I didn't go there with him.

Brooke: You saw him tonight?!? You saw him tonight. Of course. Go ahead and live your life without informing me. It's fine. I'm fine. Whatever. I'll just drown myself in rosé and mashed potatoes. IT'S FINE.

Annette: I made him some muffins this morning to thank him for...everything. And he came to the shop tonight. I didn't go looking for him.

Brooke: Bullshit.

Annette: What?

Brooke: Pardon me, ma'am, but your crockery is full of bullshit. Those muffins were like a trail of breadcrumbs.

You basically hiked up your skirt and said "come and get me."

Annette: Even if I did, he said he wants to be friends.

Brooke: Question. Did he say this with a straight face and/or a soft dick?

Brooke: Don't answer that yet. More important question: why did you get drunk at The Galley without notifying me first?

Annette: It's late. We'll talk about it another time.

Brooke: Now you have to tell me. I won't be able to sleep until you do.

Annette: Owen came by the shop yesterday.

Annette: With his boyfriend.

Brooke: Ah. I see. I'm going to extrapolate for a moment.

Brooke: Owen comes into your shop with his boyfriend and you go on a bender therefore you must've been hanging on to your Owen+Annette4Ever dreams despite compelling evidence that he doesn't prefer XX chromosomes. With that bubble burst, you got naked and handsy with the sheriff, and unloaded some part of this ridiculousness on him. Given that knowledge, he won't touch you with his ten-inch pole because first, he's a decent guy who knows better and second, he's afraid of catching your crazy.

Annette: Is there a question?

Brooke: Were you seriously holding out for Owen Bartlett?

Annette: I thought it was within the realm of possibility, yeah. Realms can be big places.

Brooke: And you failed to mention that to me at any point since I've been back in town? Perhaps because you knew I'd whip that insanity right out of you?

Annette: It never came up.

Brooke: Serenity now.

Brooke: You're not asking for my advice but I'm giving it anyway. Buckle up, buttercup.

Brooke: Go on with your bad self. Stop shaming yourself over naked shenanigans with the sheriff. I'm violently jealous over those shenanigans and I expect detailed reports on his dick. Stop trying to follow a plan. Plans are fucking useless because life will always jack that shit up. I speak from experience. Stop trying to force guys to fit your plans. Men are square pegs, and while they're all about the round hole, they're never going to stop being square. Either embrace the square or find a new one.

Annette: You want me to fuck Jackson?

Brooke: One of my favorite things about you is that you do your thing and you don't apologize. You're nice about your thing but you still do it like a badass. So, I hate that you're losing your mind over this right now. I want you to do what you want and not worry about it being wrong. And someone should be getting laid around here.

Annette: I just don't know what I want.

Brooke: Then fake it until you figure it out.

SOMETIMES, my ideas were bigger than my lady balls.

Everything sounded fantastic in my head but I couldn't quite execute those ideas. When I was in high school, I had this big idea to read one hundred books over the summer. Not any one hundred books, but the ones a fancy newspaper said everyone should read before they die. To make matters even more special, I decided I'd also analyze those books much like the newspaper's in-house reviewer did. I'd be witty, eloquent, and excessively referential, and traffic would overwhelm my clunky little WordPress blog.

I didn't make it through ten books. They were boring or pedantic or far removed from any point of relatability, and I gave up. The only person reading my reviews was my grandmother, and that only reminded me that I wasn't finding the reach I'd expected. On top of that, I was stuck inside, racking my head for pithy comments and wrangling code while I wanted to be kicked back on the beach with books I didn't hate reading.

Looking at the pies I'd baked for Jackson, I couldn't help thinking about that summer. No one knew I'd spent the night weaving strips of dough into a textbook basket weave pattern and coaxing blueberries into glossy perfection.

I could just as easily deliver these pies to Brooke's house or drop them off at the barbershop around the corner. Those boys never refused free food.

But just as I knew I didn't want to keep reading those books, I knew I wanted to see Jackson again. I wanted him to look at me like I was as delicious as yesterday's sticky buns. I wanted those things but I didn't want it to mean anything. There was a limited number of things I could manage in a given day and the expectations associated with wanting Jackson weren't on my list. I just didn't have it in me. I could do this as long as I didn't build it up into a huge project like my one hundred books and their pithy reviews.

If the expectations didn't exist, the risk didn't exist either.

Still, those pies taunted me all day. They were in the storeroom, secure in a glass container, but they taunted me from all the way back there. With every lull between customers, I found myself pacing down the sidewalk to look for Jackson's town-issued SUV in the station parking lot. Each time I found it there, I debated dashing over to deliver my pies. I figured I'd drop them at the reception desk and retreat, insisting I couldn't leave the shop unattended for long.

That was my tidy little plan, but somehow the day slipped away from me. When I finished with my last rush of customers, I glanced toward the station and found the sky streaked with pink, purple, and gold. It wasn't my typical closing time but I grabbed my pies and flipped the front sign on my way out.

I didn't stop to fix my hair or check my teeth for left-over bits of spinach from my lunch salad. I didn't need to do any of that because I was walking in and then walking right back out. No visiting. If Jackson wanted to talk about pie or anything else, he knew where to find me.

It was just another one of my mind games.

I pushed through the station doors and waved to Cindy at the reception desk. "Hi! How are y—"

She cut me off with a wobbly wag of her cane. "Go on back," she said, winking in the direction of my pies. "He'll be thrilled to see you, I know it."

I sputtered to a stop, blinking as I processed her words. "No, that's fine. I don't want to bother—um—anyone. I'm just dropping—"

"No can do, my dear," she hollered, waving that cane around like a drunk bride with a penis wand. "He told me to send you right back the next time you dropped in."

That stopped me fast. The only reason he'd say that was if he expected me to pay him visits and that—that was the kind of expectation I was trying to avoid. "He said *what*?"

"He's expecting you," she replied as she answered the phone. "Talbott's Cove Public Safety Office, you got Cindy here. How can I assist you this evening?" When I didn't move, she whacked her cane against the side of her desk and covered the receiver with her palm. "Go on. Don't stand there all night. You know the way."

I glared at the office door in the back corner of the station. It was slightly ajar. "Wouldn't want to keep him waiting," I murmured as I marched through the station. It was nearly deserted, with only two deputies busy at their computers. It didn't take me too long to slip inside Jackson's office. "Since when am I on your list?" I asked as I leaned back against the door.

Jackson's head snapped up from studying the documents on his desk and his gaze landed on me. His eyes softened a bit and the hard line of his lips melted into a smile. "Since always," he replied.

Without looking, he closed the file in front of him and pushed to his feet. His hands dipped into his trouser pockets. Another suit, the coat abandoned on the ancient rack in the corner. His sleeves were rolled up to his elbows and his collar open. No tie today.

"It's good to see you again, Annette," Jackson said. "I wasn't sure I would."

He beckoned me forward. At least ninety-four percent of my body wanted to follow his command. Maybe more. That little stronghold in my head wouldn't allow it. Instead of going to him, I deposited the pies on his desk and dropped into one of the empty chairs. He stared at me for a moment, his jaw working and his eyebrows lifting as he watched me cross my legs. "And yet you told Cindy to send me back. You must've had some idea I'd show up here again if you told her that."

Jackson reached for the Pyrex dish and pried off the lid. "What did I do to deserve this?" he murmured, looking inside.

"Nothing in particular," I said, as flippant as I pleased. I didn't know why but this man brought out my sassy side. My inner bitch, if you will. That, and the desire to drop my panties the minute he leveled me with one of those stern stares. It sounded ridiculous but one look from him and some ancient, cavelady part of me was ready to hand over my undies and take what he had to give. "Why am I on your list?"

He pointed at me with a pie. It looked miniscule in his big paw. "The better question is why wouldn't you be on my list?"

I motioned between us. "I know this is really fun, us repeating questions back to each other for five minutes and all, but I'd appreciate an answer."

"I like you," Jackson said, "even when you're busy hollering at me." He bit into the pie, sighing and murmuring his praise as he devoured it. "How do you do this? What's your secret? I couldn't bake a pie like this with the aid of ten pastry chefs and your magical back alley berries."

"Answer my question or I'll feed the rest to the fire-fighters." I reached for the dish but Jackson snatched it away. "I'll do it."

"You wouldn't dare," he replied, the dish cradled in the crook of his arm like a newborn baby.

"I would," I countered. I had to work real hard to ignore the throb of enthusiasm from my ovaries at the idea of Jackson and babies. *Oof.* "I would and I'd make you watch."

He narrowed his eyes at me. "You're cute but you're cruel. You hide it behind that pretty smile and those fuck-hot ankles—"

"Excuse me, my *what*?"

"—but there's some evil hiding under those dresses. Those fuckin' dresses." Jackson nodded as if he'd proven an essential point and popped another pie in his mouth. "You're on my list because I want you there. If you come to the station, I won't have you waiting for me if I can help it."

"Gotta get those pies and muffins hot from the oven," I said with a stiff laugh.

"If that's what you want to believe, sure, Annie," he replied. "The treats are good but you're better."

I didn't know how to respond to that, instead rubbing the pad of my thumb over my fingernails. "Okay," I murmured. "I'm happy you like them. I played around with a new recipe and that design on the crust. It's fun. Not a big deal, really. Just something I do in the evenings. I like experimenting with baking and I can't eat it all myself."

Jackson stared into the dish for a moment, his brows winging up as he studied the lattice pattern. "It is a big deal and I'm glad you came up here," he said. "I wanted to see you but it seemed like you were busy most of the day."

"How—I mean, what?" I stammered. "What do you mean? How did you know that?"

He swiveled his chair to the side and gestured to the large, wide window. "If I want to see you, I need only look out the window."

The station's slightly elevated position offered a broad perspective on the village and a straight shot to my store. It could've been creepy, Jackson observing me from atop this hill, but it wasn't. It was overwhelmingly arousing. Of all the vast and interesting things he could've watched—Main Street, the harbor, the Atlantic Ocean stretching off into the horizon—he watched me shelving books and ringing up sales. How in the world did I compare to an entire ocean?

Finally, I said, "I never realized you had such an amazing view."

He studied me, his gaze rolling over every inch as if he was remembering me naked. His eyes seemed to darken and heat. That was all it took. I had to tuck my hands under my backside to keep from flinging my underwear at him.

His throat bobbed as he swallowed the pie. I'd never thought of swallowing as a sexy action before but this man was something else. The longer I spent with him, the more I liked him. And everything about him, right down to swallowing.

"I do," he agreed, his stare bringing pink to my cheeks. "It's gorgeous."

I smiled at him in response, glancing to his lips. I was real smooth. My seduction game was on lock. "You wear that pie well," I said, gesturing toward his mouth.

That was it. The extent of my game. No wonder I was still single.

Jackson grinned, wise to my play. "Get it for me."

Drumming my fingertips on the edge of his desk, I said, "You're all the way over there."

He shrugged. "Then you should come over here."

"That hardly seems necessary," I replied.

"You're right," Jackson said, nodding. "It's hard and necessary."

"That's not what I said," I argued, a laugh taking the sting out of my words. "You know it."

Another shrug. "It's what I heard." He brought his hands together, brushing off the crumbs. "You're a mile away. Get over here so I can have a look at you."

I glanced to the door at my back, suddenly aware of the privacy afforded by Jackson's enclosed office. I pushed out of the chair and rounded his desk, my gaze anywhere but Jackson. I needed all of my attention on walking without incident.

When I reached his side, I leaned back against the desk and finally looked him over. His hands were loose on the armrests and his legs spread wide. His trousers stretched tight across his thighs and I dedicated a long, long moment to studying those thighs and the unmistakable bulge beneath his belt. I glanced up, a shy grin on my face. All I had to do was take this itty-bitty step.

"Where's your head at today?" he asked, his voice low.

"Right here," I replied. That was the best I could do. I couldn't handle anything serious. I was fresh off a long-term, one-sided, mostly imaginary relationship and I couldn't dive into the dating game and its associated bullshit right now. But I could be here, with this man who made swallowing sexy, and I could want him. I didn't have all the answers yet but I could want him and it could be as simple as that.

I leaned in to wipe a buttery crumb from Jackson's

scruffy chin, and he answered that gesture with a kiss to my inner wrist. A wave of tingles rolled over my skin and a tiny gasp passed my lips. I stood there, frozen as he pressed his lips to my pulse again. I felt that kiss everywhere. It grazed the back of my neck, tugged at my nipples, and brought a rush of heat between my legs.

"Jackson," I breathed.

"Annette," he replied with a growl.

Take charge. Take me.

As if he heard my silent pleas, he stood and hauled me close, wrapping his arms around my waist and seating me on his desk. With a hand steady on the back of my neck, he kissed me hard. He was aggressive, and I liked it. I *needed* it. My hands scraped up and down his flanks, my fingers digging into his soft tissue in silent demands to claim more of him.

His teeth scraped over my lower lip while he filled his palms with my breasts. My head fell back as I groaned and I decided I didn't care whether I knew any of the answers. I wanted this man and if the hard cock trapped beneath his clothing was any indication, he wanted me, too. And then he kissed me again, and my hands found their way to the throbbing length behind his trousers.

"Annie, I want—"

"I don't know what it is about you," I whispered, reaching for his belt.

"Whatever it is, you're welcome," he replied with a laugh.

That burst of levity turned into a frantic fumble to get rid of the layers between us. Skirt up, trousers down, panties off, his fingers on my clit. His mouth was on the pulse in my neck and his cock was in my hand, and—

"Wait," he panted. "*Wait.*"

7

GRATE

v. To reduce a food into small bits by rubbing it against the sharp teeth of a rasp.

Jackson

I COULDN'T DO THIS. There was no way I could take her on my desk. I didn't care whether it was late and most of the crew was gone for the day, we'd still have to be quiet. She deserved more than I could offer her here.

"Wait," I said, groaning. "Wait. Annie, wait."

She reared back, her eyes wide and her touch gone. "What? What did I do? What's wrong?"

"This is too quick," I argued. We were on my *desk*, for fuck's sake. I was all for indecent but this was unnecessary. I had a perfectly good bed a few minutes' walk from here. "Let me do this right. Let me treat you right."

She pursed her lips and cut her glare to the side, unimpressed. "Really? That's what you want?" She aimed a glance at the heavy erection bobbing against my belly. After a beat, she took me in hand, stroking just enough to keep me hard and hungry. "I must've misinterpreted this."

Why was I doing this? Why couldn't I follow my instincts and fuck her like I'd dreamed? Why couldn't I take what she was offering without second-guessing?

"I don't have a condom," I replied, my fingers circling her clit. She was so wet. So wet. She'd slipped off her panties but now I regretted missing out on doing it for her. I wanted the pleasure of stripping her clothes off, watching her body reveal itself to me. None of this was *right*. Not for our first time together. "If you really want this, you'll want it in ten minutes when I get you into my bed."

A cloud passed over her eyes and I knew I'd pushed her too far. I'd forced her to consider what she truly wanted again, rather than what felt good in the moment. And hell, I was all for the feel-good option but I could wait until she was certain about it for more than a minute.

"I shouldn't have—we shouldn't have done this. I should go." She dipped her chin and reached for my trousers. Pulled them up, tucked me in. "Perhaps our paths will cross some other time."

Annette went to slide off the desk but I wasn't ready to watch her go. I leaned forward, caging her in with my hands on either side of her hips, and brushed my lips down her neck. "You were going to let me fuck you on this desk two minutes ago. That requires something stronger than 'perhaps.'"

After a long pause, she tipped her face up to me, a smile quivering over her lips. "Enjoy the pies, sheriff. I'll see you around town."

She pushed off the desk, scooped up the panties she'd kicked off, and marched to the door without a backward glance.

"The next time I have you under me," I called, loud enough for her to hear but too low for my deputies on the other side of the wall, "it won't be on a desk."

She dropped her hand to the doorknob and inclined her head to the side. "Good night, sheriff."

8

CUTTING IN

*v. The process of quickly combining flour and dry
ingredients with fat, usually butter.*

Annette

"WAIT A SECOND," Brooke cried, tearing her sunglasses
from her face. "You *left*? You had a cock in your hand and
you *left*?"

"Yes?" I answered, shrinking behind my glass of
sangria. I didn't have much else by way of cover out here
on the day-drinking deck at Arundel Wharf in Kennebunkport. It was another warm July day, the sun high
overhead and a cloudless sky stretching on for miles.
That meant this harborside restaurant was packed and
everyone was hearing about my questionable dick-
juggling skills.

"I can't fucking believe you. When there's a hot cock in your hand, you fuck it. It's the law," she yelled. People around us turned to stare but Brooke waved them off. "Oh, please. You're fine," she called over her shoulder. "Learn to eavesdrop less obviously."

I folded my arms on the table and gestured her closer. "If you keep screaming about cock, we're not going to be allowed to come back here," I whispered. "Turn down the volume a touch, okay?"

Rolling her eyes, Brooke sat back in her seat. "I just can't believe you left him there in that," she started, motioning toward her crotch, "*condition*."

"Would you listen to yourself?" I demanded. "I leave one guy with blue balls and it's a crime against humanity. You leave half the men in New York City in the same condition and it's a point of pride. Please, explain to me how the situations are different."

Brooke tipped her sangria back and drank deeply. "First things first, I'm the baddest, beastiest bitch New York's ever known. I can't help it when men find that arousing and run after me with their sad little dicks hanging out. But most importantly, I didn't care about any of those guys. Hell, I couldn't even keep track of their names when I was with them."

I stared out at the water and the boats moving through the harbor. It really was the perfect summer day, the kind of day I stored up in my memories to save me in the winter. "I don't care about Jackson," I said.

"You know what's awesome?" she murmured. "How

you're so bad at lying. Say that again—about how you don't care for him. Maybe this time you'll be able to look at me while you do it. Oh, and also? Try to say it as if you believe it, too, and you're not asking me a damn question."

I shot a sharp glance across the table. "Okay, fine," I said. "I care about Jackson. He's my neighbor and I see him around town but—"

"Oh my fucking god," Brooke said, groaning. She pushed her sunnies to the top of her head and rubbed the bridge of her nose. "I love you but I also want to slap you. Really hard. Not some quick tap but a full slap, the kind that leaves a handprint on your face and knocks this bullshit out of your head."

"I'd slap you back," I muttered.

"I'd fucking hope so," she replied, tugging up the top on her strapless sundress. "Girl, what is your malfunction? Why are you avoiding that fabulous slab of man?"

"Oh, I don't know," I said, lifting the pitcher of sangria to top off our glasses. "Perhaps it's because I barely know him and I can't hook up with him and then avoid him for the rest of my life."

Brooke shook her head, sending strands of pale blonde hair over her shoulders. "You'd only have to avoid him if you do something unforgiveable. You know, like calling out the wrong name or kneeing him in the balls or passing gas while he goes down on you. You get that, right?" Not waiting for a response, she barreled on. "And don't quote me on this but I'm mostly certain you won't have to announce your sexytimes at the monthly town council meeting. I know Talbott's Cove is behind the times but I don't think it's necessary to present courtship plans to the community anymore. So, to recap, call him now and tell him you're ready to come to your senses."

"Great info. Thanks bunches."

I guzzled my drink. It was all I could do. I was out of explanations for Jackson, for Brooke, for myself. All I knew was that my head had told me to leave, my heart had been on the fence, and my vagina had screeched at me to stay. And that was the crux of it for me, this internal war of wills.

It was go-for-flight with my lady bits, of course. They hadn't been the center of someone else's attention in ages. My heart was still bruised from Owen and my poor judgment, but it also beat a little harder, a little faster when Jackson was near. But with every one of those hard, fast beats, the ache of my semi-imaginary breakup shot through my chest. My brain was taking neither shit nor prisoners. It didn't like the idea of me jumping into it with Jackson and was lobbying hard for me to take it slow, get to know him, keep my panties on.

My major organs were locked in a staring contest.

"Please, just explain to me why you dropped the cock," Brooke said. "I'm actually very curious about this and if you don't tell me now, I will probably hound you for the rest of your natural life. Maybe longer. I've heard there's a witch in Salem, Massachusetts who communicates with the dead. She might be able to tell me, once and for all, why you rejected Jackson Lau *after* you got your hands on his jewels. So, it's fine if you don't explain this shitshow to me now. The witch will get it out of you after you're gone. And that might be very soon because I'm going to strangle you if you keep pussyfooting over a man who is clearly obsessed with you."

I glanced at her, the afternoon sunlight bouncing off her hair. Her sunglasses were enormous, straight out of Jackie O's accessory drawer, and her dress's deep blue and lime green print made her skin look like buttercream. It was amazing how someone so beautiful could also be so relentless.

"He's not obsessed with me," I argued.

"Uh huh, sure, okay," Brooke replied, bobbing her head.

"He's not," I insisted. "He's a really nice guy. He's just being nice."

"Did you realize the juice wasn't worth the squeeze?" Brooke asked. "He's got the meat but not the motion?"

"I can't believe you just said that out loud," I muttered. "It's one thing to think it but entirely another to say those words in the middle of a busy restaurant. I don't understand your brain."

"Few do," she replied. "But can you blame me for asking? You're not giving me anything. You tell me you went to his office with pie—which is the pastry equivalent of come-fuck-me heels—and things quickly heated up. Then you dropped his dick like a hot potato? I can't square that circle, sister. I can't do it. Set me straight or plead insanity."

I tugged my lower lip between my teeth as I considered this. The answers, they weren't the kind of truths I could get my arms around on the first try. I wanted Jackson, there was no mystery there, but it wasn't that simple. I didn't know how to want him while guarding my emotions and I didn't trust myself with those emotions right now.

"He said he wanted to take me back to his place," I started, plucking each word with care, "and he wanted to do things the right way."

Brooke blinked at me for a solid minute. "You're not helping your case here, hun," she said. "Look, I'm all for the quick-and-dirty-on-the-desk routine. I love the Q-and-D. But him saying he wants to take you home, do it right...that's a big neon sign informing you that he wants to go downtown and spend a little while visiting each neighborhood."

"What—what are you talking about right now?" I asked. "Honestly, I'm confused. I thought I knew where this was going but—"

"Vagina licking," she roared.

That drew several surly glances from the people around us.

"I'm sorry," I called to the table beside us, motioning toward Brooke. "She's not...she's not well. It's a condition."

Ignoring me, she continued, "If he only wanted to get

KATE CANTERBARY

his dick wet, he would've fucked you on the desk. I continue to be baffled by your rejection of this guy."

"To be fair," I replied, "he said no before I said no."

"He didn't say no," Brooke argued. "He said, 'Let's go back to my house so we can play Jane and Tarzan.' The difference is remarkable." She signaled to the waiter for another pitcher of sangria. "It's worth noting that we have sufficient amounts of time and liquor to continue playing logical fallacy games but I'd love to hear the real story. The one you're hiding under a mountain of horseshit."

"I'm scared," I confessed. "I'm scared that I'm going to start things with Jackson and—"

"Hate to break it to you, honey," Brooke interrupted, "but you've already started."

"Brooke," I warned.

"Annette," she replied, matching my tone. "I'm just calling you on your shit. It's all I'm really good for."

That wasn't true but I'd deal with her comment later. "I'm scared that things are going to progress with Jackson," I started, shooting her a pointed look, "and I don't know if I'm ready for that. I don't know what I want. I don't even know him. I just don't trust myself to make the right decisions."

Brooke stared at me for a long beat and then said, "You're overthinking this. Forget about Owen Bartlett and the beautiful, fictitious babies you were going to have with him. The best remedy for that nonsense is getting laid. You're taking a simple situation and making it all kinds of extra. Stop worrying about everything. If you don't climb him like a jungle gym in the next few days, I'm going to do it."

I slammed my drink on the table as white-hot possessiveness zipped through me faster than I could comprehend. "You wouldn't."

Shrugging, Brooke continued, "I'll dig the Louboutins out, put on one of the two dresses that make me look like I have tits and an ass, and bring him some of my *pie*."

I could see it now. Her tiny waist wrapped in a mere scrap of fabric and her long legs made even longer by the most treacherous heels in her closet. She'd go for the full red lip, too. She always knew how to pull that off whereas I looked like a kid playing with Mom's makeup.

But I couldn't see Jackson's hands on her. As much as I attempted to torment myself with the sight of Brooke in Jackson's arms, I couldn't get there. In trying to mentally pair my best friend with the guy I couldn't get out of my head, I found myself toggling through the memories of his hands on me. The way he squeezed my waist when he picked me up and set me on his desk. The way he'd gripped my thighs when he'd tossed me over his shoulder. How he was rough but tender.

Despite the day's heat, a patch of goose bumps broke out on my skin. I refused to acknowledge the tightening of my nipples. They were on their own.

"Listen, girl. If you don't want to take what he's offering, someone else will," Brooke continued. "And that someone else will be me." She smiled at me, shrugging. "What? Is that a problem for you?"

I still couldn't see them together but even the thought of Brooke's hands on Jackson turned me inside out. Working hard to keep the cavelady screech out of my voice, I said, "Uh, yeah, it is." I shifted to face her. "Keep the Louboutins on the shelf and stay away from the cherry red lipstick."

"Really? Because I thought you weren't interested," she said, waving her *I had no idea* hands at me. "You've spent the entire afternoon telling me how it wouldn't work out and you didn't have feelings for him. Since you walked away and refuse to consider going back, I am left to infer that he's free for the taking."

Most people underestimated Brooke. They saw the hair, the face, the body first, and they assumed she was nothing more than a real-life Barbie doll. Head full of plastic, right? Wrong. She was whiz-bang smart and worked harder than anyone I knew. And she had the biggest heart. It was wrapped in barbed wire and kept on ice but huge nonetheless.

I tapped her elbow to grab her attention from the men a few tables away. "I'm going to say something and I need you to know it comes from a place of love."

Brooke rolled her hand, urging me to proceed. "Quickly, sweet pea. I need to get back to eye-fucking those guys."

"Sometimes you're a manipulative bitch."

She threw her head back and let out a throaty laugh.

"Sometimes? That is literally on my business cards. 'Brooke Markham, Manipulative Bitch and Hedge Fund Manager.'"

"Is that what you do?" I asked.

"For fuck's sake, Annette," she muttered. "First you tell me I can't sink my hooks into your man meat and now you're saying you don't know the basic details of my professional life? I'm beginning to think we're not friends but acquaintances who drink and complain together."

"There's nothing wrong with being acquaintances who drink and complain," I said, raising my glass to meet hers with a *clink*. "Acquaintances who say things to each other that no one else will say, and not hate each other too much because of those things."

That was the straightforward but also convoluted truth. Adult friendships were complex. Ours certainly was.

"Stop it. I don't do sentimental," she whined. "And don't forget—we're basically the only thirtysomething single ladies in town. This is friendship born from scarcity."

"Of course," I replied, nodding along with her snarked-up version of reality. "Okay, this calls for a new law. If I've had his penis in my hand, you're not allowed to go after him. Bare, not over the clothes."

"Does that allow for dry humping?" When I leveled her with a scowl, she asked, "What? It's an important clarification."

"We're too old for dry humping," I said. "We're not seventeen anymore and we don't hookup with men in the back of someone's mom's minivan."

"Fine," she replied with a dramatic eyeroll. "Care to legislate anything else?"

I shook my head, laughing. "That's all for today. I can't handle much more than Jackson."

Brooke edged her sunglasses down and peered at me over the frames. "But you'll *handle* him?" she asked, the suggestion weaving through her words.

I held up both hands in surrender. "I don't know. I don't know what's going to happen. He might not want me handling him anymore." As I said it, I remembered Jackson telling me the next time wouldn't be on a desk. I had to fold my lips together to keep from bursting into a silly grin. "You'll stay away from him and I'll take it as it comes."

"Excellent," she said. "Taking, coming. All good things. You need more of both in your life."

"Only me?"

Brooke shot me a wide-eyed scowl. "Uh, no. We both need it. The world would be a happier place if we were getting it on the regular. That's why I need to return my attention to those snacks on the other side of the deck. Let's see if we can get them to buy us some more drinks."

I glanced at the group of guys, each in a different colored pastel polo shirt. They were young, probably early twenties. Cute but far too fresh-faced for me. I needed a bit of age on a man. Some experience, some wisdom. "Starting a harem?"

"Don't you know that term is outdated and pejorative?" she snapped. "It's polyamorous love puddle now."

"Oh, right," I murmured. "Yeah, you should have one of those. Definitely. But I'm going to stick with the one dick if you don't mind."

"That's what I'm screaming about," she shouted, drawing the attention of the surrounding patrons again. She looked around, grinning. "What? I didn't even say *cock* this time."

9

MACERATE

v. To soften or become softened by soaking in liquid.

Jackson

THREE DAYS WENT by without a word—or a crumb—from Annette.

It was strange, really, having a relationship with a woman that started with her getting naked, peaked with me refusing to fuck her, and then declined to wondering whether we'd see each other again. Was it even a relationship at this point? It had to be. I wasn't entertaining any alternative designation.

I'd thought about going after her when she left my office. Who wouldn't? But there was the slight issue of my dick being harder than an iron spike and her arousal all over my fingers. I wasn't fit for public appearances. It was bad enough my station manager, Cindy, was already starting a wedding registry and drafting a list of baby names. I couldn't make matters worse by chasing Annette through the village while everyone watched from their decks and screened-in porches.

Instead of going after her, I waited...and waited. I'd held out hope that she'd drop by with some baked goods just to keep the pattern going. No such luck. Over the past few days, I'd managed to work hourly loops down Main Street into my routine.

Yeah, I was checking up on her. Part of me was hoping she'd notice me driving by her shop a time or fifty and come outside to holler at me.

Thankfully, I didn't have to wait much longer. I caught sight of her pawing through a display of fresh peaches at the local market and I wasn't too proud to admit I stared at her for a full minute or two from the far end of the produce section.

I hadn't planned on grocery shopping tonight but now I was thrilled about running out of eggs. Her dark hair spilled over one shoulder, curtaining her face while she studied the peaches. Sniff, squeeze, inspect.

I envied the shit out of that fruit.

After drinking in a good, long look at her, I was able to move again. Quick strides had me out of the leafy greens section and closing in on the seasonal fruits. I sidled up next to her, my elbow bumping hers as I reached for a peach. She glanced up at me, her automatic smile shifting into an eyebrow-arching smirk.

"Sheriff," she said, giving me a quick once-over. Her gaze swept across my shoulders, seeming to pause at the sheriff's office emblem on my sleeve. "Funny seeing you here."

"Is it? Funny?" I asked, my words innocent. "Should I take that to mean you believe I subside on your baked goods alone? Or that I haze my rookies, making them shop for me?"

"Of course not," she murmured. "It's just that I've never seen you here. I figured you used one of those delivery services as you have your hands full."

"My hands haven't been full for three days," I replied under my breath. "Know anything about that?"

"Sure don't," she replied, reaching for another peach. Sniff, squeeze, inspect.

"Well then," I said with a shake of my head. "I do my own shopping. I'm not sure any of the local markets offer delivery, and none of the big chains come out this far."

I held out a peach for her and damn near burst into flames when she leaned down to inhale its fragrance, her breasts grazing my forearm in the process.

Her eyes fluttered shut and her smirk transformed into a joyful smile. "Mmm. Yes. This one." Nodding, she took the fruit from my palm and added it to her cart.

What a treat it would be to please this woman as much as a ripe peach.

"So," I started, clearing my throat, "why all the peaches?"

Annette bobbed her head from side to side as she

reached for another peach. "I'm working on some new recipes. Scones, tarts, a few other things. I haven't been able to nail them but I think that's because stone fruit wasn't in peak season when I tried. Since the entire market smells like ripe peaches, I figured this was the time to try again."

"Need any help?" I asked.

She glanced up at me, surprised. "With what? Baking?"

"Yeah," I said. "Or anything you want. Put my hands to work."

She laughed but leaned closer to whisper, "Your hands will probably find their way under my skirt and away from the dough."

It was my turn to laugh. "Is that how it is, Annette? I can't be trusted?" She jerked a shoulder up in vague agreement as she continued inspecting the fruit. "I'll remind you that I've never had the pleasure of stripping your panties off you. Maybe I'm not the one who can't be trusted."

She'd always beaten me to it, one way or another.

"Believe me," she murmured, shooting me a side-eye glance. "I've considered that angle."

She abandoned the peach display and I was hot on her heels. It occurred to me that following Annette around the town market at this hour was bound to catch the attention of the locals. I was torn between slowing my steps and forgoing all concern for the rumor mill. In that split second, I settled on the best of both. I allowed her the space to walk without me hovering over her but accepted that anyone watching would be able to read my intentions from a mile away.

"You can't survive on scones alone. Let me cook dinner for you," I said when I caught up to Annette in the dairy case. She was loading butter into her cart. "Then you can teach me about baking."

She started to object, her lips already pursed and her curls rustling against her shoulders as she shook her head, but then she stopped herself. "How big is your oven?" she asked.

I replied with the type of conviction reserved for horsepower and dick size. "Huge."

ANNETTE MET me back at my house and piled her groceries and baking tools on my kitchen island. Once I had my firearm stowed, I stood to the side, my hands clasped behind my back, and allowed her a minute to unpack her bags and organize her goods. That seemed to be an adequate amount of time to wait before getting my hands on her.

When her materials and ingredients were sorted, I caught her around the waist. "You're coming with me," I growled, backing her up against the refrigerator.

My lips brushed hers and all the tension I'd been carrying the past few days vaporized. *Poof.* It was gone and in its place was a heavy cloud of desire. Her hands fisted in my tan uniform shirt as I kissed her, tugging me closer. I kicked her feet apart and pressed myself to the notch between her legs. There was no denying the immediate reaction I had to her kiss, her body, her presence in my home, and she deserved to know how she affected me. When we finally came up for air, she was breathless and trembling in my arms, her eyes unfocused and her lips swollen. I wasn't much better.

"What was that for?" she asked, tilting her head to look up at me.

"Do I need a reason?" I asked, still rocking against her. She felt like a dream, even through these layers.

"I guess not but we really have to stop going at each other with questions. Someone has to answer at some point," Annette said, dropping her head to the side. It offered me the space to savor her there and it wasn't long before my fingers were itching to feel her skin.

I tugged her skirt up, fisting the fabric at her hips. I was dangerously close to her panties. This wasn't what I had in mind. I figured I'd kiss her and quench my body's need to have her close. But it wasn't enough. I'd had her kisses, her embraces. I wanted more. That led me to an obvious conclusion. I wasn't walking away from this refrigerator until I'd MacGyvered an orgasm out of her.

No touching the undies, no problem.

"Here's a question you can answer," I said, groaning as I pressed into her heat. No longer was this a simple matter of friction. I was rutting on her now. We were so close, separated only by thin layers of fabric. Her panties, my trousers. Nothing else. If it was possible, this was more indecent than the moment we shared in my office. "Is this all right? Do you want me to stop?"

She shook her head and her hair cascaded around her, covering her face. "Don't stop."

"But is this all right?"

"Mmhmm" was her only response. That, and she dragged her nails up my back and over my shoulders. My shirt should've muted her touch but much like everything else between us, it heightened the sensations. The fabric teased my skin in the wake of her fingers and a hot, dizzy feeling plowed through me like a head rush.

"You're such a tiny thing," I whispered, stroking her thighs as my hips bucked against her center.

"Not really," she replied, her words low and husky, as if she'd just woken up. "I'm nowhere near tiny."

"Ah, but you're tiny to me," I said, my lips at the crossroads between her neck and shoulder. "I told you the other night, you're fragile."

She hooked her leg around my waist and canted her hips up to meet me, desperate to find the rhythm she needed. "Does that mean you're afraid you'll break me?"

I shook my head, murmuring my disagreement. "I know how to handle you, Annie."

"Tell me how you'd handle me," she said. "Please."

"You don't have to beg me. Not ever," I answered. I wrapped my arms around her, boosting her up for better leverage, and thrust into the notch between her legs. The warm spot there was growing wetter by the minute. "I'd push a finger inside you, and then another. I wouldn't have to warm you up because you're always hot for me. Aren't you, beautiful?" A broken gasp slipped from her lips as she nodded. "When I couldn't bear the sight of your round ass rocking on my hand anymore I'd get my cock out. Slide right in, all the way."

"Oh my god," she panted. "Jackson."

"Yes, Annie?" I continued rutting into that sweet spot between her legs but never delved beyond the cotton barrier. In a sense, she hadn't granted me that permission. The occasional chastity and uneven boundaries we'd established were nothing short of illogical but this wasn't the time to renegotiate. She wanted to know how I'd fuck her and I intended to illustrate that...without touching her underwear.

"I'm—I'm close," she whisper-shrieked.

"I know, beautiful," I replied, picking up speed. The refrigerator was rocking along with us now, creaking on its casters and shuffling against the adjoining cabinets. "You're going to give it to me."

"Tell me," Annette started, "what happens after you—you're inside me."

I figured I'd be shocked. I figured I'd wade in some incredulity that sweet, bookish Annette was dredging my depths for filthy stories. But I wasn't. This was Annette, sweet, smart, welcoming, generous—and dirty. To me, it made sense. I wouldn't want her any other way.

"You'd scream for me," I said, growling as my cock flexed the way it did when I was on the edge. I was ready.

So fucking ready. "You'd scream when I slammed into you and then you'd scream when I pulled out to do it again. You'd keep screaming as I held you down."

"And you wouldn't stop," she said between cries. I felt her nails scoring the skin at my collar, those little bites of pain like whips urging me forward. "Wouldn't stop for anything."

That was it. I'd held out long enough and the roughly whispered pleasure in her voice was too much. Just too damn much. "No, beautiful, I wouldn't stop until I pumped everything I had into you and you were all out of screams and until you couldn't stand on your own."

Her hands clawed at my back and shoulders, desperate to find something to hold on to. "Oh my god, yes," she panted. "I want more, Jackson. *More*."

Who was I to refuse the lady? I would not. No, not even if I was dangerously close to coming in my pants. We were rushing headfirst toward that outcome and for the first time in all my ejaculating years, I wasn't looking for an alternative. Her nails were raking down my back, her legs were tight around my hips, and her pussy was soaking straight through my trousers to my boxers. I was exactly where I wanted to be right now.

"As much as you want, for as long as you want, Annie," I vowed.

As I edged farther into her cotton-covered heat, my orgasm shot down my spine and released into my boxers. For a minute there, I was certain my brain scrambled. My vision shorted out and my ears filled with static and my hips went on pumping. I couldn't stop, even if I tried. My body was dead set on giving her everything I had and some of the things I didn't, and I couldn't stop until she was satisfied.

"But you wouldn't be finished," she said, her voice pitching high and dragging me back to consciousness. She convulsed against me, her legs tightening as she dug her heels into my ass. It hurt but it was worth it. "Would you?"

Her body pulsed under my cock as she shuddered and came apart. I kept rutting, slower, less urgent, but I couldn't bring myself to stop. As this point, I needed this as much as she did.

"Not even close. Then I'd take you into the bedroom," I rasped, "and fuck you right through the mattress. Like I want to fuck you through this refrigerator right now."

Another spasm coursed through me, a spurt for good measure, and I was done. From the feel of the vibrations moving through Annette's body, she was right there with me.

Neither of us spoke for several minutes as we caught our breath. That orgasm wrung everything out of me. I needed a big bottle of Gatorade, an entire pizza, and a night curled around Annette. Not in that order but all at once. Naked lady, food, electrolytes.

Slowly, the world around us came back into focus. The breeze was cooler now, damp. The smell of fresh peppers and tomatoes scented the kitchen air. Peaches, too. The refrigerator fan clicked on for a bit and then off.

I was a wet, sticky mess from my belly button to my balls. My grip on Annette's waist was fierce and my face was buried in her hair, and life was good.

"Whoa," she whispered, loosening her death grip on my shoulders. *"Whoa."*

"I love it when you say that." I kissed her neck, sucking a bit to draw another gasp from her lips. "Good whoa?" She laughed and the movement had me throbbing against her again. My hips still bucked lazily, not ready to abandon the cause. "Don't answer, just keep laughing. Your body feels amazing."

"Good whoa," she confirmed. "Really good."

I loosened my hold on her waist and then dragged my fingers up her thighs. I followed the line of her panties, tracing from hip to backside. I wanted to get rid of them.

"Hey, Jackson?"

I smiled against her neck. I liked this woman. I liked her a whole lot. "Yeah, Annette?"

"You're touching my panties," she sang.

"Yes, I am." I chuckled into her hair. "Am I wrong in thinking you're enjoying this?"

"Not wrong," she said on a sigh.

"That's what I like to hear," I replied.

She dragged her nails up and down my forearm. It was heaven. "But that's not the issue. You said you could touch me without going anywhere near my undies and I believe I've disproven that theory."

"In that case, I'll be wrong any time you want it." I

tucked her hair over her ears and dropped a kiss on her temple. This time, I was the one to pull away first. Given my condition, I had to. My boxers were rapidly shifting from pleasantly wet to uncomfortably soggy. "I'll be right back," I said, crouching down to catch her eyes. "Are you all right?" She pressed her fingertips to her lips, nodding. "Okay. Stay right there. Don't move a muscle. Got it?"

I stared down at her, waiting for a response. Her lashes brushed her reddened cheeks and she kept her fingers on her lips. Eventually, she inclined her head to the side and said, "Got it."

I stepped away from Annette and the loss of her heat sent a shiver through my shoulders. As I marched down the hall, I unbuckled my trousers and opened my shirt, ready to toss both in the hamper when I reached my room.

It didn't take long to clean up and change into a fresh pair of boxers and shorts, but every minute felt like one too many. I wanted to be back in the kitchen, pressed up against Annette and whispering every depraved thing I'd ever thought into her hair. She smelled like sweetness there; vanilla, sugar, spice. That scent gave me ideas, ideas that flew in the face of everything I believed. I wanted her in the kitchen, wearing nothing more than a frilly apron and her feet bare. I wanted her sitting in my lap and feeding me pie.

"I'm losing my damn mind," I murmured to myself as I zipped my shorts.

When I rounded the corner into the kitchen, I was faced with two facts.

One, Annette was still here. Given our history, I wasn't convinced she'd stick around when the afterglow faded. This was good news.

Two, she hadn't followed directions. She was busy slicing a tomato as if she owned the place. This was also good news. I wanted her to feel like she owned the place. I would've enjoyed some direction-following, but I'd survive.

Tugging a t-shirt over my head, I asked, "Didn't I tell you not to move a muscle?"

She eyed my torso for a beat, studying me as if she was deciding whether I met her criteria. I hoped to hell that I did. "You said something," she replied, waving the knife. "I don't recall the specifics."

"I'll forgive you this time." I grabbed two bottles of beer and knocked the tops off. "But only because the refrigerator is not the most interesting place to hang out."

She took the beer I offered, remarking, "Nor is it the most comfortable."

I smoothed my hand down her back and tugged her closer. "Did I hurt you? Was that too much?"

"I'm good," she replied, glancing up at me with a tight grin. Then she blinked, and a wall came down. We weren't discussing the refrigerator games any further. "Let's get this dinner going, okay? What can I do? These tomatoes were too good to miss so I got started on them."

We worked together to prepare the meal and chatted

about our days. I'd grown accustomed to living alone and this domestic back-and-forth was like speaking a language I'd learned years ago and nearly forgotten. I liked that language. I wanted to speak it more often and I wanted to speak it with Annette.

"What is this?" Annette asked, pointing inside the refrigerator.

I followed her gesture to the shelf of plastic-wrapped plates and jerked a shoulder up in response. "Food," I answered.

"Yeah, sure," she replied, still pointing. "But what's the story? These aren't your dishes."

She wasn't wrong. I had a rainbow of dishes and plastic food storage containers, none of them mine. "They are not," I replied slowly. "But I intend to return them to their rightful owners."

"But...but what is this all about?" she asked, inspecting a plate of pork chops and cauliflower. Lord, I hated cauliflower. I didn't have the heart to tell Mrs. Mulcahey that but I hadn't eaten a bite of cauliflower since I was a kid. Not even those weird purple and yellow cauliflowers my mother grew in her garden. I was no fool. Being purple didn't make it any better. "There's a story here and I don't think I can close the refrigerator until I hear it."

I set my knife down with a quiet groan. "The ladies in this neighborhood, they bring me meals. Dinner plates, zucchini breads, a Crock-Pot of meatballs. It's always something. I didn't ask them to," I added when

Annette's brows shot up. "They just come by with a plate or two."

And a story about their single daughter or sister or friend being perfect for me.

"It's more than I can eat," I continued, "but I don't want to insult them."

Annette dragged her gaze away from the chops to eye me up and down. "You seem like the kind of guy who can manage an extra plate or two without complaint," she said. "You have that eats-raw-eggs-for-breakfast look about you."

"I'm taking that as a compliment," I murmured, returning to the cutting board.

"By all means." Annette retrieved a few items from the refrigerator and set them beside me. "Should I expect Meals on Wheels to stop by tonight?"

I shook my head. "I doubt it. They've probably activated the phone tree and alerted everyone to prioritize the other bachelors this evening."

"Ah, got it," she replied, bobbing her head. "They know I'm here. I figured the mother hens would keep eyes on you, sheriff, but I had no idea they were spoon-feeding you, too. It's making me rethink the muffins and pies I've sent your way."

"Don't say that," I murmured. "I love your baking but it's a distant second to you."

She laughed and flattened both hands on the countertop. It reminded me of her hand on my cock. I couldn't help it. We'd shared nothing more than a few minutes in my office, but in my mind every second stretched on for hours. I remembered the heat of her palm, the tight curl of her fingers around my shaft, the confident way she stroked me. It was amazing—*she* was amazing—and I'd pumped the brakes.

Oh, how I'd regretted that decision. I regretted it when I went to sleep, aching and alone. When I woke up painfully hard. When I jerked off in the shower. When I glanced out my office window at her shop. Basically, all day and all night.

"Did you hear me?" Annette asked, forcing me out of my memories.

"No, I'm sorry," I said, running a hand down my face. "What did you say?"

She peered at me, her lips pursed as if she was holding back a laugh. "I said, does it bother you that people know I'm here? That they're forming their own conclusions and spreading it up and down the seacoast?"

Shaking my head before she finished speaking, I replied, "No. Not at all. Does it bother you?"

It wasn't until then that I realized I didn't mind the constant gaze of the townspeople if it meant I could steal time with Annette. Just a few days ago I was worried about keeping a squeaky-clean reputation but how could this be wrong? Sure, my thoughts were dark, filthy sins but my neighbors didn't have to know that.

I'd also considered that I couldn't court Annette's attention without getting serious as required by the "no tomcat sheriffs" rule around here. But I wasn't concerned about that now. I didn't have a different woman in my house each night and the serious part didn't scare me. Not anymore. If anything, I craved it. Seeing Annette out in the village or busy in her shop drove me mad. I could look but I couldn't touch.

I wanted the right to go to her, to be with her, to call her mine.

"It doesn't bother me because people talk about people all the time. It's just what they do around here," she said. "It's no different from anywhere else. We all know each other so it seems like everyone is meddling in each other's lives. They're not. It's the same as everyone in a circle of friends talking about each other. I don't mind the talking. I get it. It's human nature."

I blinked, waiting for the "but." Because it was coming. Her tone was too hesitant for any other word to follow.

"But"—and there it was—"I don't want to give people the wrong idea. I know I can't control anyone's ideas but I don't want anyone getting carried away with some notion that we're, you know, a thing."

I set my knife down and watched her. "And that would be a problem?"

"Maybe not a problem," she said, a little exasperated. "But a situation."

"And you're not ready for another situation?" I asked.

She gave a curt shake of her head but didn't meet my eyes, instead kept her focus on the cutting board. "No. Not entirely," she said.

I grabbed a dish towel, needing something to keep my hands occupied. "No situations," I said. I wound the fabric around my palm like a tourniquet. It was all I could do to hold back the argument burning on my tongue. "That's not a problem, Annie. I don't need any situations either."

WE ATE outside on the back patio, flanked by citronella candles to keep the bugs at bay. Annette was quiet, more than I'd expected. Then again, few of my expectations panned out when it came to her. I'd wanted her to curl up in my arms and let me protect her from everything beyond us, but she didn't want that. Not yet.

Annette pointed to a thin beam of light to the south with her fork. "That's the old Talbott's Cove lighthouse. Owen Bartlett took it over when he bought the land where it sits."

"Is that so?" I asked. Discussing Captain Bartlett—and Annette's relationship with him—wasn't my preferred topic.

"Yeah," she murmured, oblivious to my displeasure. "Up on the hill, overlooking the town, is the Markham house. You can see the roofline from here, and the flag pole, too. Their property extends way back into the woods. There's a dairy barn out there, a bunch of old cabins, even a cemetery. Their family has lived on that land for centuries. Judge Markham retired about five years ago and he wasn't thrilled about that. It's a complicated situation with him. His daughter Brooke—she's an only child—moved home from New York City not too long ago."

I allowed her to ramble as if she was telling me something new. I'd made it my business to know every patch of land and resident in this town, and enough about their comings and goings to know when something wasn't right.

I knew about Bartlett's billionaire houseguest within hours of him arriving in the Cove. I had an eye on the Nevilles' inn, too. I was still piecing together the whole story but I knew they'd survived a gruesome attack that killed Cleo Neville's immediate family years ago, and one of the perpetrators was still at large. I'd been keeping extremely close tabs on the Fitzsimmonses' property. There was no telling when their son would leave rehab and I wanted to be prepared. I was hoping for the best and rooting for the kid to kick his addiction once and for all, but I also knew the reality of the opioid epidemic. I'd seen it in Albany and I was seeing it here, and it wasn't getting any better.

"And over there is the mouth of Dickerson Creek, which used to be part of the old Dickerson Farmstead," she continued, gesturing toward the forest. "The high school kids hike up there in the summer and drink beer after Eskimo King closes down for the night. The Creek, not the Farmstead, that is."

"Thanks for the clarification."

"Anytime," she replied, tipping back her beer. "I know this is a small town but there's a lot more than meets the eye."

"Do you doubt my ability to handle the town's safety?" I asked with a chuckle.

"What? No. Of course not," she replied. "What makes you think that?"

I gestured toward her. "You've been schooling me on the people and places of Talbott's Cove for the past ten minutes and I have to assume you're doing that because you don't believe I know how to find my way."

"Oh, I—I," she started, tapping her index finger against her lip. "Sometimes I lapse into tour guide mode. It helped when I first opened the bookstore and out-of-towners would ask general questions like, 'What's good around here?' and I'd just tell them everything I could think of."

"I've heard that about you."

Annette leaned back, stared at me for a second, then nodded slowly. "Is that what people say about me these days?"

"They've said you're uncommonly beautiful, intelligent, and generous with your time and knowledge," I said.

She waved away my words. "You're confused. That wasn't me. It was one of my sisters. Or all of them, blended together and averaged out," she added.

"Excuse me, ma'am, but I'm capable of vetting my own intel," I countered. "And I'm sitting right here, in the presence of your uncommon beauty and boundless knowledge. I'd say it's a fair assessment."

"Are you flirting with me, sheriff?"

I tossed my hands up in the air. "Finally, she notices," I said to the night sky. "I'm telling you, when I first arrived, *everyone* told me you knew the nooks and crannies of this place better than anyone else. If I wanted to know what was up, they said I should get the pertinents from you."

"Oh, really?" she asked. I nodded. "Why didn't you ever stop by to get those pertinents?"

"I did," I said, laughing. "Several times. I discovered I couldn't talk to you for more than five minutes without wanting to touch you." I dragged my knuckles down her bare arm, not missing the slight sigh she released. "Why are you nervous right now? That's the reason for tour guide mode, isn't it?"

The breeze rustled her hair as she shrugged. "Yeah, it looks that way," Annette replied. "I am nervous. I've never been with someone without also having plans. I don't know what this is and I don't know what to do with it. Even with random hookups or friends with benefits, I had a plan. I knew where it was going and where it wasn't."

She glanced at me, her eyes shining bright in the near darkness. God, she was gorgeous. The kind of gorgeous that hid behind homecoming queen smiles and epic blueberry muffins and the simple act of being nice to people. The kind most people missed because she distracted them with books and stories about old farms and piles of local gossip.

"Do you need a plan?" I asked.

Annette lifted her hands and then let them fall to her lap. "I don't trust myself to make plans right now, not after everything that's happened in the last week or so," she replied.

At first, I assumed she was talking about us and everything from her naked confessions to this evening. Then I realized she was talking about Bartlett. I fucking hated that. I liked the guy but I couldn't deal with this unrequited love bullshit. Not even for a minute.

Through clenched teeth, I asked, "What happened with all that?"

She shook her head, frowning. "I don't want to get into it. It's complicated."

I leaned forward to catch her hooded gaze. "Not complicated. Not really." She started to protest but I continued, "You're a smart chick. As you just illustrated, you know everything about everyone in this town. Of all the people in the Cove, you would've known the deal with Bartlett."

She leaned back in her chair and crossed her arms over her chest. Clearly, I wasn't making the progress I'd intended for this evening.

"Yes," she started, "but—"

"Nope," I interrupted.

"But," she continued, "Bartlett and I go way back. I've

known him since forever and I wasn't really sure about—about, you know. His mom said it was a phase and—"

"Now that's fucking obnoxious," I muttered.

"And he took one of my friends to homecoming—"

"A million years ago," I said. "Here's what I don't understand."

"Oh, great," she muttered, rubbing her forehead.

"Why do you think that was good enough? I'm serious," I added when I caught her eyeroll. "Like I said, you're a smart chick and you have fuck-hot ankles. Why were you willing to rubber-stamp a relationship with a man who wasn't fighting off bears for the pleasure of your company?"

"There are no bears out here," she said, unimpressed. "Not usually. But it was good enough for—"

"Please don't finish that sentence," I interrupted. "I beg of you. Don't tell me that you'll hold out for a guy who isn't interested in you."

"Just rub salt in the wound," she said under her breath.

That stopped me. I wasn't trying to be hurtful. "I'm not trying to do that. I'm only trying to understand why you'd undercut yourself like that for Bartlett."

Annette blew out a breath and shook her head slowly. "I don't know, Jackson. I guess I need to spend some time soul-searching. Shall I leave to do that or am I allowed to finish my beer?"

Ah. There it was. The edge of Annette's patience. Even town sweethearts had one.

"Listen, I shouldn't have brought it up. You don't have to defend yourself to me. Whether you're making plans or not making plans, I can roll with it. It's your choice and I understand where you're coming from now."

Annette peered at me the way I'd probably peer at someone who made several hairpin turns in a single conversation. "What about you? How do you feel about plans?"

I reached for my beer bottle, needing something to keep my hands busy. Jerking a shoulder up, I studied the label and said, "Nah, no plans here. I should've said this the other day but I'm not looking for anything serious."

I tipped back my beer, a futile attempt at washing away the taste of my lies. If she'd asked me a week ago, it would've been true. I hadn't been looking for anything serious, anything that diverted my attention from the job and the reputation I wanted to build here. But now I understood why she was the town sweetheart, an institution like JJ growling at patrons and Bartlett pulling in lobsters. She was one of a kind, and she deserved to be treated that way.

By me.

"I'll drink to that," Annette replied, holding her bottle up to mine in a toast. "Now, let's make those scones."

10

SWEATING

v. To heat fruits or vegetables slowly in a pan with a small amount of fat so that they cook in their own juices.

Annette

JACKSON HAD IDEAS.

Big ideas. Relationship ideas. He claimed he didn't but that was a special slice of bologna.

I couldn't tell up from down right now and everything I felt with him seemed distorted, as if I was experiencing my life through fun-house mirrors. Aside from my issues—and my constant desire to dispense with undergarments while in his presence—he wanted me in a way I didn't comprehend. I'd never been on the receiving end of attention—*desire*—like this and I didn't trust it. It seemed too much, too fast, too good to be true.

Yeah, he brought out my inner stripper, the one who lived right beside my inner bitch, but sexual chemistry wasn't everything.

The reality was that I felt things for Jackson. Sexual things, emotional things, connection things. But he was the first man in ages to offer me a bit of attention, some affection. As I'd already learned, I could go for actual years with little more than a few special book order conversations. This avalanche of emotions was nothing more than Jackson tuning into me and turning me on. It didn't mean anything.

Right?

Right. Of course. I had this under control.

The scones, though, not as much. We had the dry ingredients measured and sifted—not without leaving plenty of floured handprints on each other—and most of the wet ingredients ready to roll. It had only taken us two hours to accomplish these initial steps. The operative ingredient here, the peaches, wasn't making things easy on us.

"Like this," I said, bumping Jackson with my elbow to get his attention. "Peel the skin off gently so you're not bruising the fruit."

"No bruises," he murmured, watching as I worked the skin off a peach.

This time, I nailed it. The last two tries weren't as smooth. "Now, you try it."

He held the fruit in the palm of his hand while he scored the skin with a paring knife, sectioning it into quadrants. From there, he worked his thick fingertips, of which I was intimately acquainted, along the knife's lines. He edged the skin away with care and precision, even when the fine flap slipped out of his grip or tore in uneven swaths.

But the problem I'd discovered with peaches—good peaches, ripe peaches—was the juice. A peak-season peach would sop all over your hands once cut, and this crop was no different. Just when Jackson was about to tug the last bit of skin from around the stem, the fruit went flying.

"That fucker," he muttered, grasping after the peach even as it sailed across the kitchen and landed near the back door with a sloppy *thud*. "That fucking fucker." Shaking his head, he turned to me, his hands coated in peach juice. "I'm the worst helper you've ever had, aren't I?"

I snorted out a laugh. Ladylike, truly. "You're the only helper I've ever had," I said as I went on a retrieval mission. "You might be fumbling the star ingredient—"

"Don't forget me mixing up teaspoons with table-spoons," he added.

"And that," I agreed, "but I'm not complaining. Help is help, and I'll take it."

Jackson tore a handful of paper towels off the roll and passed them to me. "You don't test out recipes with your family? Everyone's told me that your mom's quite the cook."

"Nope," I replied, an entire lifetime's worth of exclusion packed into one word. "We have different kitchen philosophies. Better to keep them separate than start a holy war, you know?"

"Let me make a deal with you," Jackson said, holding open the garbage pail while I deposited the runaway peach and the paper towels necessary to clean up its trail. "You do the baking, I'll wash the dishes."

For every action there is an equal and opposite reaction.

I didn't know why that thought burst into my mind like an annoying pop-up ad but it was there now and I couldn't force it away.

"Sure," I said, turning back to the countertop. I couldn't look at him. I didn't trust myself to meet his gaze without agreeing to his demands and that was a bridge I couldn't cross right now. "That would be awesome. I hate washing dishes. I usually fill up the sink and leave everything soaking in there for days. It's not until I need something and there are no alternatives that I'm compelled to wash anything."

Jackson slung a dish towel over his shoulder as he leaned against the island. "We have a deal," he said. "One last question for you, Annie."

Still concentrating on the peach in hand, I asked, "What's that?"

"Am I coming home with you tonight? Or would you rather I come over tomorrow to"—I swear on my life, his voice dropped a full octave and my undies fell off all by themselves—"wash you up?"

"Hmm," I started, "let me think about that."

The peach bobbled out of my grip, first popping into the air and then bouncing off my inner arm when I tried to reel it back in. Instead of containing the fruit, I volleyed it toward Jackson. Bless his heart for trying but he only made matters worse when it slipped out of his grasp and hit me square on the clavicle. It followed the line of my chest down, rolling to a sticky stop right between my breasts.

Jackson and I stared at the half-bald peach sitting just beneath the neckline of my dress before glancing up at each other.

"You're not allowed to distract me while I peel peaches," I shouted.

At the same time, Jackson said, "Now you really need me to give you a good washing."

I wagged a finger at him, and then reached in to retrieve the peach. "At this rate, we're not going to have any scones before three in the morning," I said, handing him the fruit for disposal. "This shit would never happen on *The Great British Bake Off*."

"I don't know what that is but I think we could put this stuff in the fridge and try again tomorrow." Jackson shrugged as he tossed the peach away. "It's a tough job but I'll roll up my sleeves and lick the peach juice off you." He hooked his thumb over his shoulder, toward his bedroom. "Just take off your clothes and I'll do all the work."

"You're rather gallant, sheriff," I said. I was like a three-year-old—sticky, sugary, in need of a nap. "But it's late and I should go. We have a bit more time until peach season ends."

He nodded as if he understood but I knew he didn't. To him, I was getting over a non-relationship and being ridiculously cautious with my heart. My vagina, too, but mostly my heart. He didn't understand my mind games, my mental gymnastics, my struggles to accept affection when it wasn't hard fought. But he was a nice guy, a gentleman, and he respected the boundaries I laid down.

"I'll walk you home," Jackson said, shoving his hands into his pockets. It was as if he realized the touchy-gropey-kissy portion of the evening was over. "Don't think you can argue this point with me either. You probably know everyone on this street and the location of every crack in the sidewalk but that doesn't mean I'm going to let you walk through town by yourself at this hour. I'll see you home, Annie, whether you like it or not."

I hummed in response, not confident in my ability to reply without overturning my plan to leave. Jackson was tricky like that. He seemed like the average good guy, all nice and polite with his ma'am-ing and charitable lawn mowing and collecting drunk girls from bars. But underneath the good guy veneer was a man who wanted to keep a woman as his own. He stewed with a desire to protect and serve that woman but he also wanted to belong to her. It traveled through his words and gestures, his stares and touches, and it was potent enough to run off with my thoughts. It made me believe that a man could want me—just me, just as I was—and that belief lodged a knot of confused emotion in my throat.

My head couldn't keep my heart straight—or maybe it was the other way around.

I reached for the bowl of cracked eggs but Jackson beat me to it. "I've got this. I'll have it for breakfast, since you claim I chug raw eggs," he said, gesturing with the bowl toward the epic mess we'd created in his kitchen. "Whenever you decide to revisit the scene of these crimes, I'll have everything waiting for you, and I swear I'll stay out of the splash zone until it's time to hit the pots and pans."

With my hands washed and my baking tools stowed in my tote bag, I laced my fingers with Jackson's and let him walk me home. In the harbor, sails jangled against masts. A dog barked in the distance and beetles hissed at the street lights. The midnight air was cool with a hint of damp sea breeze, the kind of air that folks referred to as "good sleeping weather." It was a blessed reprieve from the past weekend's wave of hot, humid days and equally unpleasant nights.

This would've made for the perfect weather to sleep with Jackson. I knew he'd be my personal furnace. My big grizzly. I bet he was a compulsive cuddler, too. He'd chase me right to the edge of the bed and then lock me in his strong arms all night.

I didn't know whether I was a cuddler or not. I'd never lived with anyone but my family and college roommates, and I didn't snuggle with any of them. I'd never had serious relationships either. I was always making big plans, always climbing.

Climbing didn't leave much time for cuddling.

We walked down the street and into the village without a word, and I was thankful for the quiet. It helped ground me in my decision to slow this—this flirtation. It was barely more than that, if I didn't include the nakedness and the one time in his office when we were *this close* to having sex and then the time he said the dirtiest things I'd ever heard spoken.

Just a flirtation. One that was dry humping its way out of control. *Dry humping.* My word. How did that even happen? I wasn't telling Brooke about this. She'd rake me over the seventeen-and-in-a-minivan coals.

When we reached the alley behind my shop, I gestured toward the building as if he didn't know where we were and said, "This is me."

"It is," Jackson said, bobbing his head as he surveyed the area.

"Okay, well," I said, my voice trailing off. "Thank you for the walk. And dinner. And attempting to bake scones with me." I hiked my tote higher on my shoulder, a move that separated my hand from his. "I should go. Up. Go upstairs. To the apartment. Where I live."

Chuckling at my inability to produce complex sentences, Jackson announced, "I want to see you to the door."

I lifted my clasped hands to my lips as I searched for

the words to send this man away. He was one of the good ones, I knew it. Too good.

"That's okay. I can't get lost on a single staircase," I said, regret thick in my words. "Jackson, I think"—I glanced to the sky, the moon and stars, and the dark expanse of the ocean for guidance but found none—"I think we should stop seeing each other like this."

Shocking the shit out of me, Jackson replied, "I concur."

"You do?" I snapped. I wasn't expecting him to agree this easily. If I was honest, I'd hoped for a tiny bit of protest. A lady needed hope, right?

He ran a hand down his face as he laughed. "I don't want to walk you home at midnight."

"Well, you insisted so that's not my problem," I replied, flicking my fingers at the street behind him. "I would've been perfectly fine on my own."

Jackson rubbed his brow, laughing. "I don't want to wonder whether I'll bump into you at the market," he continued. "I want to get your phone number from you and not from questionably ethical uses of my office. I want to have dinner with you and then I want to spend the night with you. I want to spend a lot of nights with you. As many as you'll give me. I want to watch you bake and then wash your dishes for you. I want to give the people around here something to talk about because the only dirty secrets we keep are the ones in the bedroom, you hear me?"

Without conscious thought, I took a giant step

toward him. It was the wrong direction but I couldn't help myself. "I want you to have that," I said, "with someone who wants it, too."

We stared at each other for the longest minute since humanity started measuring time. It stretched on and on as he stared at me, stern as always, and I did everything in my power to keep from taking his hand and walking him up the stairs with me.

It wasn't about me wanting him anymore. Feelings and expectations were wrapped up in this now, and I couldn't handle those.

"You have really big feelings and I don't know how to deal with that," I said, a little breathless. "My entire world has tipped and twisted in the past week and you're fast-forwarding ahead with these—these *plans*." Jackson gave me a slow blink but no other response. "I'm squarely in no-plans mode and you're—hell, you're picking out new dust ruffles."

Another slow blink.

"Jackson, say something or leave. Staring at people in the dark is creepy."

The sails went on clanging and that dog was still barking, and Jackson just blinked at me.

"I don't know what a dust ruffle is," he said. "I don't believe I've picked one out."

I ran my hand through my hair, sighing. "We're in different places. That's all I'm trying to say."

"I understand that you're not ready," he replied. "But

know this: I'm not going anywhere. I'm right here, waiting for you."

"I speak from experience when I tell you waiting isn't a winning strategy," I said, a rueful grin spreading across my lips. "Don't waste your time repeating my mistakes."

His eyes crinkled as he stared at me. "I don't see it that way."

"Find someone who doesn't make you wait, Jackson. It's not worth it."

Jackson took a breath and glanced away, his eyebrows inching upward. "I have to disagree with you there," he replied. "You might know this town and everyone in it, but you don't know me. If you did, you wouldn't try to change my mind when I already know it. You'd know I'm not a dumb cop fixated on somethin' pretty. You'd also know that I have enough patience to wait for what I want and enough sense to know when it's worth waiting for."

He leaned in, sliding his hand through my hair, and brushed his lips over mine. It was quick but earnest, making promises I realized he intended to keep.

"Good night, Annette," Jackson said, dropping a kiss on my forehead.

The forehead kiss hit me hard. Somehow, it was more intimate than the straightforward lip lock and it left me aching for more. And that—*that* right there—was the worst part of this. I couldn't believe anything I felt. Wanting more, wanting to leave, wanting anything; all of it came at me like the first steep ascent on a rollercoaster.

I didn't know what waited after the peak and I couldn't pry my fingers away from my face long enough to find out.

"Good night, Jackson," I replied, lifting my gaze to his. "I'll see you around town."

I already knew I was going to bake for him, see him, kiss him again. I knew it as well I knew my own name. Despite all the doubts and distortions in my mind, I wanted Jackson Lau.

And he wanted me, too.

A smirk pulled at the corner of his lips. "If I don't see you first."

Brooke: I just watched Jackson walk you home. Then he walked back to his house.

Brooke: Why, pray tell, was he doing that?

Brooke: Is it my turn with him? Is that what's happening? We're going to time share his ass? Full-on sister-wife this thing?

Brooke: If that is the case, it's in our best interest to draw up an agreement now. Terms, conditions, operational standards.

Brooke: I'll get started on the documents.

Brooke: Okay. Done. I had something similar sitting on my hard drive and it was easy enough to change the key details.

Brooke: I assume you're fine with alternating weekends

because I'm all about hard partying Saturday nights followed by lazy Sunday mornings and it would suck if I couldn't have him for those consecutive days.

Annette: What the hell are you talking about?

Brooke: Sharing Jackson.

Annette: Oh my god.

Brooke: What?!? It makes perfect sense.

Annette: I sent him home. He wants...lots of things.

Brooke: And by that you mean...anal?

Annette: OH MY GOD. Brooke!

Brooke: Am I right or wrong? I'm...I don't know how to interpret that response. It could go either way, really.

Annette: He wants a relationship. He wants something serious and official and, I don't know, long term.

Brooke: So...not anal?

Annette: It didn't come up, no.

Brooke: But you can't rule it out.

Annette: Again—OH MY GOD.

Brooke: Okay, settle down, Angel Cake.

Brooke: Remind me why you have a problem with relationships? Because I distinctly recall us drinking Moscow mules in Bar Harbor two months ago and planning our weddings.

Annette: It just seems like this thing with Jackson is too good to be true.

Brooke: You're being stupid.

Annette: Thanks, love.

Brooke: Seriously. You're letting this Owen shit weigh you down. Stop it now.

Annette: I am working on it, you know. I'm not trying to be this way.

Brooke: But you're going to see him again, right?

Annette: Yeah.

Brooke: Does he know that?

Annette: Maybe. Not sure.

Brooke: Good. It's good to keep men guessing.

Brooke: But since I have you here, could we talk about a time share arrangement?

Annette: Was I not clear last weekend? I'll fucking end you if you touch him.

Brooke: Okay, all right, fine. It's not a big deal. I'll just shred the documents I prepared.

Brooke: We really did make a hunter out of you.

11

BUN WASH

n. A sugar syrup solution brushed onto yeasted buns on removal from the oven to impart a glaze or assist in the dusting of sugar.

Jackson

I STEPPED up to the counter at DiLorenzo's Diner and tucked my thumbs under my tactical belt. Before arriving in Talbott's Cove, where the sheriff's department sported tan uniforms right out of the seventies, I hadn't worn a tactical belt in years. Once I'd climbed a few ranks with the New York State Police, I traded in the uniform for suits, but muscle memory always took me back to my earliest days on the job.

Waving to the diner's namesake, Joe DiLorenzo, I

turned down the radio clipped at my shoulder. "What's good today?" I called.

"Hiya, sheriff," Joe said. "It's all good. What? You think I'd serve you shabby chicken salad? This isn't New York."

This was our back-and-forth. I asked him about business, he made a playful jab at New York. If I was lucky, I got a side-eyed question about when I was heading back there. These locals, they didn't think I'd last.

"And thank god for that," I replied.

"I'll have your order up in a couple of minutes. Can I get you something cold to drink while you wait?" He glanced at the coffee pots and soda fountains behind him. "I've got a fresh batch of lemonade today. Some iced tea, too. What'll it be?"

"If it's no trouble, could you mix the tea and lemonade? Half and half?" I asked.

"Trouble?" he muttered. "What kinda joint would I be running if I couldn't mix a drink? You think that hack Harniczek is the only one in this town with a good pour? Please."

"I never doubted you." I stifled a laugh when Joe went on muttering about the price of an iced lemonade tea in New York. To his mind, everything outside the Cove was grossly overpriced.

Joe slid a plastic cup and straw across the counter before ducking back into the kitchen, still muttering. This time, he was fed up with taxes. I didn't disagree with him there. His absence gave me a moment of unexpected quiet.

When I visited local establishments on non-official business—namely, lunch—I often found myself bombarded with town gossip, safety concerns, and random gripes.

Today was different. The diner's lunch counter was mostly empty and the handful of patrons seated in booths were busy with their food and newspapers. They paid little attention to me beyond a quick nod or wave, and that seemed like a milestone of sorts. Rather than peppering me with questions to ensure I was tending to the town's concerns, they ignored me. Either they were too famished to leave their turkey club sandwiches or they trusted me to do the job.

"If you don't get your fine ass to that bookstore, I'm gonna fuck you up."

Alarmed, I pivoted in search of the low, smoky voice and found Brooke Markham. She stood behind me, hipshot, arms crossed over her chest, and a glare sharp enough to cut glass. I blinked, quickly taking in her impossibly tight pants that cut off below the knee and the baggy tank top that demanded I buy her brunch.

"I beg your pardon, ma'am?"

"Get your ass to the bookstore," Brooke said, biting out each word. "It's not complicated, dude. Go to her. I don't care what bullshit she fed you. She's lying. She wants to see you." She uncrossed her arms and waved them at me. "Also, she's a terrible liar. I'm assuming you're at least minimally competent, which means I'm also assuming you're capable of recognizing when Angel Cakes Cortassi lies her ass off."

"I'm sorry, ma'am," I started, but Brooke was quick to interrupt.

"Save your *ma'am* for someone who appreciates that shit," she snapped. "Perhaps the bookstore."

It was my turn to cross my arms and level the glares. "*The bookstore* isn't a fan of it either," I replied.

"The bookstore doesn't know what she's talking about," Brooke said, stepping into my space. "I know the bookstore is throttling your bandwidth. The bookstore thinks she needs time to sort through some issues." Her nostrils flared as she blew out an impatient breath. "The bookstore needs a push in the right direction because the bookstore doesn't believe she deserves a slab of prime rib like you."

"Prime rib?" I repeated, failing to hold back a chuckle.

"Oh, shut up," Brooke said, pulling a sour grimace. "You know you're hot as fuck. You're like six-five, two-fifty, jacked to shit, and your tan is a goddamn Copper-tone commercial. Aside from all that, you have hand-cuffs and say things like, 'it can and will be held against you.'"

I gestured toward her, openly laughing now. "Keep going. I thrive on positive feedback."

She rolled her eyes but the motion wasn't isolated to her face. It seemed to ripple through her entire body. Every last inch of her hummed with annoyance.

"If you don't turn around and go straight to the book-store, I will fuck you right up," Brooke said, leaning closer to stab her finger against my chest.

"Ow," I yelped, rubbing my solar plexus. "Was that a finger or a claw, Wolverine?"

"I'd call you a pussy but those things can take a beating and keep on fighting. You need to get to that bookstore. Today. Now. Run really fast, reverse time, and save me from this blasted conversation. If you don't, I'll tell everyone you don't like shellfish. They'll run you out of town with pitchforks and fire." She caught my arched eyebrow and continued, "Try me. When it comes to protecting my people and launching disinformation campaigns, I'm your worst nightmare."

"You play dirty," I said, careful to keep my voice low. This conversation needed to stay between us.

"If you think this is dirty, I won't abuse your tender mind with details of my more effective tactics. But if you ever want to know what really happened to the Sheppard Stevenson investment banking house before the housing market bubble burst, I know where the bodies are buried and I keep the shovel close by."

I studied her for a moment, taking in her white-blonde ponytail and diamond stud earrings. "The things you say, Miss Markham, they make me wonder whether I should call for a search warrant."

She reached into her tank top and retrieved her mobile phone. I didn't know whether bras now came equipped with pockets and it didn't seem like the proper time to ask.

"Do as you're told, sheriff," she murmured, busy typing and swiping.

I stared at her for a moment, not sure I understood anything I'd heard in the past five minutes. "What are you? Ex-CIA turned small town mafioso or something?"

"Worse," Brooke said, her eyes widening as she smiled up at me. "Ex-sorority president turned hedge fund manager." She regarded me as I accepted my order from Joe. "Go to her. I won't tell you again."

"Thank you for the advice, ma'am," I said. "I'll take it under advisement."

She narrowed her eyes and returned her hands to her hips. "Never speak of this conversation again."

From halfway out the door, I asked, "What conversation?"

She turned her head, just enough to stare at me from the corner of her eyes. "Very good. We'll keep you. Now, go. I have egg salad to retrieve."

12

DISSOLVE

v. To stir a solid food and a liquid food together to form a mixture in which none of the solid remains.

Jackson

DESPITE BROOKE'S ORDERS, I gave Annette space.

She needed some more time to get her head on straight and I allowed it.

Today, though, this was a different story.

Instead of dodging the station and Annette's morning rituals, I turned the tables on her. Armed with coffee and donuts, I headed to her shop a few minutes before she usually arrived. I needed that time to straighten myself out. I needed to pull it together and fortify if I was going to carry on a conversation with the beautiful book mistress.

I'd spent the past few nights reliving every moment of Annette up against the refrigerator. God damn, I needed to get her on a bed. Kitchen appliances were the wrong surface for worshipping quirky women.

I was unaccustomed to wanting a woman like this. Don't get me wrong, women were amazing and delicious, and I'd desired several over the years, but that was nothing compared to the run-through-a-wall-to-get-to-her desire I felt for Annette. This was a pull unlike any other, one that wasn't entirely comprehensible. I didn't understand how she could draw me to her, body and soul, as if she was my true north.

In reality, I barely knew Annette and she definitely didn't know me. It seemed that we'd skipped over those steps, and maybe that was the problem at play. We were operating on inadequate knowledge. We needed to talk...and stay away from refrigerators.

When the lights flipped on inside the shop, I parked myself near the door to catch her attention. But she spotted me long before she reached the door, pausing in the middle of the sales floor. Today's sundress was long and white with thin black stripes rounding the bottom of her skirt. No ankles to be seen but it was angelic and sexy as hell, all at once.

She shook her head at me but couldn't fight off a smile.

I could work with that—slightly exasperated but generally pleased to see me.

Rapping my knuckles against the glass, I called,

"Open up. I brought breakfast." I held up the cup carrier and pink bakery box as evidence. "Can't eat these by myself. It's a bad stereotype waiting to happen."

At that, she started toward me. Once the storefront window lights flicked on, the lock unbolted, and the sign turned over, she pulled the door open. The chimes tinkled overhead and I tightened my hold on the breakfast goods. It was that or risk dropping them while I dragged her into my arms because these past days and nights without her were a special brand of agony.

"Good morning," she said, stepping aside to let me in. "This is a surprise."

"A good surprise," I said, moving toward her. "Right?"

"Good, yeah," she said. It sounded like a concession. "It's also an awkward surprise."

"How so?" I asked. I was undeterred. Nothing she had to say was slowing me down.

"Come with me," she ordered.

"With pleasure." I trailed after Annette, captivated by the sway of her full hips. I was a slave for this woman and she didn't even know it. It didn't compute that I'd followed her into the storeroom until she plucked the coffees from my hand.

"Thanks for this," she murmured, taking a sip of cold brew.

I ran my hand down her back, starved for the feel of her. "I wasn't sure how you liked your coffee," I confessed. "But I asked around. Found out you like it cold and sweet."

Annette glanced up at me, her eyes the same shade as the beverage in her hand. "You asked around?"

"I did," I said, bobbing my head as I stroked her back. I didn't want to stop touching her. Not today, not ever. "Found out you like old-fashioned cake donuts, too. Chocolate."

"Dust ruffles," she murmured.

"No dust ruffles," I insisted. "You must think I'm pretty bad at my job if I can't query a local merchant without powering up the rumor mill."

Annette sipped her coffee, her eyebrow arched especially for me. "That is not my suggestion, no," she said. "You might know your detective work but I know this town, and I know everyone and their auntie will be in here this afternoon looking for juicy bits."

"Lucky for you, I picked up coffee and donuts for most of the shopkeepers on Main Street. Everyone and their aunties will have several stops on the juicy bits tour today." She rolled her eyes but she smiled while doing it. "Just doin' my part to keep the local economy chugging along, ma'am."

"Appreciated." Annette set the coffee down and turned toward the small refrigerator tucked into the back corner. "Seems like we've both put a lot of effort into donuts."

She returned, handing me another one of her Pyrex containers. I pulled the top off and stared at the powdered sugar lumps. "And these are...?"

"My awkward donut holes," she replied, pinching one

between her fingers. Raspberry jam dribbled out. Some very primitive corner of my mind found that arousing. I didn't want to understand it. "My kitchen is too small for a full-scale donut operation so I went with the holes instead. I could make regular donuts but I'd have to fry them one by one and that would take hours. It's a new dough for me, a sweet brioche. I hope they came out well."

Annette held the not-quite-round ball to my lips and I accepted, gripping her wrist to lick her fingers clean in the process. "Delicious," I murmured. "But I have one question for you."

She watched as I sucked on her index finger, her eyes hooded, lips parted. "Anything," she whispered.

"Is this awkward because we both brought donuts or because you made them for me and I trampled all over that by showing up here with your favorite old-fashioneds?"

She blinked up at me as pink dashed across her cheeks. "I wanted to work on making a good brioche," she said, a touch of defensiveness in her tone. I sucked harder. "A-a-a-and I thought you might like them. I-I knew you'd like them."

"That's right, beautiful. You know what I like," I replied. "Another question."

"I only agreed to one," Annette argued.

"I'm asking anyway," I said, lashing an arm around her waist. God, she smelled good. "If I hadn't come here this morning, were you going to walk yourself over to the station?"

"Maybe," she replied with a shaky breath. "I might've fed the firefighters instead."

"Evil, evil woman," I whispered. I took the dish from her hand and set it on the nearest surface. "You wouldn't do that, not even to spite me."

"You don't know that," she said, shrugging. "For all you know, I like making you suffer."

"Oh, I'm well aware of that fact, beautiful." With both hands on her waist, I picked her up and set her on the table. "What do you think I've been doing the past two nights?"

"Reading that book you've had on your nightstand for months?" she quipped.

I pushed her legs apart and stepped between them. "Yes, that's exactly it," I replied. "Unfortunately, it's been a worthless distraction."

Annette's hands skimmed up my chest and over my shoulders. "Sounds like you need to get between some different pages."

I leaned down, my lips a breath away from hers. "Sounds like I need to get some fuck-hot ankles between my sheets."

"Just the ankles?" she asked, shooting me a sharp glance. "Are you sure you're not some kind of serial killer posing as a small town sheriff? Seems like a good cover."

"Not a cover. Not a serial killer. Not just the ankles," I said, kissing the corner of her mouth between each statement. "I want the whole package and the peach down your dress, too. Hell, Annie, I want it so much. I just need you to want it, too."

"I made you donut holes." She inched closer, nipping at my bottom lip. "That has to count for something."

I covered her lips with mine, sighing into her as she opened for me. My tongue stroked over hers, tasting coffee and sweetness. I'd planned on coffee and conversation, but Annette annihilated my best intentions. She always did, and I was the fool who still hadn't learned my lesson.

"It counts," I said against her lips. "It would count for more if you admitted you were walking your fine ass to the station and feeding me these donut holes in the privacy of my office."

Annette paused for a moment, blinking at my neck. Then, she said, "Yeah, I was bringing them over."

I could see her there, sitting on my desk with her legs spread while she hand-feeding me her best creations. Then I'd lay her back on the hard surface and taste her sweetness until she was shaking and writhing. I'd take her right there on my desk and let her scream down the walls. No one would doubt what was happening and no one would doubt she was mine.

"Now, admit you wore this dress because it is the most unholy piece of clothing in your closet and you like making me jizz in my pants."

Her palm shifted to my crotch and she stroked me over my trousers. We could talk later. We had all the time in the world so long as she kept touching me. I wasn't much for conversation before noon anyway. I bucked into her hand, every inch of my body tightening as my head fell back on my shoulders and I let loose a growl too animalistic to be human.

I wasn't the kind of man who lost control. I didn't lose my temper or find myself at the end of my rope too often. I worked hard to keep a cool head. But a few minutes with Annette canceled it all out. I was ready to riot if it meant getting my hands on her.

"I knew you'd like it," she purred. "You love it when I wear white. That, and no one will notice the powdered sugar all over me."

"The last time you wore white, you didn't let me admire you for long," I said. "Not that I minded you getting naked at my house. If you recall, I've been inviting you to do that again."

"Ah, yes," she said, sighing. "You should know I've had some rough nights as well. I've had a lot on my mind."

"I want to hear all about that." I growled into her neck, still rocking into the heaven that was her hand on my dick.

She laughed at that, the vibrations moving through her body and into mine like an electric shock. "Ah, but some things are best left unsaid."

There were so many reasons to step back, straighten myself out, and return to the plan. Aside from the fact we were in a glorified closet, I came here to talk with Annette. I wanted to build a connection beyond our history of complicated interactions. I wanted to make it work with her.

But my cock was a single-minded master and the cradle of her thighs felt like the only place I'd ever truly belonged.

"Annie," I said, grunting as I pressed into her heat.

"Yes, Jackson?"

I pushed her skirt up to her waist and out of my way, and then dragged my hands up her thighs. With my fingers twined around either side of her panties, I asked, "Are you with me, beautiful?"

The nod came first, then the words. "Yeah. Yes. I am," she whispered, her eyes dark and hungry.

"All the way?" I continued. "We're doing this, you and me? You're not going to tell me you need time to figure things out and show me the door when we're finished?"

Her shoulder jerked up. "That depends on how well you finish."

"You don't have anything to worry about there," I murmured, tossing her undies to the floor and wrapping an arm under her backside. Her hands went to my belt while I tugged the top of her dress down to reveal her breasts. "I've been waiting to lick these tits for ages. They're like perfect cupcakes with cherries on top. Bet they taste like vanilla sugar, too."

"You're ridiculous," Annette said, laughing.

"Completely," I agreed. Goddamn. This woman was so much *fun*. "Since I have to concentrate on your tits, I'm gonna need you to get these pants off me before you cause another accident."

"That wasn't my fault," she said. "Not entirely."

She pushed my trousers down and curled her hand around my cock while I tongued her nipples. She tasted like all the things I loved about her. It wasn't a flavor, it was a feeling.

I dropped kisses onto each of her breasts before working my way back to her lips. "There's a condom in my wallet. Grab that for me, beautiful."

She reached into my back pocket and retrieved the billfold. Instead of going for the rubber and tossing everything else aside, she took a moment to study my driver's license and glance at the cards inside. All while her other hand stroked me to within an inch of sanity.

"How long have you had this?" Annette asked, pinching the condom between two fingers. "I have an IUD but I like to cover all the bases."

"It's new. You can check the expiration date," I said, the words turning into groans as her grip tightened. "With the exception of last week, I'm always prepared."

"Are you always such a Boy Scout?" she quipped, tearing the packet open with her teeth.

"Put the goddamn condom on me," I ordered, my jaw clenched. I couldn't take another minute of this hand job or her smart-ass comments. The combination was lethal. "Do it now, Annie." Her eyes widened, sparkling as if she enjoyed my rough tone. If that was the case, I had plenty more where that came from. "Now or I'm fucking you without it."

She kept her gaze steady on me while she rolled the condom down. Once it was in place, we stared at each other, our lips no more than a breath apart. She gave me the tiniest of nods and I pushed inside her.

The first moment was heaven. Annette cried out, I buried a groan-turned-growl in her neck. She rocked into me, I nearly blew it all right then. It was so good, terrifyingly good. Good because she felt like absolute perfection but terrifying because I knew I was a goner for this girl. I was gone when I started lusting over her ankles but this was some higher-level cosmic soul mate shit.

"Keep yourself still, beautiful," I barked, my hand flat on her back.

"Don't want to," she replied, her ankles locking at the base of my spine as her body rolled against mine. "Can't make me."

I dragged in as much oxygen as I could but it wasn't enough. My body was diverting all resources toward moving in Annette and as long as I could do that, nothing else was necessary.

"Yes, I fucking can," I snapped, sliding my fingers down the seam of her ass.

She clawed at my back, her nails blunted by my shirt. I hated that shirt for existing. I wanted it gone. I wanted me and Annette, and a bed and all the time in the world, and I wanted everything else to go the hell away.

I pressed two fingers to her ass. Her entire body shuddered against me. "See? I made you do that."

I slammed into her like I was trying to prove a point. Maybe I was. Maybe I wanted her to know we were better together than either of us could've guessed.

"Right there, right there, right there," she gasped.

"If you'd stop squirming for a second, I'd get you right there," I said, squeezing the cheeks of her ass hard.

"You love my squirming," she argued.

She was right. I loved the way her compact body fit with mine and how her hips matched my rhythm without faltering. And now, with her thighs clenched around me and her hands fisted in my hair, I loved the way she clung to me while I fucked her mindlessly. I was coming apart piece by piece, splintering with her every whisper and plea.

"Jackson," Annette cried out. *"Jackson."*

Her lips found my neck and stayed there as I drove into her, too consumed by these sensations to respond with more than my body's instincts. Oh, this hurt. Everything ached, straight down to my bones. My body was fevered, my blood pounding in my veins. My muscles were pumping hard, pushing, pushing, pushing. Tightening as I held myself off, spasming as I surrendered to the pain. I couldn't hold on another minute without cracking right in half.

The front door chimes sounded at the same moment I blasted into the condom, shooting hard enough that I wondered how it could stay intact. Annette pressed her palm to my mouth, muffling my roar. I went rigid, every last inch of me, as I emptied myself into her. It was like a dam bursting.

"I'll be right with you," she called, running both hands through my hair. "Just give me a minute. Or five."

The customer replied with some comment I couldn't hear over the fuzzy noise in my ears.

When the last spurt pulsed through me, I laid Annette back on the table, dropped my head between her breasts, and closed my eyes. I needed to deal with this condom but I was sleepy-sated and didn't think I could peel myself from this heaven for anything. Not when I was still half hard inside her and thinking up ways we could make this table work for us one more time.

I could pull that off. Bend her over, flip that skirt up, slap her ass, hold her down just the way she liked. Yeah, that would do just fine.

"What are these little growls all about?" Annette asked, her fingers making magic on my scalp.

"Thinking about fucking you on this table," I mumbled.

"We just did that," she said.

"Mmhmm. I want to do it again."

She traced the tendons in the back of my neck, dissolving every ounce of tension stored there. "I like that idea."

When I gathered my senses, I pushed up on an elbow and pressed a kiss to her lips. "Please tell me we have time for that. Also, I need you to tell me I imagined someone coming into the shop."

"Nope, that really happened," she replied.

I shook my head against her chest. "This wasn't what I had in mind when I came here this morning," I said, glancing at up her.

"Are you sure about that?" Annette asked, her lips pursed in the best pout ever. Loved that pout.

"Actually, yes," I replied. "But then I saw you in this white dress and you had little donuts for me, and I am powerless when it comes to you and your pastries."

Her eyebrow arched up. "My baking isn't intended to turn you on."

I gave her a quick shake of my head. "Neither are your ankles, beautiful. You just can't help it."

13

PROOFING

v. The period of time the dough must rest after dividing and rounding.

Annette

Brooke: I was on the front porch just now, staring at the ocean and wondering how my life managed come apart at the seams like the last days of Rome, and who did I see sneaking out the back door of your shop but Sheriff Lau.

Brooke: I have to assume he was leaving after a quick morning romp and I am impressed.

Brooke: I have a multitude of questions but I am still impressed.

Annette: Thank you.

Annette: And your life hasn't fallen apart. You're doing awesome.

Brooke: Don't distract me from the topic at hand but you're wrong, my life is a Shakespearean tragedy and I am never more than five minutes away from floating myself down a damn stream like Ophelia.

Annette: Why don't we unpack that for a second?

Brooke: No. No. I'd rather hear about your quickie, please. The thrill of your life is the only thing keeping me going.

Annette: I'm still processing but here's what I know for sure. It didn't seem quick.

Brooke: Ohhhhhh that's the best kind.

Annette: It was incredible. I've never had sex like this before. I'm smiling like a lunatic and my belly feels like cotton candy.

Brooke: Does this mean you've completely foreclosed the possibility of a sister-wife setup? If there were any two women who could make it work, it would be us.

Annette: I love you but if you say that again, I'll tear your eyes out.

Brooke: Fair enough.

Brooke: When are you seeing him next?

Annette: I'm not sure. He got a call and had to go check on something near the Nevilles' inn.

Brooke: That place is fucking haunted.

Annette: No disagreement here.

Brooke: You didn't articulate next steps? Didn't establish expectations going forward? He just zipped up and zipped out?

Annette: I could barely speak when he kissed me good-bye. I was in no condition to formulate action plans.

Brooke: He really knows what he's doing, huh?

Annette: My head is fizzy like sparkling water, my chin is still trembling, and I can't feel my lips. Aside from sex in the storeroom, he brought me cold brew and chocolate old-fashioneds and said really sweet things. I almost told him I loved him.

Brooke: I wouldn't blame you. I love him for you.

CONFIDENCE WAS A TRICKY THING.

For years, I'd believed my big aspirations for my tiny bookstore were within reach if I worked hard enough. If I did the right things and put in the time, people would come. Even when I only sold a handful of books each day, I kept on believing my work would pay off.

That confidence moved me forward when I was barely covering my expenses and my family wanted me to give it up for a reliable income. It pushed me out of my disappointment when I couldn't snag big-name authors for an in-store visit during their book publicity tours. It picked me up when I couldn't convince the locals to join a book club unless I was offering free food and wine.

And it was that confidence that had me nodding in smug agreement when I woke up this morning to find my sweet little shop listed as one of the best independent bookstores in the country.

The country.

At first I thought it said *county* and that seemed plausible. But then I noticed the next bookstore on the list was in Culver City, California and realized this list had nothing to do with my county. Repeated mention of works by local artists, photographers, and diverse authors I stocked here had me thinking back to Cole, Owen's deckhand boyfriend. He'd gushed about one of my Maine photography books. Bought several copies, too. With his fancy black card, the kind reserved for professional athletes and movie stars and other special people. When I followed the article's threads back to the beginning, I discovered it was first posted on a small site two weeks ago. Only days after Owen, Cole, and all the vodka in the Cove.

But I shook that coincidence off. The shop was inundated with customers today and I wanted to focus on that rather than the strange sequence of events leading to my shop being full. People came from Bar Harbor, Kittery, even Portsmouth, all touting the online article that was now trending on all the local news sites.

My shop had never seen traffic like this. I had to call in my part-time sales clerks, Jane and Yosefina, just to keep up with the mad rush. I barely had a minute to pee but I found a few moments to wonder whether Jackson was watching me from his office. I hoped he was watching. I hoped he was still thinking about me and us and yesterday morning. I wanted it even when wanting scared the shit out of me.

That confidence, it sure was tricky.

Around noon, I took a call from someone at an internet company wanting to help me develop an online storefront. I'd never considered such a thing. It came at the perfect time, since I'd spent the morning juggling customers in-store and fielding calls requesting many of the local books and gifts I stocked here.

By four o'clock, the Portland newspaper had called to schedule an interview. They were working on a series about female-run businesses and wanted to come up to Talbott's Cove to visit.

Shortly before closing time, Jackson appeared in my shop, his height and heft sucking up the oxygen around him. My gaze scraped over the long lines of his body without conscious thought. He was dressed in sheriff's garb today. I couldn't decide which look I preferred, the suit or the uniform. He seemed more comfortable in suits but more authoritative in the uniform.

As I watched him scanning the shop, his gaze passing over each customer before landing on me with an easy smile, I realized I craved both his comfort and his authority. Even when I didn't know what to believe or where to stow my trust, Jackson wrapped me up in his steady strength. I liked that. I didn't understand it or know the right way to embrace it, but I liked it.

He lifted his fingers to his head, tipping an invisible hat toward me. "What's going on here?" he mouthed from across the room.

I held up my hands and let them fall to the counter.

When I registered a pinch in my cheeks, I realized I was grinning at him like a madwoman.

I was roused from my staring contest when a customer bustled up to the counter with a pile of books the length of her arm. "Do you have the next book in this series?" she asked, holding a paperback up. "I couldn't find it but I wasn't sure if you had a special supply in the back."

"I can check. Give me a minute." I caught Jackson's eye over her head. He winked, as if he knew I was thinking about yesterday morning. I was never looking at my grandmother's old kitchen table the same way again.

Once I was alone in the storeroom, I pressed my hand to my chest and surrendered to shuddering breaths. Of all the things that had happened today, it took Sheriff Lau tossing a wink in my direction to get my heart hammering against my ribs and my lungs begging for oxygen. Not to mention the heat between my legs and the ever-present urge to drop my drawers. I stood there a moment, cataloging my body's reaction to this man.

A hat tip, a smile, a wink. That was all it took.

After collecting a few books, I returned to the counter and finished the sale. Jackson was tucked into the nonfiction corner with a new political hardcover. I watched him while he flipped through the book, stopping every few pages to skim the text. And I wasn't the only one watching him. Nearly every customer shot glances in his direction, taking in his broad shoulders and the height that forced everyone to crane their necks.

I signaled for Yosefina to take over the sales counter and then made my way to Jackson. When I reached his side, I tapped the book cover. "Getting between some new pages?"

He shifted, turning his back to the shop as he studied the shelves. From the other side of the shop, I was certain it appeared we were carrying on a quiet but book-centric conversation.

"Haven't thought of anything but getting between your pages since I left here yesterday morning," he said, his voice low and rough. "I'm sorry I had to run out like that. I've been keeping my eye on a situation and ended up dealing with it all day, and—"

"No apologies," I interrupted. "I had customers and it was nine o'clock in the morning and it just wasn't the time."

Jackson looked away from the shelves, his gaze landing on my lips and sliding down the v-neck of my blue wrap dress. "It damn well better be the time soon," he said. "I haven't been able to think of anything but bending you over that counter since I walked in."

I dragged my tongue over my parched lips. "You should tell me about it. To get it off your mind."

A switch flipped in Jackson, shutting down his cool, calm sheriff vibe and turning on the starved, sexual man I was beginning to adore. His jaw locked, his lips pulled up in a naughty smirk, his nostrils flared. He was verging on snarling bull and I couldn't help but lean closer to him.

Jackson shot a glimpse across the shop. "Turn off all the lights. Lock the doors. Get you behind the counter," he said, each statement rushing out in a huff. "Skirt up, underwear down. Wrap your fingers around the edge of the counter because you'd need to hold on to something." He dragged his knuckle from the base of my throat to the valley between my breasts. "Get my cock out and slide inside you, fuck you, lose my damn mind on you."

A choked sob slipped past my lips and I didn't try to cover it up. There was no point. My nipples were tunneling their way through the fabric of my bra and dress, my cheeks were flushed, and my chest was heaving with erratic, choppy breaths.

I turned my head toward Jackson but didn't meet his gaze. I couldn't. If I took one look at his hot, hungry eyes, I was going to climb him like a jungle gym and demand he take me right up against the boring-as-hell political manifesto books.

"This place will be cleared out in ten, maybe fifteen minutes," I said.

"And yet we could be upstairs in your apartment in three," he replied. "Decisions, decisions."

"My apartment is small," I cautioned.

I didn't know why I said that about my sugar-cube-sized apartment. It seemed like I should warn him that me and my existence were less than he was anticipating. Even if I'd wowed him with muffins and pies and a tumble on the back table, I didn't want to escalate his expectations. I didn't want to disappoint him.

"But it has a bed?" He shuffled, causing his elbow to brush my arm, and a tiny purr rumbled in my throat.

"It does," I replied.

"That's all we need," he said. "I've been waiting to get you in bed for months."

"More like weeks," I said, stealing glances over my shoulder at the remaining customers.

"Months," Jackson repeated, pressing his hand to my belly. "Believe me, Annie, it's been months."

His fingers stretched from the bottom of my bra's underwire to the top edge of my panties. He stroked me in tiny circles and lit a line of heat down my torso. I was aching for him, my core throbbing and clenching while my shoulders were strung tighter than ever before. The slightest tap could split me in half and leave me in shards on the floor.

The door chimes sounded and I shot another glance over my shoulder. The shop was nearly empty, only two customers still perusing the shelves. On any other evening, I would've been right there, chatting them up and staying open long past the official hours. Tonight, after dropping into the deep end of crazy-good publicity, I was shutting this place down.

"All right, here's the plan," I said to Jackson. "Go on upstairs. The door's open and I'll meet you there in five minutes."

"The door is open? Why would that be the case?" he asked, separating his warm hand from my belly.

"Because I left it open," I said. "I burnt some orange brioche rolls last night and needed to air the place out."

Jackson shook his head as he backed away from me. "We'll talk about that later," he promised. "The burnt rolls *and* the unlocked doors. And the pepper spray I want you to keep in your bag."

"Later," I said, holding up my hands in surrender. "We'll talk about everything."

I MANAGED to hurry the stragglers along, lock up the cash, send Jane and Yosefina home, and secure the shop in three minutes. I moved with the singular purpose of getting upstairs and getting under Jackson. It didn't matter whether it was loaded with complications or weighed down with all my doubts and issues. Right now —tonight—I was setting all of it aside. I could want Jackson and have him without getting lost in the thicket.

If I kept telling myself that, it would be true.

I climbed the stairs and pushed open the screen door to find Jackson standing in the middle of my apartment and his sheriff's belt slung over the back of a kitchen chair. He seemed too big for my cozy home, too male for my flamingos-and-pink-pineapples décor. But he crooked his finger at me and I went to him, dropping my phone, bag, and keys to the floor.

Too big, too male, too right.

"That was six minutes," he said, tracing the line of my dress's v-neck.

"I know, I know," I replied with a sigh. My fingers went to his short-sleeved uniform shirt, attacking the buttons as I groaned about my most talkative sales clerk. "Jane usually works a few weekend hours for me and was able to come in today because, you know, a million people came through the shop. Yosefina too but she's antisocial so that's good. But Jane wanted to talk about those million people and didn't realize I was trying to, uh, I mean—"

"Go home and get fucked?"

I stopped unbuttoning, flattened my hands on his hard chest, and looked up. "Yeah. Yes. That. She didn't understand that and I wasn't prepared to explain it to her."

"She didn't need an explanation. We're the only ones who need to know." Jackson reached for the tie at my waist, loosening it with one finger. When it fell away, he loosened the internal tie. My dress hung open, revealing my mismatched panties and bra. He ran his knuckles over the rise of my breasts and down my belly. "*Annette*," he rasped.

I went back to working his buttons and opening his trousers, my gaze steady on the barely covered wall of muscle in front of me. After everything we'd shared, this was the first time I was getting my hands on his naked skin. Anticipation hummed through my veins, electrifying every touch and breath.

"Mmhmm?"

"Am I allowed to touch your panties tonight?" he asked. "Because I want to. I want to twist them around my fist and rip them off."

I pushed his shirt over his shoulders, letting it fall to the floor. A white cotton t-shirt separated me from his chest and I pushed it up, driven by my need to touch him. All of him.

"Annette," he prompted.

"What?" I murmured, busy tugging the t-shirt over his head. When it was free, I smoothed my hands up the hard ridges of his abs and across his chest. There was a dusting of golden hair there, barely dark enough to stand out against his skin. But I loved the feel of those coarse strands under my palms. "Oh, this is nice."

"All right, that's it," he said, bending down and hoisting me over his shoulder. He marched through my apartment and into the bedroom, yanking off my undies as he went. "Won't be needing these."

With more care than I expected from him right now, he set me on the bed and freed the dress from my shoulders.

Jackson pointed toward my bra as he kicked off his shoes, socks. "Get rid of that," he ordered.

He pushed his trousers down, stepped out of them. Only his boxers remained, and the huge erection stabbing at the fabric.

"Annette," he said, dragging my gaze away from his crotch. "The bra. Lose it."

He dropped his knee onto the bed and my legs fell open. I reached back to wrest open the clasp then flung my bra aside. I was naked and waiting, my most intimate places revealed to him. But it wasn't self-consciousness (hello, belly rolls) or doubt (what if I wasn't good in bed?) that sent a herd of buffalo stampeding through my stomach. It was that I knew I could love him and maybe I already did.

And wasn't that hysterical? After everything I'd experienced in the past couple of weeks and all my efforts to curtail my attraction to Jackson, I was carving out a spot for him in my heart. I already knew it was a deep, yawning cavern, a space he'd grow into over the years. Yep, it was absolutely hysterical because even as I went on making room for him, I didn't trust myself to give him the keys. It belonged to him but I couldn't let him take ownership.

Not yet. Not until I understood us better, knew it was real. I was the queen of mind games, after all. I'd carved out space for a man before. I'd handed him the keys, too. I wasn't going to be so giving this time. It wasn't like we were in any rush. Nope, no rush. We had all the time in the world.

"Jackson," I said, holding out my hand. The way he stared at me, I was amazed the bed wasn't on fire.

He shucked his boxers and crawled toward me, his cock heavy and hot as it bobbed between us. I reached for him, needing an anchor. "You feel so good," he murmured, thrusting into my fist. "You're stunning. Do you know that? Looking at you now, I can't believe how beautiful you are."

"It's not like this is the first time you're seeing me naked," I said, laughing.

"It is," he replied. "It's the first time I'm looking."

A breath shuddered out of me as Jackson pressed his lips to mine. It was a sweet kiss, slow and generous, but the need vibrating between us was enough to register on the Richter scale. He knew this, too, and pulled my hand from his cock.

"No more. No more, beautiful. I don't want to come on your belly. Not this time," he whispered against my jaw. "Let me get a condom."

"We don't have to," I said, wrapping my arms around his waist to keep him in place. "I've been tested and I have an IUD and if you wanted—"

"Fuck yes. Yes, I want," he roared, his fingers finding my clit. He circled me there, unhurried at first then quicker. Much more quickly. "I don't know what to do with you right now, Annie. I want everything. I want to lick you for hours. Suck on your nipples and fuck you with my fingers. Feed you my cock. Tease you and find out what you like. Flip you over, fuck you from behind while I grab that round ass of yours. Flip you back over, wrap your legs around my waist and fuck you slow. I want it all and I don't know where to start."

I canted my hips and locked my legs around him.

"Let's start at the end of that list and see where it takes us."

Jackson took that recommendation and ran with it, sliding inside me with one magnificent drive. He stayed there, his body rigid and his breath coming in ragged pants. Then, after dropping his forehead to my shoulder, he started to move. His hips pumped in quick jabs, in and out, in and out. I dug my heels into his backside, urging him deeper. I wanted longer drags, harder thrusts.

"Like this?" he asked, pulling out and then grinding into me.

"Yes," I said, forcing that single word into thirty syllables. "You feel so good, Jackson. It's *so* good. I'm so full. Don't stop."

"That's funny," he said, chuckling against my shoulder. "You make it seem like I'd electively leave your pussy paradise."

"Is that what we're calling it?"

Jackson nodded, grunting when he rocked inside me again. He forced his arms under my back, holding me tight. "I'm not trying to be one of those guys who says it's better without the rubber but fuck me, you are fucking perfect right now. I don't want this to end."

"It doesn't have to," I whispered, my fingers scrabbling over his back, desperate to hold on to him as my body dissolved like sugar over high heat. Something about his grip on me, the way he gathered me up like I was fragile but fucked me like I was unbreakable, it tripped me into the immediate orgasm zone.

"Come on, beautiful," he murmured as the first wave of spasms rolled through me. I felt his teeth on my neck, my shoulder. Kisses all over. His cock moving in me, my muscles rippling around him. Clinging to him. His body went stiff as he sank into me again, his cock twitching and jerking as he emptied himself in me. "I've got you. Just let go."

And he did. He had me and the cavern in my heart, too.

14

CRUMB

n. The soft inner part of a loaf of bread or cake.

Jackson

"How do you bake here?" I asked. Wearing only my boxers and the lazy grin of a guy who just had incredible sex, I stretched out my arms, almost certain I'd be able to touch two walls from the center of Annette's apartment. I couldn't but I wasn't far off. "It's...it's tiny."

Annette's home was just like her: small, pink, and hemmed in with some awkward ceiling angles. And there were flamingos everywhere. Embroidered on little pillows, printed on mugs, painted in watercolor. The short, silky robe she was wearing.

"It's not that bad," she argued, twisting her hair up into a bun. "It works for me."

The kitchen and living room were separated by nothing more than a big footstep, and the dining room was a corner. Her queen-sized bed was tucked into an alcove to create the illusion of privacy. As much as I liked her, it wasn't big enough for the two of us. Or, more specifically, it wasn't big enough for me. That, and I kept knocking my head on the sloped ceiling.

"Your stove, it's tiny. The oven, too." I motioned toward the miniature appliances, the ones I'd expect to find in a child's play house. "How do you bake here? It must've taken you hours to bake all those muffins."

"Not really." She shrugged and moved toward the refrigerator. Also child-sized. "How about...hmm. Let's see what we have in here."

She opened the door and peered in while she stroked the top of her foot against the back of her calf. This common movement was sensual and intimate, and it had me crossing the room in two steps to wrap my arms around her waist.

"Hello there." She dragged her nails down my forearm. Loved that sensation. "You just can't leave me alone around refrigerators, can you?"

Kissing her neck, I murmured, "So what?"

"Just an observation," Annette replied with a laugh. She bent at the waist, forcing her backside against my cock. Without conscious thought, my hands shifted to her waist and my hips rocked forward. "Fridges really turn you on, huh?"

"It has nothing to do with the appliances," I said, a low growl rumbling in my throat. "All about you."

She didn't say anything for a long moment and I forced myself to be still, even as I craved her friction. Then, "I have cheese, rye bread, too. I made it the other night so it's not the freshest but it's good. I know I shouldn't keep it chilled but it's been so warm recently. It would've turned stale and moldy in a hot minute if I didn't refrigerate it. I also have a Sussex pond pudding with apples but that recipe didn't turn out anything like I anticipated."

I didn't know what Sussex pond pudding was and I wasn't about to ask. "Rye bread it is," I said.

"I have beer, too," she offered. "Grab some, will you?"

Our arms loaded down with bread, its accompaniments, and beer, we returned to her bedroom. The blankets and pillows were in a heap on the floor and the top sheet clung to a single corner but we nestled in with our snacks, no care for the linens.

Annette handed me a slice of bread topped with a hunk of cheddar, a dollop of sweet, spicy mustard. It looked like art. Everything she did was beautiful, thoughtfully precise. For the first time in my life, I wanted to stop what I was doing and photograph the food I was about to eat because sharing this with everyone seemed necessary. I wanted to say, "My lady made this. She made it from scratch. Isn't she something?"

And it didn't escape my notice that she served me before fixing her own slice. That was Annette's way.

"Is that okay?" she asked, pointing toward the bread. The bread I'd been staring at for a solid minute while I fantasized about Instagram captions. "I can make you a slice without mustard."

I leaned over, kissed her temple. "It's great," I said. "It's the prettiest piece of bread I've ever seen."

"Thank you for that but it's not particularly pretty," she said. "I didn't score the dough correctly and the bake was a bit uneven. I think the loaf was too big for my oven so the heat didn't distribute effectively."

"You know my oven's huge," I said, working damn hard to hit that innuendo. "You're welcome to it any time."

"Your oven is amazing," she said with a breathy sigh. My cock was interpreting that sigh as a point in its favor and I took no issue with that. "But, you know, that's—it's very nice of you to offer."

"But?" I prompted.

She was busy assembling her own slice. "But I can get along fine with my own," she said. "I don't want to trouble you."

"What troubles me is you leaving your home open for anyone to walk in," I said.

"Oh, stop it," she said, waving away my concern. "Nothing like that happens in the Cove."

I traced the line of her jaw with my index finger, drawing her toward me. "That's what everyone says until something happens. Don't leave your front door open all day, Annette. Don't leave the back door to the shop open either."

"Jackson, I've lived here my entire life. I know this town inside and out. You could blindfold me and drop me in the woods at midnight, and I'd find my way home without a scrape. Hell, I can identify most of the residents by the way they jingle coins in their pockets." She pinned me with a sharp look. "I know this town."

My finger still on her chin, I said, "I don't doubt that. I don't doubt you, beautiful. But I know a few things, too, and this town isn't as safe as you think it is."

She blinked, nodded. A flash of surprise passed through her eyes. "Okay. I'll work on it."

"And I'm getting you a can of pepper spray. You're going to keep it with you." I kissed her then, mostly because I couldn't get enough of her lips but also to head off her disagreement.

When we parted, Annette reached for the beer bottles on the window ledge. She passed one to me before taking a long drink from hers.

"What made you come here?" She ran the back of her spoon over the slice of bread, distributing the mustard to every corner. There was an eroticism to her ministrations, something captivating about the capable way her hands moved. "What about Talbott's Cove appealed to you?"

I felt my cock lengthening, hardening as I watched her drizzle more mustard over the slab of cheddar. Why was mustard drizzling sexy? What was it about the way she twirled that spoon over the bread and cheese that made me think of the kind of sex that resulted in broken bedsprings and scratched backs? It took real effort to respond to her question when I wanted to force her legs apart and taste her sweetness.

"I field this question a fair amount," I managed.

"I'm sorry," she said, biting into her slice. "I didn't mean to pry."

"No, it's fine. I like it when you pry. Talbott's Cove isn't the kind of town that brings in a lot of newcomers, and people are curious," I said. I sampled my bread—heaven. I still wanted to feast on Annette but that would keep while we talked. "I usually tell people that I wanted to work in a town where I'd know all the residents."

"But that's not the truth?" She licked a spot of mustard off her thumb and I couldn't hold back my growl. "Or, not the entire truth?"

"Yeah, not the whole truth," I admitted, staring at my beer. The beer wasn't licking its thumb or sitting cross-legged in a short robe with nothing but skin beneath. The beer was safe. "The whole truth isn't a good look for a sheriff."

"I'm sure it's a good look for the man I'm sleeping with," she said.

"Is that what I am?" I squinted at her, not under-standing her. "Is that all?"

Her words, they stung a bit. I didn't want them to but they did. I didn't know what I wanted her to say but I wanted to be more than the man she was sleeping with. And I would be. It was just going to take some time.

"Tell me your story," Annette insisted, patting my knee. "We'll save the labels for later. They go better with breakfast. I'll make you some cinnamon rolls with fresh caramel sauce."

"Fuck, yes," I said, laying both hands over my belly. "All right, well, since cinnamon rolls are on the line, I better get on with this." I laced my fingers around the bottle and stared at the ceiling, silent for a long moment as I gathered the words. "There was a missing persons case a few years back. A little boy disappeared, and the circumstances were highly suspicious. Conflicting stories from the parents, physical evidence that couldn't be explained away. Something about that case stuck with me. I couldn't let it go. Even when the evidence dried up and the trail went cold, I couldn't stop thinking about that kid and the gut sense that someone who knew him did something terrible to him. It kept me up at nights, interfered with my cases, drove me damn near crazy."

"That's awful," she murmured. "I'm so sorry, Jackson."

I forced down a mouthful of beer, trying to push images of the crime scene from my mind. Tried, failed. This job had a way of changing people, and that case changed me.

"It hit me hard when his body was discovered. Harder when the forensic evidence pointed toward the father," I said.

I'd never forget the anger that flashed through me

like a bomb blast after finding that boy's remains. The anger stayed with me, too. Followed me around for weeks, months. I'd always accepted that some violence was senseless but I couldn't accept this. For a time, I doubted whether I wanted to live in a world with the kind of savagery that had killed that boy.

"It hit me harder than any other murder investigation. I had some time off shortly after that. If I was smart, I would've seen the department's counselor and got my head straightened out, but I didn't. I hopped in my truck and drove east until I hit the ocean. Then, I headed north. It was an unintentionally scenic road trip through Rhode Island, Massachusetts, New Hampshire. I stopped in small towns along the coast, and by the time I crossed the border into Maine, I knew I needed to get out of the city for good. Part of it was the case. The other part of it was realizing I did want to work in a town where I knew every single resident."

"One small step toward saving the next kid?" she asked.

I blew out a breath but didn't respond until Annette ran her fingertips down my arm. "I realize that I can't prevent every crime, but in a town like this, I can keep an eye out for the signs." I shifted to the side, gazing at Annette. "What makes you stay here?"

A deep laugh rumbled up from her belly. "When I'm not chasing after unavailable men and getting sloppy drunk and generally embarrassing the hell out of myself,

I like it here. I like the people, the community, the way this place changes slowly but surely."

"Why are you still beating yourself up about that?" I asked. I dropped my hand on her thigh, needing some physical connection to her.

She avoided my gaze as she worked on another round of rye bread extravaganzas. "Because I'm probably banned from The Galley for life and I acted like an emotionally unstable drunk girl, and both of those things are embarrassing."

"That's not what I'm talking about," I said. "I think you know that."

Annette turned back toward me, a slice of bread in her outstretched hand. "Because I'm not so different from the town, Jackson. I change slowly but surely."

15

CREAMING

v. Beating sugar and softened butter together to form a lighter, aerated mixture.

Annette

AUGUST PEACHES WERE the best peaches.

This was the first summer I was paying attention to peach quality but I knew this month's crop was as good as it got. Last month's peaches—the one that ended up down my dress—didn't compare to the beauties coming out now. Since they were so damn good, I couldn't stop testing new recipes. My kitchen was filled to the rafters with cobblers and crumbles, crostatas and cakes. And that didn't include the pastries I'd distributed around town.

I'd shipped a peach and almond tart off to Brooke's

house on Monday and a peach and raspberry yogurt cake to the Fitzsimmonses on Tuesday. Jackson took a basket of cinnamon peach turnovers to the station on Wednesday and my sales clerk Jane got a peach and blueberry bread pudding on Thursday.

It was hard to believe I'd baked this much in one week. It helped that I had Jackson hauling in big sacks of sugar and flour for me and washing the dishes while my creations were in the oven.

As much I adored the kitchen at his house, I never managed to bring all the things I needed. Either it was the good sifter or the board scraper I always misplaced, or the paring knife I liked better than the rest. There was always something missing.

That was part of the reason I ended up back at my apartment after baking at Jackson's house. The other part was my own crazy mind game where I refused to accept I was falling for him but inventing a world of feelings based on good sex and well washed dishes. That crazy mind game was cool with the sex and the dishes but everything came to a screeching halt at the notion of spending the night at Jackson's house. That was the hard limit, the third rail.

It didn't make sense but neither did my fantasy relationship with Owen.

I allowed myself to believe it didn't have to make sense. Love didn't make sense. Hell, life didn't make sense. Why did my thoughts have to follow a logical sequence? They didn't and it wasn't worth my time to dwell on the roundabouts and contradictions in my head. Not when I could enjoy the time we had together and hope it all worked out for the best.

I hadn't planned on baking this afternoon but a thunderstorm rolled in and canceled my beach plans. I didn't take many days off from the shop but liked to reserve some Fridays and Saturdays throughout the summer. Not always the whole day but even a few hours away was worth it. Good for my tan, better for my soul.

I washed the frosting from my fingers and dried my hands on a towel while inspecting my latest bake, brown butter peach cupcakes. They stood in neat rows and columns on my cooling racks, perfect rosettes of luscious peach-scented cream cheese frosting on top.

I studied them for a moment, my hands still curled around the dish towel, then glanced to the clock. Jackson was still at the station. He'd be there a little while longer.

I stepped toward the window and looked to the sky. Only drizzle and lake-sized puddles remained. The worst of the storm was on its way north.

Seemed like the right time to deliver a snack.

I KNOCKED on the door to Jackson's office and wiggled the glass container filled with cupcakes when I poked inside.

My stars, he was a sight. Legs open as if he was giving a master class in manspreading, his tan uniform trousers pulled taut over his tree trunk thighs. Phone pressed tucked between his ear and shoulder, a pen trapped in one hand, the other wrapped around the nape of his neck. With his arm bent behind his head and that short-sleeved sheriff's department shirt, it looked like his bicep was carved from stone. And now that I'd caught his attention, his dark gaze traveled over me, his eyebrow arched.

Jackson beckoned me closer as I shut the door behind me. He usually kept his door ajar but if history was any guide, we'd want it closed. The station was mostly empty but Cindy was out there and I wasn't taking any chances.

"Are you sure?" I whispered, pointing to the bullpen behind me. "I can come back later."

"Don't you dare leave," he said, his hand over the mouthpiece. His tongue poked out, tracing his lip as he studied my white sundress printed with green palm fronds. "Stay. Let me finish up this conference call but stay."

I moved toward the open chairs but he shook his head and motioned for me to come around the side of his desk. He repeated the gesture when I stood there, staring at him.

"Why am I going over there?" I asked.

"Because I want you over here," he mouthed.

With a saucy smirk, I rounded Jackson's desk and handed him the cupcakes. "Thought you might need a treat." I crossed my arms over my chest and leaned back against his desk, waiting for his reaction.

He didn't open the container. Instead, he set it aside and tapped his palm against the wooden surface of his desk. "Sit," he ordered. I gave him an *are you serious?* head tilt but he tapped the desk again. "Sit."

With an exaggerated eyeroll, I edged myself onto the surface. Jackson responded by grabbing me by the hips and dropping me right in front of him. He leaned back in his seat, his jaw tight and his eyes hooded as he looked me up and down. It felt like an appraisal. Then he nodded, brought his free hand to my ankle. His thumb stroked half moons into my skin.

"Eat," I said, my fingers drumming on the lid.

Jackson glanced at the container but responded with a curt shake of his head. I loved his stern sheriff vibe. He was such a soft, sweet teddy bear under the stares and head shakes and that made me love the stern even more.

I watched while he listened to the call, his brows sliding together or climbing up his forehead in reaction. Every few minutes he'd chime in with a comment or reach for his pen and scribble on the pad beside me. At one point, he scowled at the phone, rolled his eyes, and then dropped his head back against the chair.

Definitely time for a treat.

I pried open the container and scooped a dollop of frosting off the lid. I held out my finger to him, not at all surprised when he curled his hand around my wrist, tugged me forward, and licked every drop of frosting. His teeth scraped over the pad of my finger, sending electricity up my spine and through my limbs.

"You were in the kitchen without me," he whispered, pressing a kiss to the inside of my wrist.

"Don't worry," I replied. "I left all the dishes in the sink."

Jackson dipped his chin as his dark gazed settled on me. "Good girl," he mouthed.

Was it any wonder I couldn't keep my undies up around this man?

He reached for his pen, poised to write something, but then dropped it to the pad. "Thank you. I appreciate any insight the Bureau can offer on this matter," he said into the phone. "That's all. We'll be in touch if this matter continues to develop. Thank you again."

Jackson slammed the phone down, shot to his feet, and shoved his fingers through my hair.

"Look at you. Coming into my office in your pretty little dress with all your sweetness. Sitting on my desk like an angel waiting for permission to sin. Just look at you."

His lips hovered over mine as he watched me, waiting for a reaction.

"I thought you could use a break," I said, my gaze shifting from his eyes to his mouth. "And I know you like cream cheese frosting."

"Don't give me that," Jackson said. "You could walk in here with an empty potato sack and I'd still want to see you, beautiful."

I tilted my head up to meet his mouth, barely brushing my lips over his. A growl sounded in the back of his throat and his hands moved over my shoulders, down my back, up my flanks. He kissed me fast, almost aggressively. The desk was hard under my backside and I heard a crack of lightning off in the distance but none of it distracted from the way his tongue rolled over mine and he branded me with his kiss.

But then Jackson dropped into his chair and ran the back of his hand over his mouth. I was wild eyed and panting like a pack mule when he pointed at my dress and simply said, "Up."

"What?" I asked, my hands pressed to my chest to keep my heart from bursting free.

"The dress," he said, pointing. "I want it up."

I reached down, grabbing for the skirt's hem. I lifted it past my knees but stopped there. "Why?"

Jackson pushed the fabric to my waist but paused, his eyes narrowing as he stared between my legs. Eventually he glanced up, saying, "You brought me a treat and now I'm going to eat it."

I laugh-gasped as he tugged my undies down and tucked them in his pocket. *Oof.* I wasn't going to recover from the gleam in his eyes when he pocketed those panties. It was confident but also a little arrogant, like he knew what he was doing and he knew I wanted it too.

Jackson brought his hands to my thighs, pushing them apart as he scooted closer. His scruffy chin scraped the tender skin of my inner thighs and I cried out. It was a strange noise, somewhere between a yelp and a moan but also a little bit of *Oh, more, please, yes.*

Jackson glanced up at me, his eyes dark as night and his grin feral, and he said, "You'll get what you need, beautiful, but only if you're quiet. Can you do that for me?"

I nodded like a bobblehead doll.

He pressed his palm to my chest, forcing me back on my elbows, and then his head disappeared between my legs. I waited for what seemed like nineteen hours before I felt two fingers trailing over me. It was the lightest touch but the anticipation had my shoulders jerking up to my ears and my head falling back. Those two fingers continued tracing me from clit to core while he showered my inner thighs with kisses and tiny bites.

Every time his teeth closed around my skin, I was certain I was going to melt into a puddle and slide right off this desk. But then he released me and a thousand itty bitty fireworks went off in the exact same spot. It was a wild rush of heat and want and explosion.

It was making me crazy.

I was ready to tell Jackson that I couldn't take much more of this teasing but then those fingers parted me and he said, "You look fucking delicious."

His tongue swept over me and my elbows gave out.

Right there, that was it. I was done. Stick a fork in me. *Done.*

"Jackson," I whispered, reaching down to get a hold on his hair. There was something I wanted to say to him but I couldn't produce words when he was sucking on my clit. Just couldn't do it.

He pushed two fingers inside me and I had to layer both hands over my mouth to keep from moaning. His fingers moved in me, teasing over that perfect spot again and again. And his tongue on my clit and his scruff on my thighs. *Oh, hell.* There was no way I could stay quiet. This was too much. Far too much.

Desperate for a moment without his tongue and fingers and beard tormenting me, I twisted my fingers around his silky hair. He wasn't having it. He shook his head as he murmured his dissent.

"Jackson, you're killing me," I hissed.

His fingers stilled. He turned, kissing my inner thigh. No bite this time. "Good killing? Or bad killing?"

"G-g-good," I stammered. "Good killing. Great killing. Gonna lose my mind killing."

Jackson nipped at my thigh, setting off another itty bitty explosion before returning his tongue to my clit. But he didn't go back to business as usual. No, he redoubled his efforts. Leaving little bites all over my legs, my mound. Sucking my clit like he wanted an imprint of it on his tongue. Curling his fingers inside me until I went cross-eyed.

He did these wonderful things but he tortured me while doing it. Backing off when my hips started rocking in a rhythm with his fingers. Lapping at my clit when I wanted more circling or sucking. Leaving kisses on my folds instead of the little fireworks I was craving.

It was possible I could stir up a thunderstorm from nothing more than the electricity coursing through my body. Everything was amazing but the type of amazing that was almost awful. This *hurt*. My core clenched around his fingers. My abs spasmed as if I was completing my hundredth set of crunches. I was coiled tight and vibrating, my body far past the point of desperation. I was convinced I was going to snap right in half if I didn't come soon.

Just when I was ready to tear off Jackson's trousers and sink down on his cock, his thumb pressed against my back channel and I went off. A switch flipped and a roar of heat blew through my body. It went on and on, one bright, burning pulse after another.

"That's right," he said, his fingers still moving as the waves rolled through me. "That's what you needed. Isn't it, beautiful?"

He gathered me in his arms and lifted me from the desk, settling me on his lap. His cock was hard against me. Hard and impossibly thick. Though I didn't believe my body was ready for rough chair sex, I loved the way he wanted me. I rocked against him, drawing a growl from him.

"I can't have you the way I need you right now, Annie," he whispered, his lips pressed to the tender skin below my ear. "But when I get home tonight, that's how I'm taking you. Understand?"

I nodded, not sure I could manage much more. This was the kind of sex that required a warm bath, a heavy blanket, and a bottle of wine afterward. I probably didn't qualify for any of those things since it wasn't technically sex, not in the traditional sense. But dammit, I was having that wine. And a moment sprawled on the sofa with my arm over my eyes, too.

"I missed you today," he said.

I sighed at that. No one had ever missed me before. "That's why I baked cupcakes for you," I said, as if that explained everything.

"Because I missed you?" Jackson asked.

I shook my head. "No," I replied with another sigh. "Because I missed you too." I shifted back to glance up at him. "But also, I had all these peaches and I had to do something with them."

"Entirely reasonable," he said, laughing. "Why don't you spend the night? That way, you won't have to miss me tomorrow morning."

My thighs burned against the fabric of his trousers, each one of those bites throbbing as the endorphins subsided.

"Not tonight," I said with a decisive nod. When he stared at me, his brows pinched and his lips turned down in a frown, I continued, "Give me tonight to miss you and just imagine the new things I'll bake up for you. I promise, it'll be worth it."

Jackson dragged his finger down the line of my jaw and said, "You know you don't have to bake me anything. Right? I don't ask to spend time with you so you'll feed me."

"I know," I said, running my teeth over my bottom lip.

I knew that. I believed it. I wasn't using pastries with Jackson the same way I used special order books with Owen. It had taken me the past couple of weeks to get to this point but I believed it now.

"But maybe," I added, cutting myself off before I could finish. "Maybe next week. Maybe I could spend the night then. Or the week after, or something like that."

That was what I needed. A due date. A timeline for ending this crazy mind game. I could figure out whether I was falling for him or falling for more of my old bullshit.

"If that's what you need, Annie, that's what you'll get," Jackson said, patting my backside.

Goddamn. I wanted this to be real. I wanted it more than anything.

16

BEATING

v. The process of thoroughly combining ingredients and incorporating air to make cakes light and fluffy.

Jackson

I WAS DRINKING coffee in my kitchen, my feet bare and shirt draped over the back of a chair when my phone vibrated across the countertop. Even though Talbott's Cove was a town built on early mornings, only a few people would call me at this hour. Either there was an emergency or my mother wanted to chat.

A quick glance at the screen informed me there was no emergency.

"Hi, Mom," I said between sips. "Up with the roosters as always?"

"I'll sleep when I'm dead," she replied. "There's no

sense lazing about. I just don't understand what people *do* in bed all morning. I can't lie there while the sun shines."

"Don't I know it," I murmured. "Since the sun has been shining for"—I glanced at my watch—"twenty minutes, what kind of trouble have you found for yourself today?"

"I don't find trouble, Jackson," she said, immediately impatient with me. "Trouble finds me."

"Don't I know it," I repeated.

My mother was born with the energy of ten rabbits, the work ethic of five horses, and the strength of two oxen. It sounded hyperbolic but it was the straight truth. Bonnie Lau was incapable of slacking off. She kept a garden that most considered a small farm, worked as a certified nursing assistant at an assisted living facility outside Albany, and regularly volunteered for a dozen or so charitable organizations. Meals for shut-ins, rides for veterans, knitted caps for preemies—she did it all.

"Well, I just talked to your sister," Mom announced, a pinch of purpose in her voice. She was in family update mode. That was preferable to interrogation mode. "Rachel decided to extend her stay in Belize through the new year and will be joining Teach For America next summer."

"Are we sure she's in the Peace Corps and not just chilling on a beach in Belize?" I teased. "If I was in Belize, I'd be on the beach."

"She's involved in important community health outreach programs," my mother replied.

"Of course," I continued, still ribbing her about Rachel's yearlong visit to Central America. My younger sister shared my mother's boundless energy and drive to do good, but she also had a touch of wanderlust. "And sneaking in a bit of beach time. Who wouldn't?"

"It's a good thing you're my favorite son," she said. "I wouldn't put up with this malarkey if you weren't."

"Only son, Mom," I replied. "I'm your only son."

I took another sip of my coffee while I prowled through the refrigerator for something to eat. If only I had some scones or donut holes...and an equally delicious woman to share them with. Unfortunately, that woman didn't enjoy spending the night here. Which wasn't to say she didn't visit. No, she was here almost every evening. She'd come over and I'd defile her on any solid surface we could find, and then we'd cook dinner together and she'd bake. But she always left at the end of the night.

She was immune to all persuasion efforts, even ones that included me on my knees with my head under her skirt. She wasn't having it and I accepted that as another one of her craggy boundaries I wasn't to cross. Even if we'd been going about the sex-dinner-baking-no-sleep-overs routine for more than a month now, it was more important for me to keep Annette in my life than break through that boundary. She'd come around in good time, I was sure of it.

"Like I said," Mom countered. "We'll have a party for Rachel when she comes home next spring. I hope you can sneak away from Maine for a few days but I understand if you can't."

I settled on a banana and resolved to bring lunch to Annette this afternoon. Given some of my meetings at the county and late conference calls, it was going to be a late lunch if I could call it that. Then, I'd bring her home with me and take another run at those peach scones.

"As soon as you give me a timeframe narrower than 'next spring,' I'll put it on my calendar. Shouldn't be a problem."

I hesitated, wanting to add that I'd be bringing a date to Rachel's party. But that was a gamble, one I wasn't certain I wanted to take. I was all for confidence but I knew my limits. Even if Annette and I found a rhythm that worked for us, it didn't mean she wanted to drive down to New York and meet my entire family.

"Might as well spit it out," Mom said. "I can hear you hemming and hawing from three hundred miles away."

"I met," I started, uncertain, "I met someone." Mom paused for a moment, drawing in a breath as if she was about to speak but then stopping and humming to herself. "What? Is it that unfathomable?"

"No, not *unfathomable*," she said slowly. "Just surprising. The last time we talked, you said you weren't looking."

I chuckled at that. "I was *not* looking," I agreed. "But someone came into my life and I couldn't look away."

Again, I paused. "If it works out and the timing is good for her schedule, I'd like to bring her home with me when Rachel returns."

I heard pages flipping and drawers closing on the other end of the line, but still no response.

"You're giving me a complex with all the murmurs and pauses, Mom."

"Jiang," my mother called, her words spoken away from the phone. "Are you working this weekend? I can't find your class schedule anywhere. It must've sprouted legs and walked off because I keep it right here and it's not right here."

My dad taught systems engineering at a technical college outside Albany. It would've been a typical Monday through Friday gig if he didn't sign up to teach during every extra session the college offered its students.

When I was a teenager, I thought he took on these additional courses because my parents were hurting for money. Around my fourteenth birthday, I had a man-to-man talk with him and promised to get a job so I could help out. He laughed at me. A good, long laugh complete with tears rolling down his face. He explained that more cash was always nice but he taught those courses because he enjoyed his students that much.

"It's right there," my father shouted in the distance. "Put your glasses on, Bonnie Marie. It's staring you in the face."

"Just tell me if you're teaching," she shouted back.

"Open your eyes, woman," he replied. "I'm not teaching but that schedule is going to jump up and bite you on the nose."

"Everything all right down there?" I asked.

"Everything is perfect, Jackson. Don't you worry," she said. "I was just checking my schedule to see if I could rearrange a few things and it looks like I can. Isn't that great?"

"Rearrange what? What's happening?" I asked around a mouthful of banana.

"We can come visit you this weekend," Mom said. "Dad's not working and I can trade shifts with Mary Louisa Thompson because she owes me several favors. We don't have to wait until next spring to meet this woman, the one you're seeing. We can meet her this weekend and that's perfect timing because we're going to the Maciases' lake house next weekend and then there's the wedding for what's-her-name's daughter, the one with the unfortunate avocado allergy. No guacamole at that wedding, I'm guessing. But this is the best timing and I can't wait to meet this lucky lady of yours. What's her name? You know what, why don't you give me her number. I'll give her a call and introduce myself. We'll get along famously, I know it."

"I'm gonna need you to slow down there, Bonnie," I ordered. "Slow way down. These are some high octane plans. I understand that's your mode of operation but I'm going to need you to dial it back several notches. Things with this woman—"

"At least tell me her name," Mom begged.

"Annette," I replied. "Things with Annette are new. I need some time before I unleash the full force of Bonnie on her."

She sniffed but I knew she wasn't offended. She wasn't one quick to take offense. "Jackson, did you hear yourself? You said she came into your life and you couldn't look away." She huffed out a sigh. "I can appreciate that you want me to slow down even if it doesn't sound like you're heeding that advice. I want to get her on the phone, have a little chat. I want to know all about her, her work, her family. So many questions. And I'd like to find out how many grandbabies she's going to give me."

I leaned my forehead against the refrigerator as I groaned. *What have I done?*

"We'd love to meet her, Jackson. Don't you think it would be great if we drove up for a visit?" she asked. "We'll take it easy, I swear. It's just that you've never said anything like this before and I want to meet the woman who caught your attention."

"This weekend might be a bit soon. I'm not sure where this is going or if it's going to last. Give me a month," I said, but quickly thought better of it. "Or two."

"You're such a pragmatist," she said, a bit exasperated.

"Someone has to be," I murmured.

"Are you sure I can't call her?" Mom pressed. "Just a quick chat to let her know how excited I am to meet her. When I'm allowed. In a month or two."

"Put the guilt trip away," I said. "When the time is right, I'll make sure you get your fill of Annette."

"It's like you don't even trust me to place a phone call," she said. "You must like her if you don't want me embarrassing you with stories about you being the fattest baby in upstate New York."

"While I'm sure she'd love a story about my baby pudge, she's really busy," I said, hedging. "She owns her own business and has been teaching herself to bake and I'm trying to take as much of her free time as she'll—"

"Oh my god, I love her already," Mom said with a yelp. "Jackson, I'm so happy for you. This is the first woman you've mentioned in ages and I just want to give her the biggest hug because I know she's special to you."

"Yeah, she is," I agreed, smiling to myself. "I hate to cut this short but I have to hit the streets and check on my town, Mom."

"Well, I'm glad I caught you this morning," she said. "I'll make sure to call around this time again."

"Oh, wonderful," I murmured.

"Tell Annette we can't wait to meet her and we already adore her," she continued. "I hope you're eating fresh vegetables and keeping your checkbook balanced."

"As always," I said, shrugging my shirt over my shoulders. "Stay out of trouble."

"Why should I start now?" she replied with a hoot.

"My mom wants to meet you," I said as we lazed in bed, our breath still ragged and the sheets tangled around our feet. I rolled to the side and planted a kiss on Annette's shoulder. "She wants to come up with my dad for a weekend next month."

She reached back from where she lay on her side, her palm grazing my leg. "We're meeting the parents?"

Focused on tasting the entirety of her shoulder, I brushed her wavy hair out of my way and kissed my way around. "If you want," I replied, as noncommittal as possible.

I was catching feelings.

It wasn't a new thing. I'd been catching them right from the start. But those feelings were bigger now, heavier. They blew right past attraction and lust and orbited around love.

Love. I was falling in *love* with this woman.

"I wouldn't mind," Annette answered as she trailed her nails down the length of my thigh. It felt amazing, like a million tiny tingles rushing out in the wake left by her touch. "What did you tell them? About me? I guess I'm assuming you told them anything at all. Maybe you didn't. That's also fine."

I dragged my teeth over the ball of her shoulder, nipping her skin just enough to draw a squeak from her lips. "I told my mother that I met someone," I said simply. "Is that all right?"

"Yes, of course," she replied. "I hope it's not a problem but I haven't said anything to my family. We have a wonky relationship. I don't offer too many details. They find everything I do problematic anyway so I try to keep my distance. It's easier on everyone that way."

My brain was still rattled from the last orgasm, but my cock didn't care. Nope, it was basking in the glory of Annette's fingers on my thigh—so close but also so far—and throbbing to life. With each pass of her nails, my body slipped into the old rhythm of rocking toward her softness, her heat. Soon I was stiff again, my cock hurting for the relief only she could offer.

"Not a problem at all," I said through a grunt. "There's plenty of time. I'm not going anywhere."

It didn't make sense that someone as devoted and generous as Annette would have a strained family life. I should've asked for details on her family situation but couldn't see through this thick fog of want. Should've pushed her to explain how a family could sustain itself with a principal member keeping her distance and rationing news of her life. Instead, I set it aside with a mental vow to revisit it later.

"Good," she murmured, her palm sliding over my ass cheek. "I like you right here."

I looped my arm beneath her, flattening my hand on her belly. *Oh, fuck.* I wanted to have her just like this, our bodies side by side and the sweat barely dried from our last round. I wanted to watch my cock shuttling into her and then dragging back, her inner muscles clinging to me as I retreated. I wanted to watch her tits bounce and sway as I thrust into her and feel the vibrations of her moans and pleas. And then I wanted to wrap my arms around her spent body and fall asleep with her.

"I want you," I said, my words spoken to her skin. "Now. Just like this."

I felt her nod before I heard her response. "I'm never making those kouign-amann cakes, am I?"

"Maybe not tonight." I pulled her leg back to rest on top of mine. "But there's always tomorrow."

I ran my fingers over her cleft, groaning at the rush of wet waiting for me. Her nails dug into my ass cheek, clawing as I circled her clit. "It's been five tomorrows," she murmured. "But I'm not complaining."

She urged me closer, her nails scratching over my backside like the strike of a match. My cock twitched against the small of her back. My skin was pulled tight over my shaft, swollen and needy from root to tip.

"Come here, Jackson," she said, patting my thigh. "Come fuck me."

Canting my hips, I drove into her with one rough thrust. This angle was glorious. It was enough to bring those three little words to the tip of my tongue and I was only able to choke them back when I closed my teeth around her skin, marking her just the same.

"Just like that," she said, her words snapping out with each thrust.

I locked both arms around her torso, holding her close and still as I pounded into her. The minute she sensed my control over her body, a flood of hot, slippery arousal washed over my cock. She wanted me to play rough and possessive but she wanted me to cherish her while I did it.

"Yeah? This is what you need, Annie?" I dragged my palm up her belly and cupped her breast, plumping it, circling her nipple.

Her answer came in the form of a purr, her body shuddering under my grasp. Her inner walls fluttered around me like the wings of a thousand butterflies and it took every last shred of strength to hold back my orgasm another second. That was all I needed, one fucking second to pump into her before I let go.

"I need you," she whispered. "You're all I need. All I want."

Her words hit a trigger inside me, a place distant and primal. I pushed into her one last time, already brainless and on my way to boneless as the first spurts blasted out of me. Goddamn, I never wanted to leave this bed. The world could burn down around us and I'd stay here, buried in Annette. I didn't want the world to burn down but I was damn interested in staying here with my woman.

"I can't believe I've never asked you this but," Annette started, her voice dreamy, "why did you get into law enforcement?"

I pressed my forehead to her shoulder. "Annie, sweetheart," I said. "I can hear my pulse right now. I can't see straight. Don't get me wrong, I'm happy for it. But I'm working on keeping myself from drooling all over you. I'm not sure I'm up for meaningful conversation." I squeezed her backside. "Not unless you're telling me how I rocked your world."

"Oh, you did," she replied. "You rocked it so hard I'm hanging off the edge of the bed and staring at your police academy graduation photo."

"For Christ's sake, Annie," I muttered, scooting back to the middle and yanking her with me. "You should've said something. You were damn near on the floor."

"I did. Just now," she said, laughing. "I figure we would've gone over together so it would've been fine."

"Yeah, fine," I grumbled. "All you need is me fucking you off the bed and then falling on top of you." Annette rolled away from me and smothered a laugh into a pillow. "All right, I'll tell you but you need to bring your sweet ass back here." I patted the mattress.

"I knew you'd be a cuddler," she said, edging closer.

I had a smartass response at the ready but discarded it as I thought better. "I haven't always been a cuddler," I said. "This is a new development."

Annette nestled her head under my chin and I looped my arm around her shoulder. "Okay. Is that your way of telling me you want to talk about past loves or is it more a matter of learning how to stay warm now that you're a Maine-iac?"

I kissed the top of her head but didn't respond for a minute. In my mind, there was no one before Annette and no one after. I was hoping to hell it was the same way for her. "Neither?"

"That's a relief because I've gotta tell you, I don't

know that I can listen to your greatest hits at the moment. Not after"—she swirled her finger between us —"everything. You might be in bed with me but that doesn't mean I want to hear about all the other women who came before me. Literally."

I kissed her head again, a broad smile stretched across my face. "Same."

After several minutes of silence, Annette leaned up on an elbow to glance at the clock. "I should head home. It's getting late."

I blinked at her, silently wishing for another hour with her. It wasn't about the sex, although it helped that we'd checked that box more than once tonight. I wanted to be with her, talk to her while we fell asleep, see her first thing in the morning.

"Sure. I'll walk you home." Annette held up her hand to protest but I swatted it away. "Don't," I warned. "I can deal with you leaving but I can't deal with you walking the streets alone at night. Say what you want about smashing the patriarchy and my toxic masculinity, but by god, I'm walking you home."

Annette tugged her dress over her head, no bra. That sight alone had me half hard again and ready to throw her back on the bed. Instead, I tucked my hands behind my head and watched her tend to her hair in my mirror. She was beautiful in the best ways. It wasn't the obvious type of beauty that anyone could spot from fifty paces. It was an easy smile and an easier warmth. It was hair that couldn't decide whether to curl or wave and did a little of both. It was thick, delicious thighs that parted like the pages of a book, opening to my favorite chapter. It was the quietly devastating way she took me into her body and turned my cock into her slave.

"Okay," she said, meeting my gaze in the mirror. "I guess I won't chip away at the patriarchy tonight."

"Thank you," I said, pushing up from the bed. My shaft slapped against my belly, still damp from her, still buzzing with pleasure. "You're sure I can't convince you to stay a bit longer?"

Aside from the chest-clutching shock of realizing I was thirty-seven years old and falling in love after less than two months with Annette, I had it good. I'd never had more satisfying sexual experiences since...ever. My belly was full of sweet pastries, my body and soul were well-tended, and life could only improve if a certain brunette book mistress would stay in my bed long after the sheets cooled.

Her eyes dropped to my cock, flaring when she realized I was primed for her. "Again?" she gasped.

"Well, you're not wearing a bra," I said, lifting my hands and letting them fall to my waist. "And you're fucking amazing, so there's that."

Annette gestured to the window, in the direction of the village and her apartment. "But I, um, I was going to..." Her voice trailed off as she glanced between my erection and the panes of glass.

"You could stay," I suggested, my words as neutral as I could manage. It'd been almost a week since the last time I'd broached this topic but I wasn't trying to rush things. As far as I was concerned, I had Annette in a manner no one else did and that was plenty for me. I didn't require declarations or anything grand, not when I knew she was pulling herself out of a bad spot with past relationships. I had her now and the rest would follow. "You have stayed here before. It wasn't so bad."

She barked out a laugh and covered her face with her hands. "That was a very different situation, Jackson."

I coiled my fingers around my shaft and gave it a light tug. "Not different at all," I replied. "This"—I tipped my chin down the length of my torso—"is exactly the same. It hurt so bad that night, Annie. So bad. Do you have any idea how hard I was for you? How much I wanted to crawl into this bed with you and feed you my cock? How much I wanted to taste you? How much I wanted to touch you and hold you?"

She stared at me, unblinking, as I stroked. Her pink tongue darted out to wet her lips once, twice. Then a new purpose flashed in her eyes and she stalked toward me. She covered my hand with hers, learning my grip and rhythm.

"My turn," she whispered, pushing my fingers aside as she dropped to her knees.

I wanted this—fuck yes, I wanted this—but I didn't. I wasn't going to come in her mouth and then walk her home. I was going to keep her in my bed, filled with my orgasms and held tight through the night. Just the way she needed.

I hooked my hands under her arms and yanked her back up. "No, I don't want that. Not tonight," I clarified.

"I thought blowjobs were always a good idea. Kind of like bacon." Stricken, Annette edged away from me. "I'm sorry."

Closing the distance between us, I reached for the hem of her dress but she pushed my hand away. "No apologies, Annie. Just stay. Please. I haven't done a decent job if you can walk out of here on steady legs."

Her gaze pinged to the ceiling, the clock, the windows. Anywhere but me. I didn't know what it was going to take for her to trust her instincts. They were in there, lurking right beneath the surface, waiting to replace this doubt with action.

"I never said my legs were steady," she whispered. "You've done a completely decent job. You've never left me with steady legs."

I crossed my arms over my chest, nodding. "All right. I'll take that. But I've never fucked you to sleep before. That's a damn shame."

Annette bunched her skirt in her hands, slowly lifting it up and over her head. "Then maybe it's time we try that."

When her dress hit the floor, I lunged for her, tumbling to the bed with her above me. I rolled her, settling in the notch between her legs. My cock, that mindless servant, flexed toward her heat as I leaned down to meet her lips, lacing a silent "I think I love you" every kiss.

v. To lightly sprinkle a dry ingredient such as flour, meal, or powdered sugar on a baked good or other surface.

Annette

Brooke: Where can I get a complete Thanksgiving dinner in the middle of August?

Brooke: I don't mean the ingredients. I'm talking about the fully cooked meal. Especially the goddamn mashed potatoes. I want to order it and have it delivered to the house. I could probably send someone to pick it up but I'd rather have it delivered.

Annette: Harris Farms might do that for you in November but I'm not sure they're taking orders now.

Annette: Why?

Brooke: You wouldn't believe me if I told you so I'm not going to tell you.

Annette: Okay. Sure. Nothing weird about that.

Annette: Do you want to meet up tonight? We could go somewhere outside of town where people don't know us and they won't ask personal questions while taking our drink orders.

Brooke: I'd love to but I can't.

Brooke: Tell Jackson to take you on a real date. You two spend too much time fucking each other's brains out at his house.

Brooke: I can't believe I just said that.

Annette: Same.

Brooke: You can't believe it because you think I say the first things that come into my mind. I can't believe it because I am now realizing I think two people can spend too much time having sex.

Annette: Jackson is at a town council meeting tonight.

Brooke: Boring. If I wasn't stuck here, I'd definitely get dinner with you tonight.

Brooke: But you should go. It'll be fun.

Annette: You just said town council meetings are boring.

Brooke: You know how to have fun with them. Bring a flask, make a game out of it.

Brooke: Better yet, make a sexy game out of it. Put on something cute and cross your legs a lot. You won't be able to walk right when Jackson's done with you.

Annette: I do have some lemon squares here...

Brooke: I don't know how that figures into my recommendation but go for it, babe.

Annette: I was experimenting with recipes last night.

Brooke: Is that something kinky? Because we can be friends and we can talk about sex but I'm going to need you to warn me if we're blowing past vanilla and discussing all the flavors.

Annette: No, dearie, it's not kinky. I made lemon, orange, and key lime curds and then made different pastries with each one. I had a lot of assorted citrus squares left over when I was done. Jackson took the orange squares to the station this morning and I dropped the key lime off with the Mulcahey's house but now I have leftover lemon squares in my kitchen. I could probably bring them to the town council meeting.

Brooke: I hope these assholes appreciate you and your squares.

Annette: They do.

Brooke: All right, then. Put on something cute. Pack up your squares. Go distract that man.

Brooke: And tell me all the dirty details tomorrow.

Annette: I always do.

Brooke: I know. It's the only thing keeping me sane at this point.

Brooke: That and the dragon blood I drink for breakfast every morning.

Annette: That's beet juice, honey.

I SETTLED into an empty spot in the last row, my lemon squares on my lap and my tote bag still slung over my shoulder, and scanned the station's meeting room. This was the oldest portion of the station by hundreds of years and had once served as the town's courtroom. The wide plank floors creaked, thick beams bisected the ceiling, and it was said these benches were older than the state of Maine.

The room held no more than twenty-five or thirty people and about that many were gathered together in small groups or bent over their phones or newspapers. Owen Bartlett and the other members of the town council were huddled together beside a long table at the front of the room. I knew from past experience they were reviewing tonight's agenda and the list of residents signed up to speak during the public comment portion of the meeting.

From the hallway, I heard Jackson's voice. "There's something going on out there. I don't know what it is but I don't like it."

"I hear you, sheriff," someone replied. "But we might be fighting the wind. The fence coming down, the noises. Probably nothing more than some strong breezes that they're hearing now because the windows are open. They're anxious folks, ya know?"

I leaned back against the bench, turning my head in the direction of the hallway to catch more of their conversation.

"It's not the wind," Jackson argued, his tone firm.

"They have every reason to be anxious. Something isn't right at the inn and I want eyes on that property every hour until I tell you otherwise."

"Understood, sir," the other man said.

"I have to step into this meeting now," Jackson said. "Update me in an hour."

Still staring in the direction of the hall, I smiled when Jackson walked through the door, his hands fisted at his waist and a scowl on his face. "I'm here and I brought lemon squares," I whispered, holding up the container.

"You're amazing," he replied, dropping beside me on the bench. He motioned for me to lift the lid. "You didn't tell me you were coming. I would've walked you over if I'd known."

Jackson helped himself to a lemon square as I shrugged. "I didn't decide until just now," I said. "Is everything all right? I heard you in the hall."

He licked the lemon curd from his fingers, his head bobbing from side to side. "Just keeping watch on a few things," he replied. "Did you lock your doors when you left?" I nodded. "That's what I like to hear."

I crossed my legs. His gaze followed the movement. "Aren't you supposed to sit up front?"

"Even if I am," he started, his attention on my strappy sandals, "I'm staying right here." He leaned forward, tucking a curl over my ear. "You know we're giving them something to talk about. Right?"

"Mmhmm." I shot quick glimpses around me, taking

stock. JJ Harniczek was in the front row, his hat on backward and his arms crossed. The Fitzsimmonses were on the far left, the Lincolns a few rows away. Neither family spoke to anyone else. The DiLorenzos were showing off pictures of their new grandson. I was surprised I didn't find Owen's boyfriend Cole among the people gathered for this meeting. Perhaps they reserved their public snuggling for bookstores. "They haven't stopped looking since you sat down and shoved your hand into my dish."

His shoulders brushed mine as he laughed. "You love it when I do that," he murmured.

"You're right," I said, grinning. "I do."

Jackson tipped his head toward the people seated in front of us. "You're all right with this?" he asked. "You're good with everyone and their auntie showing up at your shop tomorrow, digging for dirt?"

Still smiling, I nodded. They'd come. I'd smile but say nothing substantial. The Cove would light up with speculation. It would be a lot of chatter but it would also be fine. "I'm great. How are you?"

"I'm simple man, Annie. I have you and I have lemon squares. There's not much else I could ask for." Jackson sat back, his knee bumping mine as he spread his legs. "But there's one other thing I've noticed," he said under his breath, his gaze straight ahead as the council members took their seats. "Your tits are falling out of that dress."

I'd taken Brooke's advice and changed into a yellow

sundress printed with blue pineapples, one with a deep v-neck. "Oh, you noticed that?" I asked.

A growl sounded in Jackson's throat as he folded his arms over his chest. "This is going to be a long meeting."

MRS. BALL STEPPED up to the podium. There was a Mrs. Ball in every town, I was sure of it. She lived in everyone's business, found enjoyment in nothing, and didn't appear to age. She was elderly when I was a little kid—back when she gave popcorn balls as Halloween candy—and she was elderly now but didn't look a minute older than she did thirty years ago.

"There is an urgent need for a stoplight on my street," she announced, waving a spiral-bound notebook as she spoke.

"A stoplight," Owen repeated.

"It's necessary," she continued. "I've been watching the stop sign at the end of my street for the past month and I've written down the license plate numbers of each car that's failed to come to a complete stop. Thirty-four license plates. That's how many cars I've spotted rolling past the stop sign in *one month*."

Owen stared at her for a beat, then said, "A stoplight would involve hiring a surveyor to gather data on the intersection and assuming the surveyor agreed with your assessment, the public works department would dig up both Willis Point Road and Long Cove Way to run the electrical and install the proper posts. I'm talking about weeks of construction where access to your street would be limited. Once that was finished, you'd have the glare of a stoplight coming through your windows night and day. Is that what you want? Is that how you'd like us to address an otherwise safe intersection?"

Mrs. Ball paged through her notebook for a moment. "Then I'd like to know how the town plans to address the lawlessness on Long Cove," she said with a sniff. "It's clearly out of hand."

Owen shifted his stare from Mrs. Ball to Jackson. "I'm certain the sheriff will put the appropriate resources into the issue," he said. Jackson nodded in agreement. "Anything else, Mrs. Ball?"

"Not tonight," she replied. "But I'll be back next month."

"I would expect nothing less," Owen said. He glanced to the clock and made a note on his pad. "Meeting adjourned."

With that, Denise Primiani swiveled around to face us from the next bench. Her gaze swung between me and Jackson, back and forth, a knowing smile pinned on her lips.

Like most of the people at this meeting, I'd known Mrs. Primiani my whole life. I'd been close friends with her daughters when we were younger, before they moved away. She loved true crime stories. Couldn't get enough of them.

Like most people at this meeting, Mrs. Primiani was

reading all the way into Jackson's choice of seats. The only difference between her and everyone else was that she was a teacher at same junior high where my mother and sisters taught.

"How are your parents doing, Annette?" she asked. "I haven't seen your mom since school ended. Is she having a good summer?"

Well...shit. Now, I was going to have to tell my family about Jackson.

"Oh, you know," I said, nodding unnecessarily. "She's good. Enjoying the time off."

I was smiling but a pit of dread opened in my stomach at the notion of announcing my relationship with Jackson to my family. That required an uncomfortable sequence of events where I told Jackson about my very nutty, very judgey family, then told my family about Jackson, and also managed to avoid presenting him at my mother's Sunday dinner table for inspection and interrogation.

Those dinners were ridiculous. There was no singular reason why they reached the level of insanity that they did but that was how it went when my mother and sisters were together. They were loud and a little mean, and they fed off each other, every opinion bolder and stronger than the one before.

As a kid, I'd spent most of the meal ignoring the spirited discussions they carried on, focused instead on the book I'd snuck in and hid under the table. They preferred it that way. I'd always been too young to understand or I didn't know the people or topics being discussed well enough to comment. They made sure I knew that. They liked to keep me in my place.

Now that my sisters were married and had kids and teenagers of their own, the dinners were different. Still spirited, still ridiculous, but bigger and somehow louder. Still a little bit mean. Since opening the shop, I'd made a point of staying open on Sundays *and* manning the counter for the singular purpose of avoiding those dinners.

"And what have you been up to this summer?" Mrs. Primiani asked, shooting another purposeful glance at Jackson.

"Jackson Lau," he said, extending his hand. "I don't believe we've been properly introduced."

Goddammit. I tried my hardest to fight off a grin but lost that battle, smiling down at my lemon squares. Of course he'd take that opening.

"Jackson, this is Denise Primiani. She lives down on Old Sheepscot Point," I said gesturing between them. "Mrs. Primiani meet Jackson Lau, our new sheriff."

I didn't blame him. We were sitting here in front of all our neighbors, as official as a Facebook relationship status update. He had no way of knowing the connection between Mrs. Primiani and my mother and sisters, or that I was extremely conservative about the information I shared with my family.

"Looks like this sheriff has a sweet tooth," Mrs. Primiani said, grinning at my nearly empty plate of lemon squares.

"When it comes to Annette's baking, I certainly do," he replied. "You should try one."

She shook her head, scrunched up her nose. "Oh, I couldn't. I gave up sugar."

"I'm sorry for your loss," I said.

She smacked the back of the bench and let out a deep laugh. "That's a good one," she said. "I had quite the mourning period but I'm slimming down for a cruise this winter. It'll be worth it."

"I'm sure it will be," I lied. I couldn't stomach the idea of giving up sugar. "Send my best to your girls. I hope they're doing well."

"I will," she replied, sliding out of the bench. "And say hello to your mom for me. I can't wait to catch up with her."

That was local-speak for "We are going to talk about this juicy new bit!"

"I will," I said, forcing my enthusiasm. "Have a good night."

Jackson stretched his arm across the back of the bench, his fingers resting near my shoulder. After a moment, he said, "Don't you think you've tortured me enough for one night? Don't you think it's time you let me take you home?"

I turned toward him, my mind still on Denise Primiani and the pit of dread in my stomach. But when I met his dark eyes, I wasn't worried about my parents or my sisters. I didn't need to figure out how I'd tell them about my relationship or gird myself against their cutting commentary.

There was something about Jackson. It'd always been there but it seemed bigger now, brighter. And it wasn't just the desire to get naked. It was so much more.

It was as if he came upon me and took stock of me and my aggregate parts, and said, "This is nice, your calm, collected existence but wouldn't it better if we turned it upside down?"

That was exactly what he was doing and I didn't want him to stop for anything.

18

BAKING BLIND

v. The process of partially or fully baking a pastry case, such as a pie crust, without filling.

Jackson

IT WAS a great day for disasters.

I didn't make my opinions on the matter known but I was convinced the arrival of the full moon came with the surge of calamity. Most people brushed off that kind of thinking as old wives' tales or other nonsense but I was a believer. There was a restlessness in the air when the moon was ripe, one I was feeling today.

First, the innkeepers, Cleo and Rhys Neville, reported more suspicious activity on their land. Their dogs had spent the night barking at nothing, their goats and chickens were spooked, and one section of their back fence kept coming down. Once again, I didn't find any evidence of trespassers but that didn't ease their minds.

We walked their property together, righted their fence, and adjusted their motion-sensitive flood lights. I promised to keep a deputy patrolling their street for the next few days and put another call into my contact at the FBI. Even if she knew nothing, it kept the Nevilles' case on top of her mind. It wasn't much but short of razing the woods behind the inn and planting a sharpshooter on the roof, there was nothing left for me to do.

Shortly after leaving the Nevilles, a dog fell into a decommissioned well in the forest on the far end of town. The well was well off the hiking trail and required use of the off-road vehicles to bring in the proper equipment. It took several hours but the pup was rescued and shipped off to the local animal hospital to inspect his injuries.

Then I fielded a call about a group of teenagers rigging up a barge of fireworks. I found them gathered around a rudimentary raft and enough explosives to blow a crater in the beach. As it turned out, they were planning a big send-off for their friends going away to college next week. I was certain they had a cache of beer with them but didn't go looking for it. Instead, I pawned this issue off on the firefighters.

On the way back to the station, I spotted an elderly man walking along the coast road. This was the wrong spot for an afternoon stroll. The road hugged the rocky shoreline, leaving no room for sidewalks or shoulders.

Drivers found the speed limit irritatingly low but with one lane and miles of turns and bends ahead, it was necessary.

I sped up and stopped at the least dangerous spot, then jogged back toward the man. I didn't recognize him until I was a few feet away. "Judge Markham," I called. "Out for a walk today, sir?"

"No time for pleasantries," he replied, his arms pumping at his sides. He was slow going but he was going. "Lead the way, bailiff. I'm late."

The judge was dressed in pajama pants, a white undershirt, and a dark brown bathrobe. Shiny dress shoes slapped the asphalt as he walked. I fell in step with him. "Where are we headed, sir?"

Pausing then, he met my eyes with an impatient glare. "To court," he replied. "I'm presiding over an important trial today, bailiff. You should know that."

"Yes, of course," I replied, nodding as I squinted at him. Judge Markham didn't leave the grounds of his estate often. I was told he preferred keeping to himself and puttering in his garden. But this wasn't reclusive. This was unwell. "Allow me to drive you to the court-house. We'll get there faster."

I gestured to my SUV up ahead and he gave me a brisk nod. "Yes, very good. Hurry now. This trial is impor-tant. You should know that, bailiff."

After securing him in the back seat, I radioed the station. "Any missing persons reports this afternoon?" I asked, my voice low to avoid rousing the judge.

Cindy was quick to respond. "No, sir. Nothing's come up since that pupper took a bath and those kids trying to blow us to kingdom come."

I glanced in the rearview mirror and found the judge fashioning his robe's belt into a necktie. "All right," I said. "I'll be back within an hour or so. Let me know if you hear anything else."

"You got it, boss," she replied.

I followed the coast road up to the Markham estate. From the street, I spotted Brooke running across the lawn and a handful of other people spread out behind the main house. As I pulled into the driveway, I rolled down the window. "Brooke," I called.

She stopped and then sprinted toward me. "If you're here for relationship advice, this is the wrong time." She rested her hands on her hips and bent at the waist as she caught her breath. "My father took a walk around the garden but now we're not sure where—"

"I have him," I said, hooking my thumb over my shoulder. The judge was busy adjusting his robe.

She pressed her palm to her chest as relief washed over her. Then she yelled, "Oh my god, what? Where was he?"

I opened the door and stepped onto the gravel, forcing her back a few steps. I wanted to have this conversation with some degree of privacy. "He was hiking up the coast road," I said. "He tells me he's late for court."

She sagged, her eyes drifting shut for a minute. "He's always late for court." Just as quickly as she'd softened, her spine snapped straight again. "Lettie," she called. "The sheriff picked him up. Take him inside, would you?"

A tall woman wearing pale pink scrubs headed for the SUV's backseat to collect the judge. Two more women joined her. He was delivering a ruling, too busy with his recitation to notice the people shuffling him into the house.

"We need to have a conversation about this," I said, gesturing toward the cluster around her father.

"I am not obligated to discuss anything with you, sheriff," Brooke replied, her fear and vulnerability quickly replaced with her usual brand of firepower. "Thank you for finding him. There's nothing else for us to discuss."

"Brooke, I am only trying to help you," I argued. "Has he wandered off before? Is it Alzheimer's? Dementia?"

"It's none of your fucking business and I don't need your help," she replied. "I have this under control."

"Excuse me, ma'am, but you don't," I replied. "He was gone long enough to make it a mile and a half from home and in that time, you didn't report him missing."

"He's never left the grounds before," she said. "I fully intended to contact the station if we couldn't find him on the property."

"Your property covers half the town," I argued. "With all due respect, ma'am, you should've called the minute he went missing."

She eyed me up and down. "He's home now. That's the only thing that matters."

"I have to disagree with you, ma'am. He was walking along one of the most dangerous highways in the state. Aside from the fact he could've been hit by a car, he could've tripped and fallen off a rocky cliff into the ocean." I gestured to the house. "It seems like you have assistance here but it wasn't enough this time and you're fooling yourself if you think it won't happen again."

Brooke ran her tongue along her upper lip and crossed her arms. "Thank you for bringing my father home. You can go now."

I stared at her, frustrated that she wouldn't use her good sense and let me help her protect him. "The next time this happens, call me immediately," I said, stabbing the air between us. There would be a next time, I'd put money on it. If the judge found a way to give his caretakers the slip today, he'd do it again. "Whatever territorial pride issue that's preventing you from recognizing reason won't help you the next time he's gone."

"Thank you again," she said, inclining her head toward the street. "I trust you'll show yourself out."

"Does Annette know about this?"

Brooke blinked at me, unmoved. That lady was a tough nut to crack. "I'm not obligated to answer that question," she replied. "You'd do well to keep Annette out of this and keep your private life separate from the professional."

With that, she stalked into the house and slammed the door behind her.

By the time I made it back to the station, it was late in

the afternoon. I was tired and hungry, and in need of some good news. Hell, I'd be happy with no news if it meant I could grab a bite to eat.

Cindy greeted me with a fistful of messages and a folded newspaper. "Nothing urgent except Debbie Ball standing in the middle of the street yelling at cars again. She's been at it every day for the past week. She hasn't let up since the town council meeting," she said, tapping her finger on the papers. "But there's a nice write-up about our little Annette's bookstore, right here in the Portland paper. Fancy, huh?"

"Very fancy," I agreed, tucking the papers under my arm. "Thanks, Cindy."

"You got it, boss," she chirped. "I'm gonna take my break now if it's no trouble. Annette has a few books squirreled away for me. I'll only be a few minutes but I can wait if you need anything from me."

"Go right ahead. No trouble at all."

I headed into my office but left the door open. I dropped everything on my desk to scrounge for a snack. My search turned up little more than a bag of pretzels that seemed too flat to yield anything of substance.

I thumbed through the messages and returned several calls. While I listened to Mrs. Ball rattle off the license plate numbers of every car she spotted rolling the stop sign near her house, I paged through the newspaper in search of Annette.

"I'll send a deputy out to watch that intersection," I promised. "Bye now, Mrs. Ball."

Once I reached the Lifestyle section, I found Annette's smiling face. She was gorgeous as always but it was her confidence that radiated from the page. She had her arm resting on the counter inside her shop, piles of books at her back. I remembered her wearing that dress several weeks ago, the aqua one with the funky print along the hem. After the interview, I'd dragged her into the storeroom, ducked under the skirt, and offered my congratulations with my tongue.

A sidebar listed her top new releases of the past summer as well as her all-time favorites, plus recommendations for younger readers. The page was loaded with bright photos of Annette's shop and close-ups of her chatting with customers. They were great shots and Annette looked amazing. The article, that was another story.

The reporter went for the lady bookseller angle, favoring *lady* over *book*. I would've been on board with a good boost for women-owned businesses but the interview centered around her personal life rather than her career.

The reporter seemed to draw connections between Annette's favorite books and her marital status, writing, "It's no surprise this lover of all things Jane Austen is holding out for Mr. Right. When asked about her own experiences with romance, Ms. Cortassi demurred but later admitted she was 'very single.'"

I would've been all right with "single." I could've taken that punch and gone on fighting but "very single" knocked me out. I was on the ground, my eyes crossed and stars spinning over my head, and it took me a full minute of reminding myself that interview took place a *month* ago to get back up.

Blinking down at the newspaper, I skimmed the last paragraphs. Thankfully, I wasn't tempted to put my fist through a wall while reading but I still resented the hell out of this reporter. I had a mind to write a letter to the editor, complaining about that reporter's lack of professionalism. Readers deserved better than reporters who saw nothing more than a woman's bare ring finger.

And I wanted to talk to Annette about this. About the *very*. We were going to get a few things straight, yes, we were. There was no *single*, no *very*, none of it. Even if the interview hadn't aged well, I wanted to hear that from her.

I pushed out of my chair and pivoted, facing Annette's shop. It seemed like she had some customers in there but I could go in through the back door and wait until she was finished. We'd talk, we'd make sense of this impasse, and then I'd take my woman home with me. Keep her home with me.

19

CURDLING

v. The condition when a food mixture separates into its component parts.

Annette

THE LAST THING I expected to see this afternoon was my mother and sisters marching through the village like they were storming the beaches. My hands froze over the stack of books on the counter as I watched them descend on my shop in near-identical outfits: yoga pants, neon sneakers, t-shirts emblazoned with the regional middle school's mascot, a fuckton of makeup.

"What do I owe you, dear?" Cindy asked, snapping me out of my surprise-visit-induced stupor.

"Sorry about that," I murmured, blinking down at the counter. I added the last of Cindy's selections and pivoted the sales screen toward her. "Twenty ninety-seven."

She thumbed a few bills from the purse she kept belted around her waist. Some would call it a fanny pack. Cindy wasn't one of those people. She called it a cross-body bag and didn't have time for anyone who tried to correct her.

"I have twenty-one dollars and two pennies for you," she said, sliding the money toward me, "for a nickel back."

I bagged her books, my gaze continuously pinging over her shoulder at my family as they neared the shop. I was able to convince myself they were in town for reasons other than visiting with me. Perhaps they wanted ice cream from the local creamery or craved some fried fish goodness from The Galley. Better yet, they were getting their steps in with a harbor view today. All perfectly reasonable.

"I think you'll like this one," I said, gesturing to the newest in a series about a family of hunky, swoony California winemakers. "Steamy. Real steamy. But a lot of substance, too."

"I bet you're right," Cindy answered, her smile wide and her eyes glittering with the joy of getting lost in a new story. "If you don't mind, I'm just going to browse a bit more. Poke around. See if I can't blow the whole paycheck."

"Be my guest," I said with a forced laugh. I couldn't find any humor with my family on the sidewalk.

When the door chime announced their arrival, I played busy. My focus on the box of new releases in front of me, I called, "I'll be right with you. Just looking over next week's new titles. I know one of them is going to fly right off the shelves and I won't be able to—"

"We're not here to talk about books, Annette," Nella said.

"Well, not right now," Lydia added.

"But can we talk about that dress real quick?" Rosa asked, zigzagging her finger in my direction. "Because the cut is fine but the color is a crime against your skin tone. I swear to god, Annette, I'm going to clean out your closet one of these days and get rid of all the pastel. Baby shades don't work for you."

"You're right," Nella murmured.

Glancing up, I worked hard at pulling a surprised expression. It wasn't that I didn't enjoy seeing my family. I did. I also liked the time and space to mentally fortify myself for those interactions. And wine. I liked wine.

"Oh my gosh! What are you guys doing here?" I asked, holding my arms wide but staying behind the counter. Not in a million years was I acknowledging that comment about my dress. I loved this pale pink sundress and I wasn't parting with it for anything. My sisters could lapse into full-on Fashion Police mode on me and I didn't have one good shit to give about it.

I held a big smile while my sisters and mother exchanged wordless glances and tiny shrugs. It went on for a solid two minutes, long enough to catch Cindy's attention over in the romance section. She gave them a quick once-over and went back to her browsing. Whichever plan they'd hatched on the way here—because they always had plans—had gone to shit when they walked in.

Eventually, my mother asked, "Annette, are you dating Sheriff Lau?"

A shocked, breathy noise rattled in my throat, like I was gagging on a laugh. I hadn't been expecting this visit but I should've expected that question. I didn't look toward Cindy or the romance section. I couldn't meet her gaze for anything. "What? What are you talking about?"

"See? I told you it was ridiculous," Rosa said, giving my mother and sisters a sharp look. "Can we go now?"

I went back to fussing with the box in front of me. I wasn't lying, not exactly. I just wasn't confirming anything. It was an omission, for sure, but I needed more time to formulate my approach with my family. If I appeared disinterested and blew off their questions, I'd buy myself a month or two. That was what I needed to prepare Jackson for a Cortassi family dinner-slash-inquisition and pray he didn't run far and fast in the opposite direction.

"If you're not involved with him, well, that's—that's *good*," my mother said. "A relief, really."

"A relief?" I asked. I was glad I hadn't said anything. This way, I could hear what they really thought. I went on shuffling the contents of this box as if it required an extreme attention to detail. "How do you figure that?"

Rosa smiled as she stepped toward me. "We wouldn't want you getting hurt."

"Okay," I said, dragging the word all the way out. "Not sure about that but thanks."

"He's just out of your league, honey. It wouldn't work out in the long run," Rosa said. "Think about it. If you're honest with yourself, I'm sure you'll see we're right."

Ice shot through my veins, freezing me where I stood. Rosa wasn't one to make oblique comments so she wasn't saying that to hurt me. She was saying it because she believed it. Part of me believed it, too. I'd always believed it.

"And after everything that happened with Owen," Nella added. The cringe on her face said it all. She didn't have to say another word but she couldn't help but provide an annotated history of my missteps. "Where you kept trying to force it with him and he clearly didn't want that, and you didn't know how to recognize a brush-off when you saw one, and you spent a couple of years looking desperate? You don't want to do that again."

"You don't," Lydia agreed. "It doesn't matter what you two are doing. You shouldn't try to force it with the sheriff, Annette."

I jabbed a finger at them. "You're being kind of awful right now. You're welcome to rest this case at any time."

Nella folded her arms as she sent me a smug glare.

She was good at that, being smug. I couldn't say it suited her but it was certainly a skill she possessed.

"We're telling you the truth," Nella argued. "We care about you. We wouldn't be saying this if we didn't."

"I mean, there are ways to get your point across without also being awful," I said, shrugging. "I'm just saying."

"Sometimes the truth hurts. It's a lot like getting your vag waxed," Rosa said. "And you seem really sensitive for someone who claims she isn't hooking up with the sheriff."

"Your sisters are right," Mom said, leaving no room for dispute. "Whatever you think is happening between you and the sheriff, it's time to let it go. You two aren't a good match."

"Not at all," Nella insisted.

"Cool," I deadpanned. "Not sure about all that but thanks for your concern."

I wanted to argue. Tell them they knew nothing about me and Jackson. Insist I was worthy of a man like Jackson. Remind them I'd never questioned them or their relative value when they were dating their now-husbands.

I wanted to cry. Walk away, sink down into a dark corner, and cry. The door chimes sounded and I answered Cindy's wave with one of my own.

"He needs a wifey-wife and you're not into the wifey gig," Nella continued. Goddamn, I wanted to throw a book at her head. "You don't cook, you don't iron, you're not into the whole happy home thing. There are too many nice girls around here who would do that for him. Don't make him believe he should settle."

"We're only looking out for you, Annette," Mom added. "We don't want to see you following that poor man around like you did with Owen. Like Nella said, it was desperate. You don't attract a man with desperation."

Their words stung but I wasn't going to let them see that. I wasn't going to let them see anything.

I wanted to argue. Tell them they knew nothing about me or Jackson. Insist I was worthy of a man like him. Remind them I'd never questioned them or their relative value when they were dating their now-husbands.

I wanted to cry. Walk away, sink dark down into a corner, and cry. Forget all the barbs and backhanded comments—the open-fist ones, too—and pour it out.

I wanted Jackson. I wanted to get lost in him and his unyielding comfort, and I wanted him to promise me they were wrong. But now I knew what they'd think about me and Jackson, together. What they'd say when I wasn't in the room. I'd always known it would be this way but hearing it from them cemented it for me.

I also wanted to school my family on gender roles in modern society. I didn't know where they got off with this line of thinking. It was moments like these that made me question my lineage.

Somewhere in the far reaches of my soul, I found an extra store of saccharine sweetness and forced the brightest damn smile of my life. "That's enough about crazy town gossip. What's for one day," I said, shaking my head hard. "What's going on with you guys?"

Rosa fluffed her ponytail with an exaggerated groan. "We've been setting up our classrooms all morning," she said. "My room was such a disaster."

Everything made more sense now. The workout gear, the freshest cut from the rumor mill. Denise Primiani wasn't getting any baked good from me for the rest of the year.

"I can't believe how much work I have left before the first day of school," Lydia said. "I'm going to be in my classroom nonstop for the next two weeks. Goodbye, beach. Goodbye, vacation."

"It's the same every year," Rosa snapped. "Stop thinking it's going to be different because you use colored tape to organize your boxes at the end of the year."

"Why was it so bad?" I asked. It was an honest question. I didn't understand why classroom setup was such a time-consuming experience every time August came to a close.

"Oh, Annette, you should've seen it," Mom said, rubbing her brow. "The entire building was painted over the summer and everything was in a pile in the center of my room. Chairs, desks, books, boxes, everything. It was like climbing Kilimanjaro just to get started."

"I was completely convinced I was going to die in a

landslide," Nella added. "It's amazing that none of us are trapped under a pile of desks."

"It was bad but I didn't think I was going to die," Rosa said.

"The summers when they paint are the worst," Mom replied. "If I wasn't retiring at the end of this year, I would've painted the room myself and been done with it."

"That seems...difficult," I said.

"You have no idea," Nella said. She was wagging that finger again and I was working overtime to keep my expression easy. "Honestly, though. You don't know the first thing about getting a classroom ready for the first day of school. You have it so easy, Annette."

This book was practically begging me to chuck it at her.

"I sure don't," I replied. "Understand, that is. I don't understand."

Lydia dug through her purse, absently saying, "We have to go. We're meeting the rest of the English Language Arts department for vertical alignment planning and we're going to be late if we don't leave now."

"Oh, yeah," Rosa said, touching her fingertips to her temples. "Winnie Walton asked me if you could recommend some new young adult historical fiction books for her World War Two unit. I told her I wasn't sure if you knew anything about kids' books."

I could put up with some bullshit but this was one pile too many. "I do," I snapped. I flung my arm toward the left side of the shop. The one overflowing with children's and young adult books. "Plenty. Tell her to stop by or shoot me an email. I have tons of new titles her students would love."

Rosa blinked at the life-size Harry Potter cutout in the corner. "Yeah, I guess so," she murmured. "Huh. I've never noticed that."

"Rosa, you can have this conversation some other time. I'm grade chair this year," Nella said. "I can't be late for this meeting."

"Girls," Mom chided. "I'll meet you in the car." Shaking her head, she stepped away from my sisters and met me at the counter. "Annette, sweetheart, promise me you won't chase the new sheriff. If he's interested, he'll come to you."

"Mom," I said, laughing off her comment. "I get what you're saying. Loud and painfully clear. Okay?"

She tipped her head to the side, her lips folded together as she regarded me. "I want the best things for you," she said.

I believed that, too. She wanted me to be happy and have everything I wanted. The only issue was that she also believed I should lower my expectations and cram myself into a tiny, wifey box. Back when I started talking about opening a bookstore in Talbott's Cove, she insisted I'd be content working at the big chain bookstore outside town. She'd argued it would be easier, less stressful, more secure. I'd have a consistent paycheck and reliable health insurance, and I understood where she was coming from. That was my mother's way of caring—being extremely risk averse.

But it also had the effect of taking an axe to my sense of agency.

"I know you do, Mom," I replied.

She straightened a display of greeting cards and postcards before stepping back. "All right. Angie Dixon's son is moving back home next month. I'm sure you remember him. Since you're *not* dating anyone," she said pointedly, "I'll talk to her about setting you two up."

I reached out, trying to snatch that idea away from her. "Mom—"

"Don't worry about a thing. I'll take care of it all," she promised.

I stared after my mother as she exited my shop and hiked across the village. With her went a wave of adrenaline and I slouched against the counter. It wasn't always like this with my family. Most of the time, they ignored me, going about their inside conversations without noticing the outsider. But there were occasions when I had a clan of mothers, each one intent on babying me in her way.

It wasn't just the babying though. It was the minimizing, the way they confined me to that tiny cube and told me it was all I could have. Everything else, it wasn't for me. Too big, too small, too ambitious, wrong league. It left me hollowed out.

Abandoning the new releases, I trudged toward the

storeroom. I needed some water and a brownie because brownies made everything better.

Instead of a brownie, I found Jackson leaning against the table. It was a casual pose, his arms folded across his chest, his long legs stretched out before him and crossed at the ankles, but it was his expression that had me frozen in the doorway. His head was tipped down, his gaze steady on the floor but distant, his jaw clenched. His collar was open at the base of his neck. I stared at the golden skin there for a long moment.

"I dropped by to say hello because I wanted to talk to you," he started, his tone sharper than any knife, "and I learned you're not dating anyone and your mother is fixing you up with other men."

I clasped my hands together and tucked them under my chin, the only shield I had from this war on two fronts. On the one side was my family and their insistence I wasn't meant for a man like Jackson. I could scrape the black-tarred stick of their words away—and I would—but I'd always know they believed he was settling with me. That he could—and should—do much better than the bookish chick who didn't own an iron. It didn't matter that they were wrong or that I'd discarded that notion as soon as they floated it. They'd never look at me and Jackson with anything less than exasperated hand-wringing and I wasn't sure I could continue scraping that away without leaving myself tender and raw in the process.

On the other side, Jackson wanted so much more

than I could fathom. He wanted all the relationship bells and whistles but I didn't know how to operate the most basic bell and I couldn't find my whistles. He was ready for all these things and I was busy constructing a bridge of spun sugar. It was a thin, fragile connection between me and all of my doubt and issues to his boundless belief in us.

In the middle of it all was me and the creeping notion that I wasn't meant for this man. What had I done to deserve him? Nothing. He happened to drag my drunk ass home one night and I'd employed my limitless talent of making it awkward. If not for that run-in, we would've gone along without seeing each other naked. I'd forced this, just as I had with Owen.

He pushed away from the table and paced toward me, all six-foot-something of him towering over me. I knew he wasn't attempting to intimidate me but I already felt so small after my family's visit that I couldn't help but shrink even further.

"If we're not together, Annette, would you care to explain to me what we are?"

20

PUNCHING DOWN

v. The process of pushing dough down, pulling the edges in on itself, and flipping it over after it has reached the point of doubling in size.

Jackson

"If we're not together, Annette," I started, gazing down at her, "would you care to explain to me what we are?"

She dragged her teeth over her lower lip and asked, "How much of that did you hear?"

"Is that the best you've got?" I asked. "I had to read about you being very single in the Portland paper and then I listened to you dodging every question about our relationship. I need you to do better."

She shook her head and pressed her clasped hands

to her mouth. "I'm sorry. I am so sorry, Jackson. I wish I had the right thing to say but you've caught me at a bad moment and I'm fresh out of the right things. All I have is wrong. Actually, I came in here to gorge myself on chocolate. That's how much wrong I'm working with today."

I shoved my fingers through my hair as I stared at her, desperate for more. Just a bit. I only needed a hint that we were on the same team but I wasn't getting it. "Then help me understand," I replied. "Tell me why your mother is setting you up with Angie Dixon's son and you're not refusing. I want to understand this. I want a reason to stay instead of walking out right now."

Annette started to reply but stopped herself, her hands holding back the words. She blinked away, her gaze darting to the table behind me, the door, the boxes in the corner. I didn't understand what was going on here but I couldn't climb out of my mad to figure it out.

"I don't think I can give you what you need," she said eventually. "Not right now, maybe not ever. I mean, I don't even iron. I'm sorry. I'm sorry about everything."

"Were you planning to go through with that date?" I asked, my patience far past frayed. "At least tell me that much."

She buried her face in her hands. "My mother is always trying to set me up with people. I smile and nod, but nothing comes of it."

"Is that what you're doing now? Smiling and nodding, and letting me believe we're in a really fucking intense relationship? Because that's what it seems like today."

We stared at each other for full minutes but didn't move an inch closer to comprehending anything. And perhaps that was my biggest issue, beyond the very single, the refusal to acknowledge that we're together, the blind date. We didn't understand each other and we couldn't fuck our way out of it anymore.

That realization sank in my stomach like a stone. I couldn't stay here, not when I wanted to wrap her up in my arms and snap her out of that fifty-yard stare. And wasn't that a bitch? Even as she was pushing, pushing, pushing me away, I wanted her more than ever.

"If you ever figure out what you want, give me a call," I said, backing toward the door. With one hand on the knob, I raised the other in a wave. "And god help me, Annette, keep this damn door locked."

21

FERMENTATION

n. The chemical change in a food during the baking process in which enzymes leaven a dough and add flavor.

Annette

I SPENT the rest of the day flying on autopilot. I didn't remember the people who came through the shop, what we talked about, or which books I sold them. But I made it through without spending more than a stray minute or two acknowledging the day's bruises.

When the storefront was closed for the evening, I dropped onto one of the toadstool-shaped pouf pillows in the children's section. There, in the shop's darkened quiet, I felt those bruises. The ones from my family barely registered. They were the mauve-gray shadows that came and went without much notice.

The one from Jackson—the one I'd caused—that was different. It was deep blue with angry red around the point of impact. I'd feel it in every breath and movement. The ache would rouse me from sleep. It would take months to fade and even then, the pain would pang through me without reason.

I thought about calling Jackson, explaining the mess he'd walked into this afternoon. But this fight wasn't about the mess. It was about me and all the trouble I had accepting love. Not just accepting it but cultivating it, defending it, keeping it. I knew that now, sitting on the toadstool in the dark long after he'd left be in the storeroom, but I didn't know how to fix it.

Knowing was one thing. Solving was a different one altogether.

I could call Jackson or go to his house and say, "Oh, hi there. Just so you know, my family verbally bitch-slapped me this afternoon and they'll always think you're too good for me. Needless to say, I was in a wonky place when you dropped in. Also, I'm kind of a mess because I can't make heads or tails of real, true affection and I don't know how to take what you're giving in a healthy way. Can you bear with me while I figure it out?"

I could do that but I didn't think I could manage if Jackson said no. And after the way I'd reacted to him, how could he respond with anything other than a resounding no? My family was awful to me and I was awful to Jackson. All that awful needed somewhere to go and I'd dumped it on the one person who *knew* me, *cared* about me, *chose* me.

Instead of reaching out to Jackson, I picked my phone up from the floor beside me. Swiping it to life, I found several messages from Brooke. Nothing from Jackson—my whole reason for keeping the device nearby—but that didn't surprise me. He'd made it clear he was waiting for my move.

Brooke: Can we talk?

Brooke: I can't leave the house tonight. Would you mind coming here?

Annette: Do you have wine?

Brooke: Of course.

Annette: Okay. I'll head over in a few minutes. I have to put myself together.

Brooke: Don't pretty yourself up on my account.

Annette: I wasn't planning on pretty but I do have to get off the floor and find my purse.

Brooke: Why are you on the floor?

Brooke: No. Don't answer that now. Just come over. I'm out on the porch with a bucket full of screw-cap pinot and cheese.

Annette: Bless you.

Brooke: To clarify, the cheese is on a plate with crackers and nuts. The wine is in the bucket. I don't eat cheese out of buckets.

Annette: That's probably for the best.

Brooke: Probably.

"Bottoms up," Brooke said as she clinked her glass against mine.

As I sipped my wine, I stared out at Talbott's Cove. It wasn't dark yet but that shadowy space between evening and night that forced you to stop, look at the sky, and wonder how any other moment in a day could be so grand. Even now, as I sagged into this wicker rocking chair to lick my wounds and numb my emotional exhaustion, I couldn't help but love this little town.

"Nice night, huh?" Brooke remarked.

"Yeah," I said, motioning toward the horizon. Some summer nights in the Cove were unpleasant. *Unbearable* didn't begin to describe the combination of heat and humidity. But this, tonight, was the best the summer had to offer. Cool air with a gentle sea breeze. The scents of ocean and woods mingling together. Dragonflies swooping from flower to flower in the garden. Pinprick stars winking in the sky. "You have an incredible view up here."

"I'm sorry I haven't invited you to visit recently," she said, busying herself with the brie. "Things have been complicated since I came home."

I nodded. "Family is complicated. I know all about that," I added.

After a long pause, Brooke said, "I screamed at your

boyfriend today. Maybe it wasn't screaming but it was a more assertive conversation than my usual."

"I'm not sure he's my boyfriend at the moment," I murmured.

"Wait. What? What's going on?" she asked, leaning on the arm of her rocking chair. "Is it because I yelled at him?"

"I don't think so," I replied, "but why were you yelling at him?"

She held up one finger. "You tell me your story and then I'll tell you mine."

"My mom and sisters paid me a visit this afternoon. It was one of their usual 'we love you so we're going to say terrible things' shows. I rolled my eyes so hard, I burned calories."

"About what?" Brooke cried. "I want to know about these terrible things so I can dispute each one."

"They've heard rumors about me and Jackson," I said. "They don't feel we're well matched."

"And why the fuck not?" Brooke asked, her brow crinkled. "Aside from being jealous that you snagged the prime rib while they have to go home to their ground beef, what's the complaint?"

"They claim Jackson needs a wife to iron his shirts and make casseroles for dinner." I pointed at myself. "And I'm not qualified on either count."

Brooke waved a hand in front of her face as she blinked, processing my response. "I'm sorry, I'm so confused right now. Are we saying that Sheriff Lau, the former badass lieutenant from the New York State Police, is capable of neither dressing nor feeding himself? Is that a correct summation of the facts as presented?"

I held up my hands. "Apparently, yes. They want me to get out of the way of the women who can do that for him, and also, I'm pathetic and embarrassing because all I do is follow around guys who don't want me."

I'd tried to keep a cavalier attitude about this. Tried to shake those barbs off. But my voice caught on those last three words and tears surged to my eyes. I refused to cry, not because I couldn't be vulnerable with Brooke but because my sisters didn't deserve that much of a reaction from me.

"And they hate this dress," I added.

"Honest to god," Brooke said, holding up her hand. "I want to throw rocks at them. Can we go now? Please? At least let me slash their tires. I've always wanted to do that."

"Maybe then you'd get arrested and I could force an interaction with Jackson," I said, sniffle-laughing.

"I'd get arrested for you any day. Twice on a day when Jackson was doing the cuffing," she said. "Okay so you've told me about the evil stepsisters—"

"They're not *step*sisters," I argued.

"I don't care," Brooke replied. "They act like evil step-sisters. You're their Cinderella. It's obnoxious and I want to go slash their tires after you explain why this means you're on the outs with Jackson."

I reached for the wine and topped off our glasses. "He

overheard some of it. The part where I didn't object when my mother decided she was going to fix me up. Probably more. With my luck, I'm sure he heard the whole damn thing and tallied up all the times I let my sisters believe nothing was going on between us."

"Yeah, that was a brilliant move," she said.

"Thanks. Really, thank you. I needed someone to crystalize it for me."

Brooke leaned back in her chair and crossed her legs. "I'm just wondering why you didn't tell them to get the fuck out of your business. Even if Jackson hadn't heard anything, it would've addressed the issue of your people being shit-stirrers drunk on their own stew."

"Because it's easier to ignore them than engage," I replied. "Every family has its issues. Mine is chronically miffed by everything I do. Does it mean I'm going to cut them off, never talk to them again? No. Does it mean they're going to listen if I raise hell and insist they knock their shit off? Also, no. I have to make peace with who I am and who they are, and stop letting their issues impact me. It doesn't matter what they think about my clothes or my work, and it doesn't matter whether they think I'm good enough for Jackson."

Brooke traced the rim of her glass before saying, "The only difference between you and Cinderella is that Cinderella actively tried to get the fuck out of the attic when the prince came around with the glass slipper. You're sitting here with me and the bucket of wine. Seems like you've chosen poorly."

I gave her a bland face. "You asked me here to talk. Have you forgotten that part?"

"Not at all," she said. "But if you'd mentioned that you were due to follow up on some pressing matters with Sheriff Prime Rib, I would've understood." She brought her hand to her chest. "*I'm* a good person. Unlike those sister bitches of yours, *I* actually care about you. I'm also living vicariously through your adventures with the man meat but I'm still a good person."

"A good person who yelled at Jackson today," I added. "What was that all about?"

Brooke glanced away, picking at the cheese plate between us. She blew out a breath, sipped her wine, then turned her attention back to the plate. She was quiet for a minute or two, focused only on freeing the grapes from their stems.

"I yelled at Jackson because he told me my dad isn't okay," she said slowly. "He's right. That's why I yelled at him. Dad isn't okay and I don't know what to do."

I reached over and gripped her hand. "I know, but we'll figure it out."

The details were hazy but I knew enough to fill in many of the blanks. I used to see Judge Markham in the village every day, but over the past two years, he seemed to fade away.

He used to walk down, pick up a newspaper, and read it cover to cover at DiLorenzo's counter while eating his standard order of fried eggs and with a side of pancakes. He'd always attended the town council meetings, often piping up with minutes-long monologues about laws and regulations, local history, and the ways things used to be around here. But he'd retreated into his gardens, ate his breakfast at home, skipped meetings. And then Brooke returned to the Cove, leaving a big career and a big life in Manhattan. As close as we were, she had yet to mention the reason for her return.

But it didn't matter whether I had the full story or not. Brooke was my friend and I could support her without getting a complete accounting of the issues.

"Are you sure?" Brooke asked, her voice watery.

"I am. I'm sure. Between the two of us, we can solve any problem," I replied.

"And Jackson. We need him," she added, blinking away tears. "You're gonna have to make things right with him because he's rather handy and I will continue to push for a sister-wife arrangement."

"I'll see what I can do," I said.

"You can do better than that," Brooke snapped. "You're fucking fabulous and when you're fucking fabulous, you take what you want without apology."

We stayed there, our hands clasped tight against the home-front battles ahead of us, and drained two bottles of wine. We ducked inside for the bathroom at one point, more cheese at another. We never circled back to her father, Jackson, or my family, instead devoting our time to discussing our shared affection for a retired collection of lip colors and whether we should make time to go shopping in Portland next month. She needed something fancy for her computer, I needed a deeper pie dish. It was the most superficial of conversations but we needed this kind of mindlessness tonight.

If friends were good for anything, it was softening life's hardest edges by doing little more than being there with a bucket of wine and easy chatter.

"I'm sad that sundress season will be ending soon," I said. "But I'm also excited for boot season. And long sweater season. It's more complicated than sundress season but it's basically a game of mixing jeans and leggings with boots and sweaters. Boots and long sweaters are the best."

Brooke gestured toward her faded orange running shorts and ratty Yale t-shirt. Only she could make that look like a style worth replicating. "Yeah, same."

"We'll get you some full-length yoga pants," I said. "Some boots, too. We'll call it shut-in chic."

"Speaking of shoes, I want to go back to that prince and the glass slipper," Brooke said, holding up a finger. "Can we talk about that? Not the part about you feeling like you deserve your sisters shitting on your love life or you pushing Jackson away because you've bought into their bullshit but the actual slipper. Who in their right mind would wear a shoe made of glass? Have you ever broken a heel?" She didn't wait for my response, instead barreling on. "It's fucking disastrous. It's like a high-speed blowout. One minute, you're cruising along. The next, you're swerving across five lanes of traffic and probably rolling over into a ditch. Add a glass heel to the mix and I'm done. Honestly, the most unrealistic part of Cinderella is not the fairy godmother or the sewing birds or the dude who doesn't recognize a woman he hung out with all night, it's the goddamn glass slippers."

"You feel very strongly about this," I said, laughing.

"Yes! My biggest fear is stepping on glass. Why the fuck would I put myself in a position to willfully stab myself in the feet?"

I grinned at her, shrugging. "It's just not your fairy tale, honey. Doesn't mean you won't get one."

22

CATALYST

n. An ingredient that helps bring about change without itself being changed.

Annette

THE SOUND of sirens pulled me from a deep sleep. I bolted upright, blinking into the darkness as I tried to remember where I was and how long I'd been asleep. It came back to me in pieces. The walk home from Brooke's house. Flopping onto my bed, fully dressed. Promising myself I'd get up, wash my face, and change into my pajamas after I cried for a few minutes. It seemed like a fair bargain since I hadn't cried once today.

But instead of shedding some dainty tears and moving on with life, I fell into spine-shaking sobs. It wasn't about Jackson or my family or the issues facing

Brooke, but everything, all the hurts I'd socked away. I wasn't sure all that crying yielded anything more than a good emotional purge and accompanying headache, but that was fine. It was out and that was better than holding it in.

Pushing off the bed, my palm flattened against my forehead to keep the pounding at bay, I went to the window. It was unusual to hear sirens unless there was a fire but the engine doors were shut. Then I noticed lights flashing in the distance. Three SUVs raced out from behind the station and through the village. My heart flipped and then my stomach followed suit. Knowing Jackson was in one of those SUVs and rushing toward something potentially dangerous had me wide awake.

Since I was still dressed, I slipped on a pair of flip-flops, grabbed my phone and keys, and headed out. I wasn't alone. Sirens didn't blare at three in the morning without bringing the entire town to the streets. We were a nosy lot here in Talbott's Cove. And I couldn't go back to sleep without laying eyes on Jackson. I needed to know he was all right.

I made my way toward the station, exchanging confused shrugs and yawns with my neighbors. No one knew what was going on but everyone had theories. Car accidents, domestic disputes, wild animals at the back door. All of it was plausible.

Cindy lumbered over to me with a walkie-talkie clipped to the neck of her sweatshirt and her cane in hand, and held out a shawl. "Come on, now. Take this. You'll catch your death out here, dear."

I accepted the shawl and linked my arm with hers. "Thank you," I said. "Do you know anything?"

Her lips folded into a faint line as she shook her head. "Nothin'," she said. "But I know our sheriff was on patrol tonight, him and the other boys, too. He wanted all hands on deck."

"Does he do that often?" I asked, scanning the crowd again.

Cindy hummed to herself. "He's only been here a short time," she said. "I'm still learning his methods."

In other words, no.

"Don't pull that face," Cindy chided. "It took me twenty years to learn the last boss. I'm a slow study. Not like you, picking up new things like magic."

"Magic?" I asked, laughing. "No magic here."

"Don't be silly," she said, whacking my arm. "You taught yourself how to start a business and now you've been at it for how long? Six, seven years?"

"Almost seven," I replied.

"And don't forget about the baking. Good gravy, I've gained an extra love handle since you started visiting the sheriff. If you marry him, I won't fit into my bikini anymore."

"I've given up on mine," I said with a laugh. I wasn't touching that marriage comment with a marble rolling pin. "No one's complained yet."

"You've got yourself a good one," she said with a

knowing grin. I started to joke about the firefighters lusting over her but she whacked my arm again. "Your sisters are boring and they wear too much makeup. What's with all the bronzer? It's just silly. Don't listen to them."

I glanced at her, studying the laugh lines around her mouth and eyes. "I try not to."

"Don't listen to your mother either. She's just as bad with the bronzer and she has a twig up her rear end. I don't know where it came from since your grandmother is such a saint but it's lodged way up there," Cindy continued. "But that sheriff of ours, you go on and listen to him. He knows his mind and he knows you're one in a million."

"I'm working on it," I said, bumping my shoulder against hers.

Flashing lights tore open the night as a caravan of law enforcement vehicles drove through the village. "They're coming back," Cindy said. "I'm going to head inside and put things in order. Who knows what they'll need when they get here." She stepped forward, her arm still linked with mine. "Let's go. You can stay in the sheriff's office. He'd hate it if I left you out here in the cold."

"Cindy, there's barely a breeze," I argued. "I'm fine out here."

She flapped her hands, nearly putting my eye out with her cane. "He'd want you inside."

Before I could respond, Jackson's SUV pulled into

the parking lot with four deputies' vehicles immediately behind him.

"Time for me to skedaddle," Cindy called. She shot me a baleful glance and hobbled away. "Come on in when you're ready."

The crowd closed in as Jackson stepped out of his vehicle. He seemed well and unharmed, all limbs accounted for and no blood in sight. I gathered the ends of the shawl in my fist, holding it as tight as possible to keep me from falling apart with relief.

Jackson flattened his hand against the backseat door while he conversed with the deputies assembled around him. They seemed to be strategizing, motioning between themselves and toward the public safety building. It was the wrong time to fixate on the way his uniform trousers hugged his ass and thighs but I was doing it anyway. His posture—strong and assertive with his feet spread and shoulders back—made me salivate. I wanted to go to him and fix everything right now. I also wanted to rip my undies off but that was nothing new when it came to Jackson.

From behind me, I heard someone say, "It could be the Fitzsimmons boy."

"That's what I thought," another agreed. "Nothing but trouble, that one."

"He was never a nice boy," someone else chimed in. "Problems with him right from the start."

"It's these parents nowadays," a fourth voice added. "Too permissive. Always wanting to be friends. In my time, we said 'spare the rod, spoil the child.' No spoiling in my house and my boys turned out just fine."

"He's in rehab," an irritable neighbor said. It sounded like JJ Harniczek but I was too busy watching Jackson to turn around and verify my suspicions. "You should give the kid some credit. He's workin' at it, he's tryin' to kick the habit. Not easy shit. You think you're all so good and holy, why don't you save your judgment for your next talk with god, huh?"

After a pause, someone said, "Maybe it's Lincoln. I love the guy but he's an angry drunk."

"Nah, that's not true. I've never seen anything like that."

"Everyone knows there are problems in that house. Always fighting, always storming out. He put his fist through a window a few years back. You remember that, don'tcha?"

"It's not Lincoln," the irritable neighbor snapped. "You people need to knock this shit off. Might as well go back to bed so you can piss and moan in comfort."

"Who can sleep with all this noise? And the lights? My god, do they need to make such a racket?"

"Why won't they just open the door? What are they waiting for?"

"I heard they found him at the Nevilles' inn. Didn't get inside the house or anywhere near their baby, thank heavens, but had weapons on him."

"Those poor people. They've been through so much."

"I couldn't go on, knowing one of the men who killed

my entire family was still on the loose. Couldn't do it at all. The stress alone would take me."

"Might not be loose anymore."

"The sheriff's been spending a lot of time out there recently. At that inn. He's kept a good eye on that place. Probably saved that family from another tragedy."

"I had my doubts about this sheriff but he's a good egg. Just hope he lasts."

"Quiet, quiet, something's happening," someone hissed.

The deputies closed in around Jackson while he opened the backseat door and reached in to collect the prisoner. They headed toward the station, Jackson walking with one hand on the prisoner's cuffed wrists, the other on his shoulder.

The questions and murmurs continued around me but I stopped listening when Jackson's gaze met mine for a heartbeat.

For that single second, everything was good and right and he was coming back to me and I'd fix everything.

But he looked away, turning his hard gaze and equally hard jaw toward the station and all my doubts returned. Then he disappeared inside.

The crowd lingered outside the station for a bit, trading theories and rumors as news trickled out from the Nevilles' neighbors. Some claimed the perpetrator was inside the inn, others insisted he was apprehended near the inn. It was said there was a cache of guns and knives found in the woods. It was also said there was a bag of rope and duct tape. There was talk of calling in the FBI, and then a hearty debate about keeping the feds out of our town.

No one knew all the details but one thing was decided: Talbott's Cove was keeping Jackson Lau. Any doubts the townspeople might've harbored toward this out-of-state transplant sheriff were gone. He was ours now.

And all I wanted was to call him mine.

·

23

LAMINATION

n. A preparation consisting of many thin layers of dough separated by butter, produced by repeated folding and rolling.

Jackson

I WAS dead on my feet. Hadn't slept in two days, couldn't remember my last meal or shower, and didn't know whose shirt I was wearing. My scruff was crossing into beard territory. I was shuffling along, coffee and adrenaline serving as my only sources of energy. There was no other description for my current state of existence.

Even if I managed to drag myself home now that the dust was settling, I couldn't bear an empty house. Every room was scented with memories of Annette and I couldn't go there without walking out and heading straight for her. I wanted Annette's comfort more than anything. I wanted it but I wasn't certain I could have it, claim it as my own.

I went on shuffling, pushing forward as best I could.

Prior to settling in Talbott's Cove, I believed life here would be slower. Without the mad hustle of the city, it had to be. Small towns like this didn't experience ongoing cycles of crime and violence.

To a degree, I was right about the pace of life. Instead of investigating assaults and homicides, my days were spent mediating neighborly disputes and fishing dogs out of wells. That change made all the difference for me. But this small town wasn't immune from anything.

The team of FBI agents parked in my conference room proved that.

They were busy collecting forensic evidence from the inn, poring over the logs of my recent visits with the Nevilles, and interviewing damn near half the town. They'd already transported the prisoner to a federal facility in Vermont, which was one burden off my small office. Talbott's Cove didn't have the type of high-security facility necessary to jail a suspect who'd twice slipped out of state custody.

I passed the conference room on the way to my office, saluting the agents with a brief wave. Some of my residents disagreed but I was thrilled to have the feds here. No pissing contests from me. To my mind, they had a broader set of resources at their disposal to build the case against the Nevilles' attacker and they were best suited to handle the matter.

A call came through just as I dropped into my seat. In the two days since apprehending the attacker, my phone hadn't stopped ringing. Between reporters thirsty for details and state officials offering assistance or insisting I make Talbott's Cove my home for the long haul, I'd talked myself hoarse. I appreciated the wave of support from outside the town but it was the local backing that truly mattered. I hated that it took the thwarting of a deadly attack to rally the Cove around me as sheriff but I wasn't complaining.

"Sheriff Lau," I answered.

"Listen up, sheriff, because I'm only going to say this once," boomed Brooke Markham's voice. "Get off your ass and go to her."

A surprise laugh burst from my lips. "Excuse me?"

"I told you to listen," she chided. "Honestly, if you weren't Grade A man meat, I'd be done with you right now."

"I see," I replied, not knowing what else to say. In need of a prop to occupy my hands, I reached for my lukewarm coffee.

"Actually, you don't see a damn thing," she said. "You don't realize that you and Annette are rowing at different speeds and instead of moving forward, you're turning in a circle. That doesn't mean you need to stop rowing, bro. It means you need to match her pace, let her build up the strength and stamina to meet you at your level. Stop focusing on her shortcomings and start acknowledging her progress."

I sipped the coffee. It tasted like dirt. "Thank you for this insight, Brooke."

"No. No, that's not how this is going to pan out," she said. "You're going to fix this shit."

On a sigh, I leaned my head against my palm. "How would you recommend I do that? If you haven't noticed, I'm in the middle of a major investigation here."

"My sources tell me the FBI has it under control and they'll be packing up by the end of the day," she replied. "You did your part, sheriff. You caught the guy. Now, go get the girl."

"Brooke, I admire your tenacity and loyalty to Annette—"

"You want to talk loyalty?" she interjected. "I'll tell you a little story about loyalty. Annette is my best friend in the whole world. She's my sister, maybe not by blood but by every other standard that matters. Believe me when I say I'd kill for her."

"Don't tell me that," I said, groaning.

"It's true," she cried.

"You still shouldn't tell me that."

"I'm just saying, I'd do anything for that girl. But her actual sisters? They're miserable, jealous cows. They went to her shop the other day and had full-on baby tantrums because they heard you two were together."

"Why would that matter to them?" I asked, sitting up straighter. "Why would they be unhappy with her?"

"Like I said, they're miserable, jealous cows," she replied. "They know you're prime rib and they don't want Annette to have you. They said shitty things about her being pathetic and desperate for chasing after you, and how she needed to get out of the way because you needed someone with a decent tuna noodle casserole recipe. And that, my friend, is why you heard Annette telling her mother you two aren't in love and getting married and having all the babies."

I slapped my hand on the desk as I pushed to my feet. "That's horseshit," I snarled. "Her sisters? Her *sisters* said this?"

"And this brings me back to my original point about loyalty," Brooke said with a cluck of her tongue. "I know I can call her on *her* worst day and she'll still show up for me. There's nothing I won't do for my girl and that's the reason for this call."

Pausing, I turned to gaze at the village outside my window. The sun shone at an angle that obliterated my view into Annette's shop but I still watched, waiting for a glimpse of her. I hadn't allowed myself that much since storming out the back door and now I couldn't look away. I was drawn to her like a force field, a magnetic pull I hadn't been able to ignore since my first morning in this seat. What made me think I'd ever be able to resist it? Resist her?

I couldn't and I didn't want to. I loved Annette all the way through and back again. I loved her warmth and the joy she found in things as simple as a beautiful blueberry or finding someone the right book. I loved her sweet and her fire, my very own Fireball shot. I loved the way she poured herself into her baking and her bookstore and her friends. And me. I loved that way she gave herself to me and asked nothing in return.

But that was the catch, wasn't it? She asked nothing in return. She expected nothing. Either she didn't know how to demand it or she didn't think she deserved it, and I'd failed to right that wrong in the most critical moment.

I wasn't about to fail again.

"Tell me what to do."

A throaty laugh came across the line. "Very good. Let's get started with short-term tactical responses and move on to longer-term strategic solutions. You'll want to write this down."

24

PARTIALLY SET

v. To refrigerate a mixture until it thickens to the consistency of unbeaten egg whites.

Annette

Brooke: Let's go to The Galley tonight.

Annette: Can't. I'm banned for life.

Brooke: No one has ever been banned from The Galley, certainly not you. Meet me there around 7, okay? Don't make me drink alone.

Annette: I love you but I'm not suited for mixed company. Maybe wine at your place?

Brooke: I want to be around people tonight.

Annette: And I wanted to try out a cream pie recipe tonight.

Brooke: Wait, did you talk to Jackson?

Annette: Not yet. Why?

Brooke: I mean...

Annette: Yes?

Brooke: Never mind. I've spent too much of life in the company of frat boys.

Brooke: Don't even think about ditching me. I'll go to your place and drag you out of the kitchen.

Annette: Understood but please be aware you're buying the drinks tonight.

Brooke: You got it, babe.

BEFORE LEAVING to meet Brooke at The Galley, I flipped through my calendar and counted the days since my last visit. Forty-two. I should've been able to estimate that without tapping my fingertip against each uniform square but I couldn't believe so much time—and so little —had passed since that night.

I remembered the chin-quivering ache that sent me in search of liquid pain relief. It'd seemed like a real, palpable hurt, something I could wrap my hands around. And maybe it was. Looking back on it, I could barely reach those feelings of sadness, loss, humiliation. They were there but they weren't the same as the rough stab of regret I experienced every time my thoughts wandered to Jackson.

I should've handled things differently. I knew that now. It was possible I knew it in the moment but I'd been rubbed raw by the interaction with my family and didn't say the right things. Rather, I ran in the opposite direction of the right things and now I was busy charting my way back.

There were no plans, no recipes for fixing things with Jackson. I'd spent the past couple of days paging through cookbooks and browsing foodie blogs to find the pastry that said "I'm sorry and I want to fix things but I'm also scared and don't know how."

Food was magical like that. With a single dish, one was able to say a million different things. *Welcome home. Congratulations. Marry me. Happy birthday. My condolences. Feel better. I'm sorry. I love you.*

I'd tested a few recipes last night in the hopes of stumbling onto the perfect combination of heart, comfort, and sweet. Chocolate zucchini cake, banana bread, éclairs. None of them were quite right and I couldn't go to Jackson until I had it right. Until I'd folded my love for him in with the dry ingredients and knew he'd be able to taste it in every crumb.

Before closing the shop for the night, I noticed a text from Brooke.

Brooke: Running late. Grab a seat at the bar and I'll be there soon.

Annette: Is everything okay?

Brooke: Fine. Dealing with stuff at the house.

Annette: We can reschedule. Or I can go there. Whatever you want...

Brooke: Stop it right now. I'll be there soon. Ish. Soonish.

WITH THAT KNOWLEDGE, I grabbed two new cookbooks and tucked them into my tote bag. Perhaps I'd find the Rosetta Stone of pastries in one of them. Once the shop was locked up, I headed to the scene of the original crime—The Galley. I returned, my head held high, and Owen and Cole showed up not more than two minutes after I settled into a seat at the bar.

Of course.

But it wasn't just my former fake flame and his boyfriend. The entire town—or so it seemed—was at The Galley tonight.

JJ Harniczek tossed a coaster in my direction, the cardboard square spinning across the bar top. "Long time, no see," he remarked. "Did it take you all this time to shake off the hangover?"

I reached into my bag for one of the books and set it in front of me. "I'm going to read my book until Brooke gets here," I said, tapping my palm against the cover. "We don't have to talk about vodka and other bad memories."

"Bam Bam's coming?" JJ asked with a hoot. "I'm really gonna need the sheriff tonight. One of you, well, that's one kind of trouble. The two of you? That's a lot more trouble. Should I call him now or wait until you're nice and sloshed?"

I didn't want to meet Jackson on these terms again. I didn't want him coming to my rescue and putting me back together when I was capable of rescuing myself, putting myself back together.

I gave JJ an unimpressed stare and opened my book. "Make yourself useful. Go pour me some pinot grigio," I said, flicking my hand toward the bottles lined up behind him.

JJ dropped his forearms to the bar and leaned forward. "You used to be a good girl," he said. "All prim and proper, keepin' your shoes shined and your nose clean." He eyed me, as if he was seeing me for the first time. "You're not so good anymore, are you?"

"I'm pretty sure pinot grigio is the official drink of good girls everywhere," I replied.

He shook his head as he pushed away from the bar. "You've changed since the last time your behind warmed that seat," he said. "Not so good anymore."

I didn't refute JJ's comment. I didn't want to address any changes—real or otherwise—that I'd experienced in the past forty-two days. Instead, I paged through my book, sipped my wine, and tried my best to keep from staring at Cole and Owen. Trying didn't equal succeeding.

I wasn't watching them out of morbid fascination or pointless jealousy. I was watching because I felt nothing for them. I had no emotional or romantic connection to Owen, not now and not then. There was little more than familiarity between us and my misplaced hope that familiarity would blossom and bear fruit.

That I'd survived for so long on so little only served to remind me that I was used to begging for scraps. I'd accepted those scraps as proof of affection, fondness, maybe even the inklings of love. I'd settled for those scraps, convincing myself they were plenty. That I could stitch together threadbare rags and form a connection worthy of my heart, my soul, my body.

When you were used to scrounging for scraps, real affection was tough to swallow.

Shortly after I requested a refill, Brooke arrived. She waved to me but found herself snared in a conversation on the opposite end of the bar. It wasn't uncommon for my neighbors to ask after her father and wax on about the time he said one thing or did another. She was always polite about it, answering questions with a pleasant-but-fake smile, nodding along as they reminisced about events she didn't recall. I didn't know how she did it, carrying the world and all its secrets on her shoulders. She made it seem effortless but I saw the cracks in the foundation.

I ordered a glass of wine for her and returned to my books. The minutes ticked by while Brooke kept that hollow smile plastered on her face and JJ peppered me with vague comments about behaving myself tonight, and then silence swept through the tavern. Glancing up,

I found Cole and Owen cozied up in their booth, their heads bent together.

I smiled at them, wishing them well in this small gesture. They didn't need my acceptance or approval to love each other but I still wanted them to know we were good. No hard feelings, no awkwardness.

Returning to my cookbook, I got lost in an intricate linzer torte recipe that started with a detailed accounting of the cake's history and permutations through the centuries. It wasn't until the main door clattered that I looked up and found Jackson darkening The Galley's doorway. On a gust of wind, the door banged behind him again, drawing the attention of everyone in the tavern.

He stood there a moment, his shoulders nearly broad enough to brush the doorframe as he scanned the room, and then his gaze fell on me. His golden arms were bent at the elbows, his hands loosely gripping his duty belt. That pose had the fabric of his short-sleeved sheriff's shirt straining around his thick biceps and my lips parting on a sigh.

I found a deep store of confidence, one I wasn't sure I had anymore, and smiled at him. This wasn't how I'd imagined I'd see him again but here we were, no baked goods in sight and the entire town our audience. He blinked at me, once, twice, thrice before allowing the corner of his lip to turn up in response. I tipped my head toward the empty seat beside me, the one reserved for my best friend, and raised my eyebrows.

It was an invitation, one I hoped he'd take even if I

didn't have the haziest idea what I was going to say or do if he joined me.

Jackson strode across the tavern, certain and bold, as if sent to collect me. It occurred to me that he was here for that exact reason. I peeked at JJ, who was reading the back of a whiskey bottle like it revealed the secrets to a long life.

"This will come back to you, Jedidiah," I hissed. "Don't think I'll forget."

"Can't imagine what you're talking about," he replied, watching as Jackson stopped at my side.

"Annette," Jackson said, his deep voice raking over my name. "I'm taking you home."

"Not until you settle up your tab," JJ called.

Jackson dropped some bills on the bar and pushed them toward JJ without taking his eyes off me. "I'm taking you home," he repeated.

"Can we talk first?" I asked, gesturing to the empty seat.

He shook his head once, a curt movement that had my edginess rising. He didn't want to sit, didn't want to talk...what was I missing?

"I am taking you home, Annette," Jackson said, each word crisper than the one before. Then, softly, "Please, beautiful. I need you right now."

And that was it. That was all I required to hop off the stool and gather my books.

"Give me that," he ordered, reaching for my tote bag.

I snatched it away with an exasperated frown. "I've

got it," I said, swinging the tote over my shoulder. "It's two books and I can't let you pay for my drinks and carry my bag all on the same night. These people are going to think I'm a kept woman or something."

Jackson brought his hand to my lower back and bent to brush his lips over the shell of my ear. "That's exactly what I'd like them to think."

25

GLAZE

v. To brush food with milk, egg, or sugar before baking in order to produce a shiny, golden finish.

Jackson

I HADN'T EXPECTED to march through The Galley and claim Annette with the whole town watching us over their grilled swordfish, but Brooke was right. It was the best way to kill a whole lot of birds with one stone.

There was no credence to the suggestion Annette was the one doing the chasing, not when I made it clear to everyone watching she was mine.

There was no denying we had a history, one that transcended our roles of sheriff and bookseller.

There was no hiding the relief I felt when she

climbed off that stool and I was certain everyone saw it on my face, too.

She'd played her part well with that flare of fire when I'd tried to relieve her of her bag. No one could argue there wasn't heat between us.

I knew Annette's family wouldn't be at The Galley but I also knew this would get back to them. And I wasn't done. No, we had another stop on our route before heading home.

"Jackson," Annette said slowly, glancing up at me, "can we talk now?"

I led her across the street, toward the alley behind her shop, and took her in my arms. I'd never believed the touch of another could soothe me down to my core but Annette, she was my balm.

"I missed you today," I whispered. "Yesterday, too. I don't want to miss you anymore."

She nodded, her head rubbing against my chest as she moved. "I missed you, too," she confessed. "But I have a lot of things to say and I think I should say them."

"Can you talk and pack at the same time?" I asked. "Because I meant it when I said I was taking you home now."

Annette stared at me for a moment, her wide, dark eyes blinking up at me as if I'd spoken another language and she needed time to translate. Eventually, she said, "I can't. I can't talk and pack, I have to say this now."

"Okay," I said. "Go ahead. I won't rush you."

She brought her hands to my chest, her gaze locked

on the buttons running down my shirt. She bit her lip, hesitating before she spoke.

"I'm just learning how to do this. I'm—I'm going to make mistakes. I'm going to push you away because I don't know what to do with big feelings and big love but I want to get better at it. At this." She tapped her chest and then mine. "At us."

"I'm going to pull you right back," I said, scooping her up in my arms and backing her up against the building. I wanted her body pressed to mine but I also needed some help staying upright. "I'm going to want everything with you and you're going to have to tell me when to slow down. I can handle it, I swear. Just tell me what you need and promise you'll give me a chance to adjust."

"I love you," she whispered, a deep valley of awe in her words. "And I want to let you love me, even when it's scary and overwhelming."

"I've loved you since the first moment I set eyes on your ankles," I replied. "I saw you from my office and my heart broke free from my chest and climbed into your hands."

I kissed her then, fast and hard, just like we'd fallen for each other. She tasted like wine and comfort, and I found myself rocking into the heat between her legs. I was exhausted and in desperate need of sleep but my cock was ready to go all night.

"Isn't this illegal?" she asked against my lips. "Public indecency or something?"

"That's why I'm trying to take you home," I said,

groaning as the friction spiraled through me. "Quick. We're running upstairs and getting all the things you need for the next day or two. Your favorite whisk, the rolling pin you favor, aprons with flamingos on them, a few of those white dresses I like so much. Just the basics. Panties are unnecessary."

"Whisks, rolling pins, aprons," Annette repeated. "What am I making with those things?"

"Anything you want," I said. "Anything at all. I want you with me and not just for one night. I want you to stay. Stay for a long, long time, Annie."

She ran her teeth across her bottom lip, humming to herself. I was prepared for an argument, braced against her certain refusal.

"But no panties? Is that your way of getting around previous restrictions on touching my underwear? This is one conversation we can have while we pack, you know. We don't have to do this up against my building."

No argument. No refusal. Just me and Annette, trying our damnedest to do this thing. With or without undies.

"If you insist." With regret, I set Annette on her feet and let her lead the way to her apartment. "I'm just throwing out some ideas here but I think we can live happily with a no-panties rule. Seems mutually beneficial to me."

Annette shook her keys at me when we reached the landing outside her door. "See? Keys. For the lock. The one on the door."

I brought both hands to her backside and squeezed.

"What? You think I'm going to reward you for seeing to the most basic safety procedures? No, beautiful. Not happening."

She hooked a glance at me over her shoulder, her eyes a pair of inky pools in the darkness and her lips pressed together in a pout. I couldn't resist that face. It was the same one she used on me that first night, when she didn't want to be alone in my bed.

"What if I asked nicely?"

I squeezed her ass, harder this time. "You better pack fast."

Annette pushed open the door and I followed her into the narrow apartment. She handed me a reusable grocery bag and gestured to the baking pans and tools piled high on the kitchen table. "You work on the kitchen goods and I'll grab some clothes. Don't mean to break your heart but I will be bringing undies. Not everything can be fun and naked games."

I pointed at her with a muffin tin. "That's false. Fun and naked games are the gift of adulthood."

She moved toward me, her saucy expression crumbling with each step. "I am sorry." She ran her hands from my shoulders down to my wrists before tangling our fingers together. The muffin tin clanged to the floor. "I didn't say what I meant and it hurt you, and I'm sorry."

I leaned forward, pressing a kiss to her forehead. "I didn't say what I meant either. Not what I truly meant. I'm sorry I left."

Annette nodded, her grip tight on my fingers. "You

look tired," she said, her brows furrowed. "Jackson, tell me you haven't been working around the clock since that situation at the inn."

"I could use a good night's rest," I admitted. "It will be better with you."

"Give me ten minutes," she said.

"Then we can go home?" I asked. "We can do this?"

"We're going home." She bobbed her head, a wide smile telling me everything I needed to know. "We're doing this."

26

CARAMELIZE

v. To heat sugar until it is melted and brown.

Annette

"WHAT IS THAT?" Jackson murmured, his words vibrating against the tender skin at the junction of my neck and shoulder. "What is it and how do I make it stop?"

It took a minute to hear anything other than my need for him. We'd only just set my things down inside his home when we reached for each other and we hadn't been able to let go since.

After another trill, I leaned away, blinked, and glanced around his kitchen. After a long moment of concentrated listen-staring, I placed the noise. "It's my phone," I said, peering around him to see where I left my tote. Grocery bags loaded with kitchen tools littered the countertop, and my tote was hidden beneath it.

"The only person who needs you now is right here," he said.

"I know," I said, busy loosening his shirt buttons. "I'd rather ignore it but it just keeps ringing."

With a grunt, Jackson scooped me up and set me on the countertop. He kept one hand on my backside and used the other to dig through the bags and then upend my purse. He sifted through lip balms and tampons, coins and hard candies to find my phone trilling under my wallet.

"Where is the pepper spray I gave you?" he asked, holding the phone out of my reach. Brooke's picture flashed on the screen.

"I didn't have room for it," I said, grabbing for my phone. The ringing stopped but then quickly started again. "She doesn't know how to back down. She'll just keep calling. Better yet, she'll show up at the door."

"You didn't have room for it," Jackson said, still staring at the contents of my purse. "You have room for six different lipsticks but not one pepper spray." He turned his attention toward me, his eyebrow arched. "We'll talk about that later but don't doubt we'll talk about it."

"I'm sure we will," I said, taking the phone from him. "Hi, Brooke."

She didn't bother with pleasantries or preamble, instead launching right in. "Are you with him right now?

I saw him walking you to his house with a bunch of bags but I need more information. Tell me everything."

"Yes, I'm with Jackson." I smiled up at him and his impatient scowl. "He took me home and I'm staying here. Me and all my stuff."

The scowl softened into a smile I couldn't help but return. "It's about time you came around to those facts," he said.

"It's my turn with you. Tell him to cut out the sweet sentiments for a minute," Brooke said. "What did he say? What did *you* say? What's happening now? I need to know!"

Jackson stepped between my legs, pushed my skirt up to my waist. "Wrap it up," he said under his breath.

"Are we still on for wine and lunch this weekend?" I asked.

"Wine, yes. I can live without food," she replied. "But don't think you're leaving me hanging until then. I need all the details. Living vicariously through you is the only thing keeping me from going full-metal Kate Chopin and *The Yellow Wallpaper*."

"I think you mean Charlotte Perkins Gilman," I replied. "You and Kate Chopin have other things in common."

Jackson dragged his fingers up my inner thighs, grinning as if he was unwrapping the gift he'd always wanted. He did that to me, he made me believe I was worth treasuring.

"Okay, whatever. Give me the literature lesson later,"

Brooke said. "Please get to the good parts. I'm growing old and weary over here."

With my gaze locked on Jackson, I said to her, "You were at The Galley. You saw him drag me out of there."

"Yes, kicking and screaming," she replied.

"I'm probably going to get naked in his kitchen. I might even spank him. Then we're going to bed where we plan to sleep."

"At least for a little while," Jackson murmured.

"This is completely unacceptable as far as key details go," Brooke seethed. "You better choose me as your maid of honor after all the shit you've put me through with this man. I'm going to give the sloppiest, sappiest toast at your wedding and I'm going to make those evil stepsisters of yours my bridal party bitches. And you're definitely buying the wine this weekend."

"Happily," I said, a giggle-moan ringing in my words as Jackson's thumbs brushed along the edge of my panties.

"Okay, all right, that's enough," Brooke said. "I can put up with a lot of things but I don't want to listen while he fucks you."

"He's not—"

"I don't care," she interrupted. "Something is going on over there and I don't need to be involved in it. We can talk *about* sex but we can't talk *during* sex."

"Love you, babe," I said.

"Love you back," Brooke replied.

I ended the call and set my phone aside before looking up at Jackson. "What happens now?" I asked.

I meant *right now* but I also meant everything after *right now*.

"Anything you want," he said, still stroking the edge of my undies. "Ask me for anything, Annette. I'll give it to you."

I brought my hands to his face, cupping his strong, square jaw and running my thumbs over his cheeks. His eyes were heavy and exhaustion pinched his brow. "It's my turn to put you to bed," I said, sealing that promise with a kiss. "And when I need it, you'll do it for me."

"That's all?" he asked.

"That's everything," I replied.

27

STRAIN

v. To separate solids from liquids

Annette

Two months later

"It happens like this every year," I murmured, my chin tipped down as I tugged up my coat's zipper. "One day it's lovely and wonderful with cool, crisp autumn air and sunny skies"—I gestured to the dark sky overhead with my gloved hand—"and then there's a cold snap and the next ice age begins. That's the real problem with having homecoming in the fall. It needs to be a springtime deal so people aren't turning into icicles out here. I don't care if that screws up everything with football. It's what I believe."

Jackson murmured in agreement as he wrapped a flamingo scarf around my neck. He was in uniform tonight, wearing a thick, dark sweater over his tan shirt, and a coat over the sweater to ward off the wintry chill. That sweater—with the sheriff's office insignia embroidered on the arm and his name over his chest, worked like a charm for me. I wanted to rake my fingers down the knit, slide my hands under it—I wanted to peel it off him. I wanted to toss it to the floor and get my hands on his skin and keep them there until he couldn't take any more. And then I'd slip into that sweater and see how long it took him to rip it off me.

"I won't let you turn into an icicle," Jackson said, patting the scarf then untying it again. "You look cute. I like seeing you all bundled up."

"Don't get me wrong," I said. "I live for boots-and-long-sweater season but it's the transition between wearing sundresses and sandals all summer to wearing, you know, socks and jeans and then to coats and hats and scarves and mittens. The hats really get me. They fuck up my hair."

"Believe me," he murmured, his concentration locked on the scarf, "I'm suffering the loss of your sundresses, too." He met my gaze with a small smile. "But your ass is on fire in those jeans. I can't figure out whether I should pinch it, spank it, or bite it." He glanced up and down the sidelines. "There's also a fourth option but I'd rather not mention it here."

I waved toward the high school's football field and the cheerleaders warming up within feet of us. "Good call, sheriff. Tuck that one away for later. We don't need to stir up any more attention than necessary."

He followed my gaze to the stadium stands where my family sat, decked out in the high school's colors. "Fuck that," he whispered, bending toward me. "Let them watch."

He tipped my chin up and brushed his lips over mine. There were no secrets about us being together but I wasn't entirely steady with the eyes of the entire town —and my family—on us. I wasn't so self-centered that I believed all these people cared about the minutiae of my life but I was standing on the sidelines before the home-coming game, wrapped up in this big grizzly bear of a man's arms, all while the back of his coat proudly announced his title.

When we parted, I ran my gloved finger over his bottom lip to tidy up the shiny lip gloss left there. "You're a bad influence, sheriff."

"I am." Jackson ran his palms down my shoulders and arms before gripping my hands. "Where's Brooke tonight?"

I shook my head at him, gave him an *if you only knew* face. "She doesn't attend football games. She has a complex relationship with our alma mater."

"Knowing Brooke, that is unsurprising." Jackson

brushed some stray snowflakes from my shoulder. A squall was in tonight's forecast. "We don't have to stay for the whole game."

I snickered at that. "No, we need to stay for the entire thing. Every last minute," I insisted. "It's the homecoming game. You have to do the coin toss thing. I have to crown the homecoming court. We have to stay through the end and we probably have to go back to someone's house for a little post-game potluck, too."

"I don't want a potluck," he grumbled, seizing my waist in his hands. "I haven't seen you all week. I want to take you home."

It had been a busy week. Jackson was in Augusta for a three-day law enforcement meeting, I had two evening events at the shop, and Brooke and I met up for dinner and drinks last night. I worked hard at making time for my friend, even when it would've been easier to cancel on her and spend the evening snuggled up with my man.

But I was determined to avoid that. She was there for me before Jackson I wasn't leaving her on the back burner now that I was with Jackson. She was the sister I chose and I wasn't about to forget that she chose me, too.

"You're seeing me right now," I said.

"Yeah, Annie, I am," he said, his voice gravelly. "And I'm wondering whether I was wrong about your fuck-hot ankles now that I'm seeing you in jeans. Goddamn, girl. The things you do to me."

I started to explain my fascination with his official sheriff's uniform sweater but I spotted my mother and sisters headed straight toward us. I wasn't sure where they'd left my dad and brothers-in-law but those men seemed to follow the old adage of being seen but not heard. Sometimes they went above and beyond with silence *and* absence.

"Oh. This is special," I murmured, stepping out of Jackson's embrace. I didn't go far but I didn't want them to see me pawing at him. They'd file it under my repeated acts of desperation and never let me forget it.

While I hadn't shut my mom or sisters out after their visit to my store a couple months ago, I wasn't seeking them out either. I accepted that there was a world of difference between me and the rest of my family and I wasn't about to change any of that. It didn't matter whether that difference sprung from choosing this profession over theirs or the tremendous gap in our ages or even my failure to be born a boy. It didn't matter at all.

Jackson swung his arm over my shoulder, tugging me closer. "Don't say a word. I've got this," he said under his breath.

"Got what?" I whisper-shrieked.

He shook his head once and held out his free hand to my mother. "Mrs. Cortassi. It's a pleasure to see you this evening," he boomed.

She accepted his hand but couldn't tear her consti-pated stare away from his hold on my shoulder. "The pleasure is all mine." She glanced away from me and gestured to my sisters. "I don't believe you've met my daughters. Rosa, Lydia, and Antonella."

He nodded toward each of them. "I've met my favorite," Jackson said, pressing a kiss to my temple.

My mother blinked at us for a moment as she struggled to process the picture before her. For my part, I was struggling to hold back a giggle. "Oh, yes," she said, eyeing me. "Yes, you have met Annette."

"Not only have I met her but I've spent the summer falling in love with her," he said. "Long before she knew it, months ago, I was falling for her."

In place of my bones was jelly. Even after two solid months of Jackson telling me he loved me—*and* saying it back—the accompanying rush of bone-melting heat hadn't faded.

"Oh my god," Nella muttered, curling her fist in front of her mouth.

My mother recovered, cooing, "Sheriff, you're such a sweetheart. We must have you over for Sunday supper. How about next weekend? Yes, next weekend. You're coming over. It's settled."

I wasn't sure whether my invitation was implied or they were hoping to get alone time with him.

Jackson glanced down at me, his hungry stare concentrated on my lips. "Does that work for us, beautiful?" he asked.

"It's fine," I said, my cheeks warming under his study. "I think. Probably."

His eyebrow arched up in question and I gave a quick shrug in response. I couldn't refuse with an audience.

"Now that I think of it, Annie and I have plans next

weekend," he replied, turning back to my family. "Yes, I just remembered. We'll have to take a rain check." He motioned toward them. "Why don't we have you over to our place?"

"You and An-Annie," my mother repeated, stumbling over Jackson's nickname for me.

"Your place?" Nella asked. "You have a place? Together?"

"When did that happen?" Rosa asked.

Jackson smiled at me, nodding. "Back in August," he said, still staring at my mouth. "I'm not too proud to say I begged. I couldn't spend another night without her and I begged her to come home with me, stay with me." He patted his belly and shot them a quick grin. "And her baking, my god. I can't function without her pastries. But I'm sure you know all about her talent in the kitchen."

There were a great many wonderful things about Jackson. The list was long and remarkable, not unlike his...ahem. But the trait I most admired in him was his willingness to make a bold move on behalf of another. He looked after me when I was drunk and sad. He listened to the Nevilles when others had dismissed their concerns. He confronted Brooke about her father's issues despite her history of tearing those who crossed her in half. And now he was picking off my family's shady comments and straitjacketing them where they stood.

"Annette, you've been holding out on us," my mother chided.

Jackson blew out a sharp breath before saying, "Not at all. Everyone in town is a fan of her baking."

"Speaking of the town, how are you finding Talbott's Cove, sheriff?" Nella asked.

"It's a great place to call home," he said, his words wide with certainty. "But it wouldn't be half as great without this lady right here. I don't know what I'd do without her. She keeps me on my toes, I'll tell you that. But I'm not saying anything you don't already know, right?"

Nella looked like she was witnessing a live-action atrocity. Hands fisted at her sides, mouth hanging open, eyes bugging out. I loved my sister but it was amazing to see her furious over something as simple as this man professing his love for me. And my muffins.

"Sure," Rosa murmured, bobbing her head. "I guess... I guess I can see that."

Lydia had the decency to appear bored with the whole conversation, craning her neck around the stadium. "I wonder if they're selling nachos at the concession stands tonight," she mused, tapping a manicured finger to her lips. "I really want nachos."

My mother clapped her hands together. "About that Sunday supper," she said, her gaze swinging between me and Jackson. "We really must have you over. Give me a date. There has to be one Sunday when I can get you two at my table."

"That's very kind of you," Jackson replied. "But we'd be happy to host you. It would give us a chance to show you the house we're buying and the plans we have for remodeling. I'm sure you want to see the new displays Annette has at the shop, too."

I shifted a bit, pressing the side of my face into Jackson's chest to smother a laugh. My family had never once visited my shop to see new storefront displays. I rubbed my cheek against that sweater I liked so much and sucked in a lungful of his scent. He truly was one of the good ones.

"Yes, of course," my mother agreed. "How about—"

"Wait, wait, wait," Nella interrupted. "You're remodeling a house? Where?" She pointed at me. "Why all the secrets, Annette? What are you trying to hide?"

Jackson's chest rose and fell under my cheek. Rose and fell. "As I'm certain you can see, we're not hiding anything," he said.

Still directing her comments toward me, Nella continued, "Then why haven't you told us about any of this?"

Jackson and I glanced at each other, our half smiles mirror images of each other. "We didn't hear back about our offer on the house until yesterday so it's as new to you as it is to us. And Jackson was in Augusta and I had that author event on Wednesday, and we've been busy," I said, still looking at him.

"Really *busy*." He pressed a kiss to my forehead, my cheeks, my mouth. "Since Annette doesn't require your approval, I can't imagine you'd be anything but thrilled for her. Isn't that right?"

"We can be thrilled and ask questions at the same time," Nella argued. "The two are not mutually exclusive. This has happened rather quickly. Wouldn't you agree, sheriff?"

A low growl sounded in Jackson's throat as he tightened his hold on me. I had to hide my face again.

"Oh my god, Nella," Rosa murmured. "Can you stop trying to prove a point for a freaking minute? You don't have to be a bitch all the time."

"Who are you calling a bitch?" Nella snapped.

"What are we talking about?" Lydia asked, her eyes narrowed as she looked between us. "Never mind. Someone will tell me later. I'm going to get nachos."

My sister turned and walked away, not troubling herself with pleasantries.

"I want to hear about this house," my mother said, holding both hands at her side as if to hold down my sisters' comments. "Where is it? When will it be ready?"

"We put in an offer on the old Dickerson house," I said. "It's in bad shape but the land is incredible."

Incredible and private. When we started tossing around the idea of finding a place together, something new to us, one of the top requirements was a home that afforded us a degree of privacy. Our days were spent interacting with the community and sharing ourselves with this town but we also needed a place to close the doors and be alone.

We hadn't expected to find something as fast as we did but we couldn't pass up the ancient farmhouse with the woods at its back and the ocean shimmering in the front.

"And the view," Jackson added, his chin brushing the crown of my head. "The view's the best."

"The work will take several months but we figure we'll be moved in come springtime," I said. "Maybe summer. We'll see how the winter goes."

The school's marching band launched into the fight song as the players jogged onto the field. My mother gestured between her ears and mouth, indicating it was too loud to talk right now. She dropped a quick kiss on my cheek and gave Jackson a one-armed squeeze. She gathered up Rosa and the still-fuming Nella, and headed back to the stands.

When the referee beckoned to Jackson to lead the coin toss, he took my hand and led me to the center of the field with him. I hadn't expected to join him for this portion of the festivities but I didn't mind. If there was anyone left wondering about my man's relationship status, this moment cleared it right up.

Several players from each team huddled around us, watching as he popped the coin into the air and then slapped it down on the top of his hand. Instead of looking at the coin, he hooked his arm around my neck and pulled me in for a kiss.

Jackson's lips a breath from mine, he whispered, "Didn't seem like the right time to tell your family that you've come to your senses and agreed to marry me. We'll tell them when my parents come to visit in a few weeks. We'll have to invite Brooke, since she's been sitting on this info since last weekend. That will be fun. They can all be hysterical together."

A smile stretched across my face as I remembered us hiking around the Dickerson Farmstead, marveling at barely-standing barns, rows of apple trees marching into the woods, stone bridges over deep streams. We'd followed a path that led to a seaside cliff and watched the ocean rush over the rocky shoreline below. I was too busy counting the wild blueberry bushes lining the path to notice Jackson had dropped down to one knee.

I didn't remember his exact words but I remembered feeling chosen. *Worthy*. Those sensations didn't swamp my system like a bath in warm honey because he wanted to spend a lifetime with me but because I finally believed I deserved it.

I was worthy of a big, full, messy love.

I was worthy of living the life I'd imagined for myself.

I was worthy of skipping over the scraps and taking everything I'd ever wanted.

If I had it to do all over again, I would've remembered what Jackson said as he knelt before me, but I wouldn't have traded that burst of confidence—of knowing what I wanted and accepting it, too—for anything.

THANK you for reading *Hard Pressed*! I hope you enjoyed Annette and Jackson. If you loved the heat and heart, steam and sass in Hard Pressed, you'll love Matt and Lauren in *Underneath It All*.

ONE HOT ARCHITECT. *One naughty schoolteacher. One crazy night that changes everything.*

MEET LAUREN HALSTED.

It's all the little things—the action plans, the long-kept promises—that started falling apart when my life slipped into controlled chaos.

After I fell ass-over-elbow into Matthew Walsh's arms.

MEET MATTHEW WALSH.

A rebellious streak ran through Lauren Halsted. It was fierce and unrelentingly beautiful, and woven through too many good girl layers to count. She wasn't letting anyone tell her what to do.

Unless, of course, she was naked.

UNDERNEATH IT ALL *is available now! Read on for an excerpt.*

. . .

JOIN *my newsletter for new release alerts, exclusive extended epilogues and bonus scenes, and more.*

IF NEWSLETTERS AREN'T *your thing, follow me on BookBub for preorder and new release alerts.*

VISIT MY PRIVATE READER GROUP, *Kate Canterbary's Tales, for exclusive giveaways, sneak previews of upcoming releases, and book talk.*

IF YOU ENJOYED this visit to Talbott's Cove, you'll love Cole and Owen in *Fresh Catch*.

Take a vacation, they said. *Get away from Silicon Valley's back-stabbing and power-grabbing.*

Recharge the innovative batteries. Unwind, then come back stronger than ever.

Instead, I got lost at sea and fell in love with an anti-social lobsterman.

There's one small issue:

Owen Bartlett doesn't know who I am. Who I really am.

~~

I don't like people.

I avoid small talk and socializing, and I kick my companions out of bed before the sun rises.

No strings, no promises, no problems.

Until Cole McClish's boat drifts into Talbott's Cove, and I bend all my rules for the sexy sailor.

I don't know Cole's story or what he's running from, but one thing is certain:

I'm not letting him run away from me.

FRESH CATCH IS AVAILABLE NOW!

BEFORE GIRL

A SEXY NEW STANDALONE FROM KATE CANTERARY

She's the girl next door.
He's the guy who's loved her from afar.
They're in for an unexpected tumble into love.

She'll juggle your balls.
For Stella Allesandro, chaos is good. She's a rising star at a leading sports publicity firm. She's known throughout the industry as the jock whisperer—the one who can tame the baddest of the bad boys in professional sports without losing her signature smile.

But Cal Hartshorn is an entirely different kind of chaos.

He'll fix your broken heart.
This ex-Army Ranger and now-famous cardiothoracic surgeon fails at nothing...except talking to a woman he's adored from afar. Whether on the battlefield or oper-

ating room, he's exacting, precise, and efficient, but all of that crumbles when Stella is in sight.

Cal always knows—and gets—what he wants, and now he wants all of her.

His *forever* girl.

But Stella isn't convinced she's anyone's forever.

Read it now!

EXCERPT FROM UNDERNEATH IT ALL

Fog wafted over Atlantic Avenue as Matthew and I embarked on the short walk to his building. Dipping my toes in the coupled pond—even if it was just for tonight—was wonderfully satisfying. I expected some relief from the constant fix-up attempts, but I never expected to feel so whole, so completely and thoroughly myself standing next to Matthew. But for every ounce of satisfaction, there was an equal amount of hesitation.

"I like your friends." Matthew shrugged, and he couldn't hold back a smug smile.

While most of my friends expressed some appreciation for the beauty that was Matthew Walsh, only Elsie set my teeth on edge. She went in for the hug instead of the handshake, and wrapped her hands around his bicep while she talked about some remodeling she and her husband, Kent, were considering.

I had no business being possessive or territorial or

even jealous, but I was. At this moment, Matthew was with me, and she was a little too grabby for my liking.

I rolled my eyes. "My friends liked you, all right. They wanted to drag you out back and take turns on you. Do you always have that effect on married women?"

Matthew stopped in front of the marina outside his building and wrapped his arms around my shoulders, his face taking on a happy, serene quality that seemed unusual for him. "Marry me and find out."

"For the love of tiny purple ponies, Matthew."

I laughed and pushed out of his arms. If I didn't get out of these shoes soon, I was taking them off and walking down the street barefoot. According to the Commodore, that was the best way to pick up gangrene and lose a foot, and a girl needed both feet and all ten toes. He was also fundamentally opposed to my heels (too difficult to flee when the situation demanded it), necklaces (an invitation for strangulation), and long hair (something else attackers could grab).

"Is that a yes?"

"You really are a caveman," I said. "I'm tired, I'm cold, my feet hurt, I have to pee, and I want to be out of this dress and eating this cake"—I held up the leftovers from the party—"in the next ten minutes, and we agreed to drinks."

"And my cock in your mouth." He stretched his arm and peered at his watch. He nodded, and said, "By the way: when will that be starting?"

"Sometime after I change and go to the bathroom. And I really do want this cake."

He sighed. "Then we need to talk about citrus fruit."

Grabbing his hand, I towed him inside. "I'm not even going to ask what that means, Matthew."

He leaned against the elevator walls and crossed his arms, his brows pinched in thought. He didn't speak again until we reached his floor. "But I'm a little wounded you turned down my proposal. That shit was heartfelt."

Underneath It All is available now!

ALSO BY KATE CANTERBARY

Standalone Novels

Coastal Elite
Fresh Catch
Hard Pressed
Before Girl

The Walsh Series

Underneath It All – Matt and Lauren
The Space Between – Patrick and Andy
Necessary Restorations – Sam and Tiel
The Cornerstone – Shannon and Will
Restored — Sam and Tiel
The Spire — Erin and Nick

Also By Kate Canterbary

Preservation — Riley and Alexandra
Thresholds — The Walsh Family

Get exclusive sneak previews of upcoming releases through Kate's newsletter and private reader group, The Canterbary Tales, on Facebook.

ACKNOWLEDGMENTS

The Great British Bake-Off is the perfect antidote to the world today. It's happy and punny and generally wonderful. Annette wouldn't be who she is without the Bake-Off.*

To the readers who've loved Talbott's Cove (and Boston and Montauk), thank you. I couldn't do this without you.

To the people who listen to me fret and perseverate and doubt and linger in the bottom of my teacup...you know who you are and I appreciate every single one of your wellness checks.

To my husband, who told me it wasn't crazy to finish a book while packing up our home and moving into a new one...thank you for that. And everything else you do.

ABOUT KATE

Kate Canterbary doesn't have it all figured out, but this is what she knows for sure: spicy-ass salsa and tequila solve most problems, living on the ocean—Pacific or Atlantic —is the closest place to perfection, and writing smart, smutty stories is a better than any amount of chocolate. She started out reporting for an indie arts and entertainment newspaper back when people still read newspapers, and she has been writing and surreptitiously interviewing people—be careful sitting down next to her on an airplane—ever since. Kate lives on the water in New England with Mr. Canterbary and the Little Baby Canterbary, and when she isn't writing sexy architects, she's scheduling her days around the region's best food trucks.

You can find Kate at www.katecanterbary.com

50780024R00200

Made in the USA
Columbia, SC
11 February 2019